GEEK GIRL

PICTURE PERFECT

HOLLY SMALE

HarperCollins *Children's Books*

First published in Great Britain by HarperCollins *Children's Books* 2014
This paperback edition first published in Great Britain by
HarperCollins *Children's Books* in 2015
HarperCollins *Children's Books* is a division of HarperCollins*Publishers* Ltd,
HarperCollins Publishers
1 London Bridge Street
London SE1 9GF

The HarperCollins *Children's Books* website address is
www.harpercollins.co.uk

5

Geek Girl: Picture Perfect

ISBN 978-0-00-748948-0

Printed and bound in England by
Clays Ltd, St Ives plc

model [mod-l] noun, adjective, verb

1 A standard or example for imitation or comparison

2 A representation, generally in miniature

3 An image to be reproduced

4 A person whose profession is posing for artists or photographers

5 To fashion something to be like something else.

ORIGIN from the Latin *modulus*: 'absolute value'

1

My name is Harriet Manners, and I am a girlfriend.

I know I'm a girlfriend because I can't stop beaming. Apparently the average girl smiles sixty-two times a day, so I must be statistically stealing somebody else's happiness. I'm grinning every thirty or forty seconds, *minimum.*

I know I'm a girlfriend because I'm giggling at my own jokes, singing songs I don't know the words to, hugging any animal within a hundred-metre radius and twirling round in circles with my hands stretched out every time I see a small patch of sunshine. Thanks to my brain drowning in the love chemicals *phenylethylamine*, *dopamine* and *oxytocin*, I've basically morphed into a cartoon princess.

Except one with an astronomically high phone bill and a tendency to look up 'symptoms of being in love' online when her boyfriend isn't looking.

Anyway, the final reason I know I'm a girlfriend is this, written on the inside back page of my new bright purple diary:

GIRLFRIEND

I did it, obviously. It would be a really weird thing to doodle on someone else's private stationery. There's a sketch of me and it's timed and dated to commemorate the precise moment – four weeks and two days ago – that Lion Boy and I became an official item.

That's right: Nick and I are finally a proper duo.

A couplet. A twosome never to be divided, like salt and pepper or cheese and tomato. We are the human versions of seahorses, who swim snout to snout and change colour to demonstrate how much they like each other, or Great Hornbills, who sing in duets together to show the world how utterly in tune they are.

And it's changed everything.

After the Most Romantic Summer Ever together (MRSE™), all that's left are rainbows and sunsets and good-morning texts and good-night phone calls and somebody to tell me when I've got chewing gum stuck to the back of my hair and I'm gummed to the bus seat behind me.

For the first time in my entire life, I wouldn't change

a single thing. There are 170 billion galaxies in the observable universe, and I wouldn't alter a jot of any of them. My life is exactly as I want it to be.

Everything is perfect.

2

Anyway, the truly great thing about being so *chipper* all the time is that nothing can really upset you. Not an early-morning start when you're used to a summer of lie-ins. Not your dog, Hugo, moulting all over your brand-new Special Outfit. Not the prospect of seeing your nemesis again after ten blissful weeks without her.

Not even the fact that it's the single most important day of your life and *nobody has remembered*.

Nope. I am a paradigm of calmness and maturity.

Like Gandalf. Or Father Christmas.

"Good *morning*," I say as I float into the kitchen. That's how I travel these days, by the way: in a magical, joy-filled bubble. "What an *auspiciously* lovely day, don't you think? Almost *propitiously* sunny, you could say. A day for *great things* to happen."

Then I stare optimistically at my snoring parents.

It looks like somebody tried to destroy the house

overnight and then gave up and filled it with sleeping gas instead. The room is dark except for the glow from the open fridge door, and cups and plates are everywhere. Dad's leaning back in a chair with a tea towel over his head, and my stepmother Annabel is slumped over the breakfast table with her cheek resting gently on a piece of buttered toast.

Tabitha is lying in her cot, making cute snuffling sounds as if she's not the bomb that keeps going off.

I clear my throat.

"Did you know that it's actually called *August* after the first Emperor of Rome, Augustus? It was his most successful month. How significant is *that*?"

Silence.

It's a good thing I am newly shiny and happy on a permanent basis, or I'd be throwing a hissy-fit round about now. Instead, I abruptly pull the curtains open so my parents can see the epic day in its full glory.

"*FIRE!*" Dad yells, whipping the tea towel off his head and peering at me through his fingers. "Ugh, worse. What have we told you about daylight, sweetheart?"

"It's 9.21am," I point out. "You're not vampires."

I don't say that with a *lot* of conviction. My parents have grey skin and red eyes, they're up all night, rarely eat and seem to communicate without actually talking. The signs aren't looking good.

"Mnneurgh," Annabel mumbles, propping herself up slightly. The toast is still stuck to her face. "How long were we asleep?"

Dad sticks a finger in the cup in front of him. "Not long enough –" he sighs and waves a hand in front of his face – "nope, Elizabeth Hurley is gone."

"Oh, God," Annabel sighs and squints slightly. Her normally perfect fringe is sticking up like the crest of a blonde cockatoo, and there are crumbs stuck in her eyebrow. "I need to get the laundry on, the bathroom cleaned..." She slumps down again. "This toast is surprisingly comfortable."

Yup.

It's been exactly seven weeks since you last saw us, and anything resembling domestic order has totally disappeared.

At an average of 125 decibels, it turns out my new sibling is slightly louder than a rock concert (120dB) and only very slightly less loud – and painful – than being shot repeatedly by a machine gun at point-blank range (130dB). Apparently the word 'infant' comes from the Latin word *infans*, which means 'unable to speak', but all I can say is: the Ancient Romans obviously never met Tabitha Manners.

Much like somebody with a fully automated firearm, my tiny sister is capable of expressing *exactly* how she feels.

I pick Tabby out of her cot and she opens her eyes and beams back at me. That's just one of the plethora of things I love about my sister: we're like peas in a pod. Except luckily her pod is in my parents' room, on the other side of the house.

Plus I have very high quality ear-plugs.

"Does anyone happen to remember what day it is?" I prompt. Maybe I should show them today's pie chart. I can't stop the anxious butterflies, but I can at least put them in the right ten-minute time slot.

"Tuesday?" Dad attempts. "Friday? 1967? Could you give us a ball-park figure?"

"Lift the green towel on your right, Harriet," Annabel murmurs, eyes still shut. "And the dishcloth next to it. We'll be awake in a second."

I step over a couple of large boxes and suitcases lying open on the kitchen floor.

Then I tentatively move the towel with my fingers. Underneath is a brand-new red leather satchel with a sale sticker still attached and the letters HM engraved on the flap. When I open it, it's packed to the brim with new pencils and pens and rulers and books.

Under the dishcloth is a home-made chocolate cake shaped vaguely like a robot that reads 'GOOD LUCK HARRIET' in white buttons down the front, and '(NOT THAT WE BELIEVE IN LUCK – YOU ARE THE MASTER OF YOUR DESTINY)' in almost illegible blue icing on the feet.

I beam at them.

See what I mean? My life is going exactly to plan. Even my parents are following my cake-and-gift related schedule, despite being asleep when I told them about it.

"Awww," I say happily, zooming Tabby over as if she's a wriggly aeroplane and giving them both a kiss. "Thank you so much, sleepyheads. You're the best."

"I'm just going to go tell Liz Hurley that," Dad murmurs, closing his eyes. "Be back in a minute."

"Say hi to her from me," Annabel says, yawning and rubbing a bit of butter off her face. "If she wants to come over and do some washing-up, tell her to knock herself out."

And my parents go straight back to sleep.

Right.

According to today's schedule, I now have six and

a half minutes left. Just six and a half minutes to put my purple flip-flops on, pick a couple of chocolate buttons off the cake, smudge the icing so my parents don't notice and get to the bench on the corner of the road where my best friend will be waiting for me: eager, bright-eyed and ready to confront our mutual destinies.

I have it timed to absolute perfection.

Unfortunately, I obviously forgot to show the plan to my little sister. Because as I kiss her tiny nose she gives me one bright, adorable smile.

And vomits all over my head.

3

Seriously.

Just *once* I'd like to start an important day without being covered in the partially digested contents of somebody else's stomach.

This was *so* not on the pie chart.

Anyway, while I'm scrubbing baby sick out of my hair I may as well update you on what else has happened in the last seven weeks:

1. I *still* haven't turned sixteen. My birthday is the last possible day of the academic year, which according to recent newspaper reports means I am statistically likelier to fail in life.

2. I've had quite a lengthy go at my father for making me statistically likelier to fail in life.

3. My Best Friend Nat and I have spent plenty of time together, despite me being in my First Ever Relationship. This is because friends should *always* come first.

4. And also because my model boyfriend spends quite a lot of time working abroad and isn't around very much.

5. Toby has spent a lot of time with us too. Despite not always being invited. Or encouraged.

6. Or actually seen for big chunks of it. His stalking skills are really improving.

7. Dad is still out of work. Unless you count playing 'Galloping Major' with a baby as employment.

8. My grandmother, Bunty, left. She managed five days of Tabitha screaming, and then found a Buddhist retreat in Nepal and decided she might be more 'useful' in a 'country very far away'.

9. Which surprised nobody, least of all Annabel.

10. I haven't done any modelling.

Since quitting my job with fashion designer Yuka Ito, I've done nothing even vaguely related. *Nada*. Zilch. Zip.

It turns out Yuka and my flamboyant agent Wilbur were single-handedly keeping my career alive between them, like two Emperor Penguins raising their runty, dependent chick. Without them there to feed it every few hours and protect it from Giant Petrels, it couldn't survive.

Except in this situation the Giant Petrel is less an enormous arctic bird of the *Procellariidae* family, and more an agent called Stephanie who replaced Wilbur at Infinity Models six weeks ago. She's very stern, very professional and she doesn't remember who I am.

I know this because she rarely answers any of my calls and the one time she did I heard her say "*Who*?".

I haven't heard from the agency since.

Honestly, I hadn't realised quite how much I enjoyed getting painted gold, or wrestling octopuses, or jumping around in the snow, or pretending to be the world's most elegant Sumo wrestler until it was taken away from me.

Literally.

Infinity Models told me to send back by FedEx the

gold shoes Yuka had let me keep.

But there's nothing I can do about it. I've got other things to focus on. Sixth form starts in ten days and I am so ready for it.

I have a brand-new red satchel.

I have an expensive calculator that does graphs and integration and quadratics and natural logarithms, whatever they all are.

I have a set of non-uniform clothes bought to be worn to my new classes. Almost none of which have cartoon animals on them.

I've stalked all of my new teachers on the internet and created a bullet-point summary for each of them, so I can win them over and/or force them to like me.

And – most importantly – I have a brilliantly conceived and carefully structured plan.

I have four A levels to ace, and a boyfriend and Best Friend to juggle properly for a healthy and balanced lifestyle. I have a stalker to keep away from bushes with thorns in them. I have my one and only sixteenth birthday to organise. I'm going to be the busiest I've ever been, so I've planned it all in minute detail.

The only problem is: every single bit of it depends on how I've done in my exams.

Which is exactly what I'm about to find out.

4

I recently read an interesting article about a twelve-week-old abandoned monkey in China who was taken to a sanctuary where it formed a strong and intense friendship with a white pigeon. Despite having nothing at all in common, they immediately became inseparable.

Sometimes I wonder if my Best Friend Nat and I look as ridiculous together as they do.

Now is one of those moments.

By the time I've hastily pawed at myself with a damp cloth and kissed my comatose family goodbye, I'm more than fifteen minutes off schedule and hyperventilating with panic.

And Nat looks like she couldn't be less bothered.

She's sitting on the bench at the junction. Her new fringe is perfectly straight, black eyeliner is identical on both eyes and a stripy dress is hanging off one shoulder as if she totally means it to.

François may be long gone, but something about her French exchange must have stuck.

Nat looks like she should have English subtitles.

"I'm sorry I'm late," I say breathlessly, handing her a chocolate button and then realising I've smudged brown icing all over my T-shirt and it looks disturbingly like something else. "Do you think the results are out yet? Do you think we've both passed?"

"This is an *awful* way to start a day," Nat says, looking up from a copy of *Vogue*. "Harriet, what are we going to do?"

I smile at her in relief.

Obviously I totally misjudged my Best Friend. We will navigate these terrifying academic waters together.

"Don't worry," I say in my most reassuring voice as I start tugging her towards school. "I'm sure it's not going to be as bad as you think."

"No, it's *worse,*" Nat says. "Harriet, what does this look like to you?"

She yanks at her dress.

I think it might be a trick question.

"Umm. That's a..." *Shift. Robe.* "Frock, isn't it?" Then inspiration hits me. "A *gown*?"

"It's *stripes*, Harriet. I've gone and worn *stripes.* But

Vogue says the hottest trend this season is miniature prints and florals. I wish they'd give me a bit of *warning*."

This is what it's been like ever since Nat got her official welcome letter from the Design College down the road. I haven't seen her this focused since the blue-glitter frenzy of Year Two. For a few epic weeks, we both looked like Christmas tree decorations.

In a moment of inspiration, I grab a floral elastic band off my wrist and hand it over.

"Oh my God, how did you *know*?" Nat says, throwing her arms around my neck.

"I am very up to date on sartorial trends," I say, nodding wisely. Plus a stylist left it in my hair once and I've been using it to keep my pencils together ever since.

My phone beeps, and I whip it out of my pocket with the speed of a technological ninja.

Ha.

I *knew* Nick hadn't forgotten about me this morning. I *knew* he was just as supportive and romantic as a boyfriend should b—

Much congratulationings, Harry-chan! May your big day be full of cloud tens and elevens. Rin x

*

I grin – I'm glad Rin is making creative use of the *Colloquial English Dictionary* I sent to her home address in Tokyo – and then wait in case somebody else wants to make contact.

He doesn't.

So I put my phone back in my pocket and nimbly change the subject.

"Nat, I've got each of our timetables cross-referenced and colour-coordinated so we know where the other person is at all times. Do you want to see them?"

This is how I've spent the last few weeks: carefully constructing an in-depth way of maintaining seamless contact with Nat when she's at college and I'm at sixth form. We haven't actually shared a class in five years, so it just requires a little extra imagination.

It also requires hanging out with Toby Pilgrim every day for the next two years, but let's be honest: I've been unintentionally doing that forever anyway.

"Don't be daft," Nat laughs, tying her hair into an enormous top-knot. "I'll just ring you after college and we can do coffee or something."

Do coffee or something?

"Did you know that coffee can actually kill you in high doses, Nat?"

"I wasn't suggesting 1,000 cups at once, Harriet."

"Just a hundred will do it," I say darkly. "Scientists have done tests."

I'm just about to tell her that coffee was actually discovered by an Ethiopian goat herder who realised his goats were eating the berries and going totally mad, when we turn the corner and both fall silent.

Ahead of us, school looms exactly like it always has.

Except something is different. Inside that building at this very moment are our entire pasts and our entire futures. That building simultaneously represents the beginning and the end.

A little part of me suddenly wants to sit down on the pavement, dig in my heels and refuse to move.

Except I know from experience people don't like it when I do that.

So I probably won't.

"Can you believe this is the last time I'll ever walk through those gates?" Nat says happily.

"Mmm."

"The last time I'll ever have to wear my hair in a ponytail for gym, which is totally inappropriate for my face shape."

"The last time you'll ever block the entrance with your insanely boring conversations."

We both turn round.

"Hi, Alexa," Nat sighs. "Great to see a long break has really brought you a sense of inner peace and compassion."

"Whatever," my nemesis says, flicking her newly highlighted hair and whacking me with her shoulder as she saunters past. "Such a shame you're leaving, Natalie. What are we going to do without you?"

"Collapse and die, probably," Nat says, folding her arms. "I live in hope."

"Maybe then I'll smell as bad as Harriet." Alexa glances over to where I'm standing, still rubbing the top of my arm. "Hey, loser," she adds. "Looks like this year it's just going to be you and I."

And – just like that – my summer is over.

5

In fairness, I've had a good run.

If you take away all the holidays and weekends, we actually only have to be at school for 195 days a year. Add to that night-times, mornings, a few field trips, an hour for lunch every day plus two fifteen-minute breaks and the potential for getting sick now and then, and I won't have to see Alexa for more than 1,118.5 hours this academic year.

That's only a full 46.6 days.

A month and a half of solid Alexa Roberts.

On my own.

Oh, God. I'd really rather get it all out of the way at once. Maybe I should ask if she wants to move in with me.

"This year it's just going to be *you and me*," I correct quietly as Nat kisses my cheek and runs through the school gates towards the office.

Then I stare at the shrieking crowd of girls she's

now surrounded by.

They look strangely unfamiliar, and it takes a while to work out it's because for the first time apart from field trips that we're not in our school uniforms. Laura has a leather jacket, and Lucie is almost unrecognisable wearing bright red lipstick. Anna has blue feathers wound into the back of her ponytail, as if she killed a bird and ceremoniously attached it to the back of her head. It's like seeing a fully dressed theatre production when you've only seen the rehearsal before.

The boys are all wearing jeans and T-shirts and have clean faces and short hair.

I look down at the Spider-Man T-shirt I bought last week and then touch my new bob haircut. I think it's obvious which camp I fall into.

Maybe I'll just make the most of it, grow a moustache and hide in the boys' toilets this year.

"Harriet Manners." A thin boy in orange corduroys and a Spider-Man hoody taps me on the shoulder. There appear to be tiny cartoons of goldfish on his socks. "How coincidental that we match perfectly today. One might call it fate. Destiny. Serendipity."

It's none of those things. He was hiding behind a clothes rack when I bought my T-shirt.

"Morning, Toby," I say as he wipes his nose on his

sleeve and stares at it in fascination.

Then I see the opened white envelope in his hands.

There are ten times more bacteria in your body than there are actual body cells, and I can suddenly feel them: squirming all over me.

"Is that..." I swallow as my entire body begins fizzing. "Is that *them*?"

"Yes," Toby says. "Or no. That's a very vague question, Harriet. They wouldn't let you into the FBI with that kind of approach. I've checked."

"One day," Nat sighs, returning from the office, "you're going to answer a question like a normal person, Toby, and we'll all pass out with shock."

"So..." I swallow. "How did you do?"

"14 A*s," Toby says, carefully tucking the piece of paper into a folder with TOBY'S EPIC ACHIEVEMENTS written on the front. "Those Mandarin and Classical Civilisation evening classes were not the waste of time and money my parents said they were."

My stomach spins and I take my phone out of my pocket.

"Here," Nat says, thrusting a large envelope at me. "Stop thinking about Nick. You know he's on a shoot in Africa: he's probably busy having a staring contest with a hippo or something. This one's yours."

I stare at it, and then try unsuccessfully to lick my lips.

One way or another, everything in my life is about to change. *Be calm, Harriet. Be Zen-like in your acceptance of the roller coaster of life and all its ups and downs and—*

"Stop whispering at your results, Harriet," Nat laughs. "Ready?"

"Mmmmmn."

"Steady?"

"Uh-huh."

"Now GO!" Nat yells.

And together we rip open our futures.

6

At any typical moment, your brain will be using twenty per cent of the oxygen that enters your bloodstream. Mine must have got greedy, because my head suddenly feels so light it could float away like a balloon.

I passed.

In fact, I passed with *flying colours*.

I don't want to boast, so all I'm going to say is: I got one more star than the Chamaeleontis constellation and one less than Orionis.

I also got a C in technology, but if I ever need a pine box or a red plastic wall clock that looks like a badly sanded hummingbird, I'll just go to the shops and buy one.

Nat is spinning on the spot in tiny circles.

"College here I come!" she yells, giving me a high five on every revolution. "I failed history but who cares, I'm going to *college*!"

Then she stops spinning so we can stare at each other.

My head promptly floats away.

"*Sugar cookies*!" I squeak, jumping up and down. "We *did* it!"

"*Massive sugar cookies!*" Nat shouts.

"UBER *sugar cookies*!"

"STELLAR *sugar cookies*!"

"IMMEASURABLE, BOUNDLESS *SUGAR COOKIES*! Our cookies have gone into orbit!"

"*Ah*," Toby says, getting a small green book out of his bag. "I was under the impression that *sugar cookies* was a negative expression but I will now make a note that it can be used either way."

Nat and I bounce and giggle hysterically and then gradually start half-hopping out of the school gates.

All this talk of cookies has made me hungry. Maybe my parents will have baked me another cake: a strawberry one, with 'CONGRATULATIONS' written in marshmallows and Smarties for the dots on the 'i's and—

"Oi," a voice behind us says. "Did one of you losers drop something?"

And every last bounce and giggle suddenly drains out of me.

Because:

a) there's a big group of girls standing directly behind us

b) Alexa is in front of them

c) in her hand is a bright purple book.

7

I read somewhere that a fully grown octopus is flexible enough to climb all the way through a human's intestines. From the feeling in my stomach right now that is exactly what's happening.

Is that… my *diary*?

It can't be. My diary is at home, next to my bed. Safe and private and protected by a carefully placed ginger hair, exactly as it's supposed to be.

Except… I can see a British Library sticker on the spine, and the row of gold stars I gave myself at the bottom, and the corner Hugo chewed in a huff when I wouldn't let him have a bite of my sandwich.

It can't be, but it *is*.

Everything I've written in that book over the last seven weeks hits me so hard my entire body is suddenly full of cold, squirming, slippery sea creature.

No. No. No no no no *no no NO.*

I run towards Alexa, but it's too late: she's holding it

high over her head and opening the front pages.

"Mr Harper, physics," she reads loudly. "Divorced. Secret fan of Zumba. Member of Royal Horticultural Society. Note to self: learn more about Latin dancing and plants. And marital problems."

Behind her are a few snorts of laughter.

When you blush, it's not just your cheeks that turn red: the inside lining of your stomach does too. I'm so hot, I think I've accidentally cooked the octopus. How is this happening? What the *sugar cookies* was my diary doing in my bag?

Oh my God.

Annabel must have thought it was my school diary and popped it in my satchel. She's so tired she probably didn't notice the words INTENSELY PRIVATE written in silver pen on the front. And it must have fallen out when I was jumping around like an idiot.

This is *exactly* why I never do any kind of physical activity.

"Miss Lloyd, advanced maths," Alexa continues in glee. "Inappropriate Facebook photos. Subtly offer to edit her online networking privacy settings."

Teachers milling around the school entrance are starting to glance in our direction. I recognise Miss Lloyd in the distance. This is going to end my sixth form academic career before it's even started.

I start leaping for the book, but Alexa continues flicking through with her other hand on my forehead while I scrabble frantically at her like a cat in a pond.

"Give it back," I beg desperately, making another lunge for it. "Please, Alexa. It's private."

Nat is fishing around in her handbag. *"Hand the book over,"* she yells, blotched with fury. *"Or I swear to God this time I'm going to scalp you."*

"Until the day it inevitably becomes a bestseller," Toby concurs, "it is Harriet's intellectual property, Alexa."

But it's too late.

Alexa has turned to the back of the book and is staring at the last page.

"Girlfriend?" she says. She looks almost speechless. *"Girlfriend?* Are you kidding me? *You?"*

The octopus in my stomach is about to die from heat exhaustion. "Yes."

"Who?" Alexa looks around. *"Him?"*

"No," Toby says, in answer to her pointing finger. "We discovered this summer that we lack the chemistry of physical lust and also that Harriet needs to work on her kissing skills."

The octopus promptly goes BANG.

Alexa looks back at me. "Are you telling me a real live boy – other than this weirdo – actually wants you?"

"Yes," I say again in a small voice.

I try to lift my chin, but all I can smell is a pungent cocktail of baby puke, damp dog hair and out of the corner of my eye I can still see brown icing on my boy's clothes and stuck in my boy's hair.

It suddenly seems pretty unbelievable to me too.

Alexa shrieks with laughter.

"OMG, this is *priceless.*" She turns to the group behind her. "Can you *imagine* the geekiness levels? I bet they're *off the chart.* I bet he's short and greasy and hasn't learnt to shave yet." She starts giggling. "Bet he – *haha* – studies physics and smells of Brussels sprouts and farts every time he bends down. *Hahahaha.*"

I think of Nick's big black curls; his coffee-coloured skin and slanted brown eyes; the huge grin with the pointed teeth that breaks his face apart. I think of the mole near his eyebrow; the green smell of him and the tilt at the end of his nose.

I think of how he laughs at the wrong bits in the cinema; how he leans his cheek against mine when he's sleepy; the way he tucks my feet between his knees when they're cold and I don't even have to ask him to.

I think of how extraordinary he is.

"H-he's not," I say in a tiny voice. "And he doesn't."

"Actually," Nat snaps. "Harriet's boyfriend is a successful international supermodel. So stick that in your cauldron and smoke it."

Alexa starts giggling even harder, and rolls her eyes at her underlings. "Of *course* he is."

"Show her," Nat demands, flushing and pointing at my satchel. "Show her a picture of Nick, Harriet."

"I... don't have one," I admit. "It's a new bag."

Alexa takes a step closer. "An *imaginary* boyfriend," she says. "That's pathetic, even for you."

"He's real," I say, except it comes out as two tiny mouse squeaks. "And I'm not pathetic."

"Oh, you are. Or should that be '*you-apostrophe-r-e*'?"

My whole body goes cold.

On the last day of exams I grammatically embarrassed Alexa in front of a lot of girls in our year. I had hoped maybe she'd forgotten.

She hasn't.

"Do you expect me to believe," Alexa says, "that anybody would want *you,* Manners? You're the most boring person I've ever met. You're a nobody. A *nothing.*"

I blink at her. For some reason I can't fathom, I wish she'd just stuck with *geek*.

"I told you I'd get you back, Harriet," Alexa adds, giving me a final shove backwards, putting my diary in her bag and closing it with a *click*. "Reading can be *such* an education, don't you think?"

And she storms out of the school gates, with her minions scuttling behind her.

8

Apparently horses and rats can't vomit.

Unfortunately, I am neither a horse nor a rat. It's taking every bit of focus I have just to make sure I don't get sick on myself for the second time today.

"Are you OK?" Nat says, putting a hand on my arm.

"Mmm," I say chirpily. "Sure. It'll be fine. Just fine. Fine."

Then I bite my lips. *Stop saying 'fine', Harriet.*

"She doesn't sound fine," Toby observes, tugging his rucksack back on to his shoulders like a broken tortoise. "I don't think Harriet sounds fine at all, Natalie."

"Shut up, Toby," Nat says kindly, and then she puts her arm round me. "Don't worry, Harriet. I mean, it's just a few scribbles. How bad can it be?"

"The way I see it," Toby adds cheerfully, "the more

information people know about you the better, Harriet. Personally, I'd like to know *everything.* I'm hoping she makes photocopies and distributes them around the classroom."

I flinch.

My diary isn't the 'today it rained, I stroked a cat, we had spaghetti for dinner' kind of report I kept when I was five and I thought every day was riveting and unprecedented.

Everything I am is in that book.

My hopes and dreams; my worries, my doubts. My most precious, perfect memories of me and Nick, written in unnecessary, humiliating detail. My lists; my plans; the bit where I attempted to rhyme *Nick Hidaka* with *big squid packer.*

My process of falling in love, page by page.

In short, I've just given Alexa the strongest weapon she's ever had against me:

Myself.

Nat starts gently leading me away from the school fence. I can't really feel my legs any more: I feel like I'm being rolled forward on rubbery wheels.

"Forget about it," she says firmly and shakes her head. "Anyway, we should be celebrating."

I blink a few times.

Celebrating. Exam results. It already feels like a billion years ago.

This is like when that guy leaked classified National Security Agency information that revealed operational details of global surveillance and threatened to take down all of America. Except that instead of the US spy programme, it's my personal secrets that are going to be spread around the sixth form.

And instead of temporary asylum in Russia, I'll end up in a cold corner of the classroom.

"I think," I say slowly, "I should probably go home. My parents are going to want to know my results straight away."

This is a lie, obviously. If they're even awake it'll be a modern-day miracle.

"Are you sure? Because Mum promised she'd take me shopping for new college clothes and I thought you could come with us."

"Ooh," Toby says. "Yes please. I think I need to buy new boxer shorts."

"Never," Nat says, rolling her eyes, "talk to me about boxer shorts again."

"Briefs?"

'No."

"Swimming shorts?"

"Why would you be wearing swimming shorts when you're not even swimming, you weirdo?"

I'm subtly edging away from my best friends in a little sideways crab shuffle.

"Shopping sounds great, Nat," I lie again as cheerfully as possible. "Maybe another time?"

"Sure. I mean, I'm going to have lots on with college and stuff. But we've still got weekends, right?"

"Right," I say in a tiny voice.

And I spin round and run home as fast as my legs will carry me.

9

Which is faster than it used to be.

Nothing makes you take up jogging quite like a brand-new baby and nowhere to escape to apart from the garden shed.

"Annabel?" I say as I open the front door and Hugo barrels towards me, tail wagging. I bend down and give him a cuddle. "Dad? I thought you might like to know what I—"

And then I stop.

In the last hour and a half, the house has totally transformed.

The curtains are wide open, the kitchen is almost clean, and there are half-filled cardboard boxes lying at random points around the hallway. Piles of shiny plates and saucers are in stacks on the table, and the mugs are out in neat, organised lines as if they're getting ready to break into an impromptu can-can.

The air smells of air freshener, and sunshine is

pouring in through the window on to the huge suitcases still lying on the kitchen floor.

This is more like it.

My parents have finally decided to give my special day the respect it deserves and spring clean in my honour.

Although they could have just used drawers and cupboards like normal people. Lining everything up on the table seems a bit excessive.

"*Harriet?*" Annabel yells down the stairs. Tabitha has decided to recommence screaming. It only takes 100dB at the right pitch to break glass, and for once the windows in our house aren't just in danger from my door slammings. "*Is that you?*"

"Who else is it going to be?" Dad says, wandering in from the laundry room. "If *only* strangers would consider politely breaking in with keys. Maybe they'd dust while they took our valuables."

His arms are full of tiny pink things: little towels, trousers, onesies, cardigans, socks, bibs. It takes another glance to realise that they aren't supposed to be pink. There's a lone red sock on top of the pile.

Dad gives me a look that indicates he knows just how much trouble he's about to be in.

"*Harriet?*" The screaming goes up a notch. "How

did you do?" Annabel appears at the top of the stairs and Dad quickly lobs everything into a cardboard box and closes the lid.

"It went really well," I say as the screeches get louder.

"*What?*" Annabel transfers Tabitha to a different arm and jiggles her up and down. "Say it again, Harriet."

"My exams went really well," I say, holding my thumbs up in the air. "Better than expected, actually."

Dad climbs the stairs two at a time and takes Tabitha out of Annabel's arms. "Pipe down, junior," he says firmly, and my sister immediately goes silent.

Annabel crumples against the wall as if she's just been popped.

"You're like some kind of Baby Whisperer, Richard."

"Albert Einstein, Isaac Newton and Charles Darwin were all premature babies like Tabby," Dad explains. "Genius recognises genius."

I hand Annabel my results and she looks at them and then beams at me. "Brilliant. Well done, sweetheart. You worked incredibly hard for them."

"Hard *schmard*," Dad says, fondly scruffing up my hair. "*Both* my daughters are geniuses. I genetically gave them my fierce intellect, fantastic cheekbones and the ability to make great spaghetti bolognese."

"Marmite," he adds, turning to the side and sucking his cheeks in. "The secret is Marmite."

"Did you genetically give them your laundry skills too?"

There's a long silence. Then Annabel lifts an eyebrow and looks at the tiny pink sock stuck with static to the side of Dad's trousers.

He coughs.

"Maybe," he admits. "We'll have to wait and see."

I look around briefly at the tidiness of the house.

It's a lovely gesture of support and encouragement, but I think they're overestimating how much I value seeing carpet. I haven't seen the rug in my bedroom for weeks.

"There's quite a lot of extra space in my wardrobe," I say, tucking my results back in my satchel. "If you need it."

Dad and Annabel look at each other.

"Huh?"

"I've got a spare drawer too, if you want it for some of Tabitha's stuff. There's no point boxing it while you clean."

"Umm, Harriet..." Dad starts, clearing his throat.

"Thank you, darling," Annabel says, raising her

eyebrows at him whilst putting her arm around me. "It's *your* big day. How would you like to celebrate?"

I think about it.

Starting the day again and making sure I do my satchel up properly doesn't seem appropriately upbeat.

"I'm going to go upstairs and speak to my boyfriend," I say instead. "I bet he's been trying to call me all morning."

"Young love," Dad grins at Annabel as I start heading towards my bedroom.

They lean over and give each other a little kiss.

"Scientists have said that romantic love is only supposed to last a year," I mumble, "due to diminishing levels of neurotrophin proteins in the blood. You guys are just making a mockery of statistics."

And, with my parents giggling away, I walk into my bedroom and close the door as quietly as I can behind me.

10

It takes a computer with 700,000 processor cores and 1.4 million GB of RAM forty minutes to map just one second of human brain activity.

Forty minutes.

No computer in the entire world can do what we each do in our own heads every minute of the day. No computer is as complicated or as interesting.

I bet they don't get into anywhere near as much trouble either.

Or write diaries and then drop them in the playground.

The first thing I do is pull my T-shirt over my head and slide down the back of my bedroom door. Then in the stuffy, deodorant-scented darkness I pull out my phone and stare at the blank screen.

No texts.

No missed calls.

No emails or Skype messages.

Not a single light flashing anywhere to say Nick has tried to reach me. I turn it upside down, just in case any incredibly romantic and supportive texts want to fall out.

They don't.

This afternoon, for the record, was supposed to go like this:

Harriet's Epic End of Exams Celebration (HEEEC)

- *Ace my exams.*
- *Squeal with Nick, who magically rings me at precisely the moment I open my envelope.*
- *Eat lots of chocolate cake.*
- *Celebrate with Nat by choreographing complicated dance moves and shouting our results jubilantly out of the window at people walking past.*
- *Squeal with Nick again, because he's just SO PROUD OF ME he can't stop calling.*
- *Tell Nick I need to focus on having fun with my Best Friend and gently imply that he needs to stop being so needy.*
- *Put on a startlingly original choreographed dance*

show with Nat for my parents.

Instead – on yet another pivotal day of my life – I'm hiding under a T-shirt on the floor of my bedroom.

I *knew* I shouldn't have used my new calligraphy pen to write the list. All the curly Es took *ages.*

My phone beeps, and my stomach does a sudden unexpected backflip like a maverick seal on YouTube.

You have such a vivid imagination, weirdo.
Can't wait for next week.
A

And it's as if somebody has thrown a pebble straight into the middle of me: panic starts rippling from it in small waves.

They start in my chest, and then they spread outwards. They spread to my shoulders, then to my arms and fingers. They spread through my stomach, into my legs and knees and toes until I'm full of undulating, pulsing ripples.

The waves get bigger and stronger and the pebble gets heavier and harder until everything inside me is threatening to spill out.

Which in a way it already kind of has.

Apparently thirty-nine per cent of the world's population uses the internet, and Alexa is on every social networking site available. With a few clicks of a button, she has access to *everyone*.

There's a knock on my door.

"Harriet?" Annabel says gently. "I just downloaded a meerkat documentary narrated by David Attenborough. I thought you might quite like it."

Meerkats have really thin fur on their bellies so they can lie flat like sunbathers and warm up in the sun, and I'm intrigued to see what David has to say about that.

But right now, I just don't care.

So I do the only thing I can.

"Oh, *Nick*," I shout as loudly as I can into my dead mobile. "The monkey did *what*? How *funny*! Tell me more about it! You are just so *hilarious*."

"Say hi to Nick from me," Annabel calls through my door.

I don't know why parents always want to send greetings vicariously. I think it's their way of making sure they're still watching us.

"Annabel says hi," I tell nobody. Then I wait a few seconds in horrible silence. "Nick says hi back."

"Great. I'll go prepare your father by explaining

that a meerkat is not, in fact, a real cat."

Annabel retreats down the stairs, and I grab a slice of the chocolate cake she's thoughtfully left on my dresser.

Eating cake on my own on my bedroom floor is not exactly how I planned to spend one of the biggest afternoons of my life.

But it's the only thing left on my list I can still tick off.

11

The rest of the day is spent:

a) eating cake
b) lying flat on my back, trying not to be sick
c) attempting to get brown icing off my duvet.

When I was in Japan I learnt that Buddhist monks in training must eat every single grain of rice in their bowl or it represents ingratitude towards the universe.

I'm pretty sure the same thing applies to chocolate cake.

The next thing I know, it's 7am and the doorbell is ringing.

I sit up groggily and rub my eyes.

I'm still in my Spider-Man T-shirt, and there is a melted chocolate button stuck to my forehead. My phone is still in my hand, from where I fell asleep gripping it like a small, hard and square stress-ball.

"Annabel?" I shout. "Dad?" The doorbell rings again.

There's a silence so – grumbling slightly – I grab my dressing gown off the back of the door and start plodding down the stairs: heavily, so my parents know that on the Day After My Big Day I cannot *believe* I am expected to get out of bed and operate as some kind of family doorman.

Then I swing the door open and stop scowling.

I *knew* Nick hadn't forgotten about me. I *knew* the big romantic gesture was coming: I just had to be patient and wait for it.

I beam at the postman, and at the huge package he's holding. Maybe it's exotic flowers. Maybe it's a carved African mask with a fascinating history, or indigenous jewellery with our names carved into a heart and—

"Are you going to take it or what?"

"Sorry?"

"I've got a lot of things to deliver, missy. Please sign here and let me get on with it."

I don't think this postman appreciates the level of grand romance he's participating in.

"Approximately 360 million items are sent by post

every year," I say sympathetically, scribbling my name. "You must be very tired."

The postman lifts his eyebrows. "I don't deliver them all, love. I'm not Santa Claus."

Then he marches off down the pavement without even looking back to appreciate the joy on my face.

The stamp is beautiful and exotic, and on the front is written in large, curly writing:

The Manners Family

Which is a bit weird.

Nick gets on really well with my parents, but I think this might be taking integration a little too far.

I rip open the package, and pull out a small piece of yellow fabric that says:

A prayer flag for Tabitha.

A string of red beads that say:

For Annabel. To keep track of your daily mantras.

A tiny pair of silver cymbals, engraved with a dragon.

For Richard. To create a cleansing sound that totally empties the mind.

Which sounds a bit dangerous. I'm not sure my father needs any help in that area.

Finally, I pull out a beautiful little engraved golden bowl with a cloth-covered stick.

For Harriet: a traditional Nepalese Singing Bowl. It stimulates the brain to produce alpha waves that will help you relax.

This is the most inappropriate gift a boyfriend has ever sent *anyone*.

What on earth was Nick *thinking*?

Then I tip the package upside down and a card falls out.

Kittens, I'll be back on Friday so leave the keys under the bush outside. Have a fabulous adventure, darlings!

See you next year.

Bunty xxx

12

Nerve impulses bring information to the average brain with the same speed as a high-powered luxury sports car.

Right now, mine feels like a milk float.

I turn the card over four times, just in case I've missed a pivotal piece of information. A code or perhaps a translator.

I'm just turning it over for the fifth time when there's a heavy shuffling sound behind me.

Annabel pauses in dragging another suitcase down the stairs and flushes slightly. "Harriet, I didn't expect you to be awake so early."

I look at the suitcase, and then at the hallway. There are even more boxes everywhere; the bookshelves have been cleared; the taps in the kitchen are shiny. Dad's loudly singing the wrong lyrics to 'Don't Stop Me Now' by Queen, which is what he always does when he's cleaning the oven.

"What's going on?" I say, thrusting Bunty's card at her. "Why is Grandma coming back? What *adventure*? And what does she mean by *next year*?"

Annabel goes a darker shade of pink and mutters, "Oh, God. Nice timing, Mum." Then she clears her throat.

"Well, we were going to tell you yesterday, Harriet, but it was your big day – it's all been very last minute – and..." She pauses. "Richard? Can you get out here, please?"

My eyes widen. Annabel never asks for Dad's help in anything. *Ever.*

Through the kitchen door I see Dad use the cooker to pull himself up.

"Ouch," he says, staggering into the hallway. "Maybe I should start doing yoga. Or pilates. Which is the most manly, do you think? Which would Batman do?"

"Can somebody please just tell me what's going on?"

"Well," Annabel says, going even more red. "There's this thing... The fact is... Actually, you wouldn't believe what's... We were just thinking that..."

I've never seen Annabel unsure how to word anything before. It's like watching a tiger paint its nails.

I look at the suitcases.

Then at the bulging cardboard boxes. The clear shelves. The cleanness of the kitchen. The masking tape and marker pens and Tabitha's crib, dismantled and propped up against the living-room wall.

Oh *sugar cookies*.

They're not cleaning at all.

They're *leaving.*

"We have news, Harriet," Dad confirms, grinning and putting his arm around my shoulders. "Massive news. *Epic* news. In fact, it's the most epic-est news that's ever happened ever."

Epic-est?

"*Will you please just tell me*!"

"Harriet," Dad shouts, exploding into the air like a firework: "WE ARE MOVING TO AMERICA!"

13

We each blink approximately 15,000 times a day. In the following silence I use up a week's worth, minimum.

I'm desperately trying to piece that sentence into an order that makes sense, but it's not working. AMERICA TO MOVING ARE WE. TO AMERICA WE ARE MOVING. WE TO AMERICA MOVING ARE.

With the best grammar skills in the world, they all kind of mean the same thing.

"B-but you can't just leave me here," I stammer. "I don't know how to work the oven properly. I don't know the code for the burglar alarm."

"31415," Dad says promptly.

"The first five numbers of *pi*?" At least that should be easy to remember.

"You're coming with us, Harriet," Annabel says calmly. "How ridiculous do you think we are?"

Dad has a piece of burnt pizza stuck to his knee.

I'm not going to answer that.

"But there isn't time," I state stupidly. "School starts next week."

"It's not for a holiday, sweetheart. It'll be for six months, at least."

"I got a job!" Dad shouts, jumping into the air again. "I'm going to be head copywriter at a top American advertising agency! I am no longer a draining sap on the life-source of this family!"

I thought Dad quite enjoyed sitting around in his dressing gown, losing his temper at people on the television and eating red jelly out of a big bowl.

"But *when*?"

"Tomorrow afternoon," Annabel says, face getting blotchier by the second. "Sweetheart, we didn't have a choice. It was that or they'd give it to another candidate. We're leaving a lot of stuff here and Bunty's going to take care of the house."

I don't think 'Bunty', 'house' and 'care' have ever been put together in a sentence before. She's going to sell it, or burn it down, or cover it with glitter paint and glue feathers to the windows.

I'm definitely going to have to hide the cat.

"Your father's new company is getting you a tutor," Annabel continues gently. "That way you won't miss anything and you can slip straight into sixth form when you get back."

I blink at her a few more thousand times.

"Your father has to take it, Harriet," Annabel adds when I still don't say anything. "He's been out of work for nine months, and New York will give him the break he needs. Plus –" she clears her throat – "we've, umm, run out of savings. We can't afford for both of us to be out of work any longer."

"New York? The job is in *New York*?"

What am I supposed to say?

That I've spent the entire summer making carefully laminated plans and timetables for the next academic year?

That I have a pencil case full of brand-new stationery I haven't used yet?

That their timing couldn't be worse and I hate them I hate them I hate them?

I'm just opening my mouth to say precisely all of that when I see a familiar expression on their faces. The Harriet's-About-to-Throw-a-Tantrum look. The Hide-the-Breakables look. The We'll-Need-to-Buy-New-Door-Hinges look.

And then I see what's underneath it.

Under the nerves, they both look sad. Worried. Tired.

Dad's excitement suddenly doesn't look so real any more. It looks like he's faking it, to try and make us all believe in it. Including him.

They don't want to leave.

They *have* to.

"I think," I say, taking a deep breath. "That I may need a few minutes to think about this."

And – trying to ignore my parents' astonishment – I turn my back, grab Hugo out of his basket and quietly walk upstairs to my bedroom.

14

OK, I am never laminating anything again.

Ever.

The first thing I do is lie on my bed with my nose in Hugo's fur and try to slow-breathe, the way Nick taught me to for times like this.

i.e. when I'm about to throw a wobbler.

Then I sit up, grab a pad off my desk and slowly write:

Reasons to Move to New York

Frankly, this should be the easiest list I've ever written.

It's the eighth-biggest city in the world. It has 8,336,697 people and 4,000 individual street-food vendors. It has been the setting for more than 20,000 films, and it has the lowest crime rate of the twenty-five largest cities in America. The rents are some of the highest in the world, and the wages totally insufficient.

How do I know all this? Because I'm fascinated by the city, just like everyone else. And because every time I watch reruns of *Friends* I go online to try and work out how they all survive, financially.

This could be an enormous adventure. Bigger than modelling. Bigger than Moscow. Bigger than Tokyo. In six months, I'd become a local. A resident. *One of them.*

And I mean that quite literally. Thirty-five million Americans share DNA with at least one of the 102 pilgrims who arrived from England on the *Mayflower* in 1620. We're pretty much blood relatives anyway.

Plus I'd get my very own tutor, who I will refer to as my 'governess'. I could learn to speak Latin and sing about whiskers on kittens or spoonfuls of sugar and be gently guided by the hand through my formative years, learning to embroider.

But for some reason, I can't make myself write any of that down.

Instead, I chew on my pencil and scribble:

Reasons Not to Move to New York

My life is here.

This is my *home*.

Everything I love is here.

Nat and Toby are here. Nick is here, albeit sporadically. My dog is here, my school is here, my bedroom is here. My memories are here: the corner of the garden where Nat and I used to build forts out of bed sheets, and the washing line I trained Hugo with when he was a puppy, and the area that used to be an expensive plant before I ran over it with my tricycle.

My books are here, my fossils, my photo-montage wall, the cold dent in the wall I lie against when it's hot in the middle of the night.

The road where Nick and I ran through the rain.

The bush outside where Toby waits for me.

The bench where Nat waits for me at the end of my road, in exactly the same position.

I love my life as it is, and I just want everything to stay exactly the same.

I chew on my pencil and stare at the wall.

Except… it's not going to, is it?

Alexa has my diary, and humiliation levels at school are about to reach unprecedented levels. For the first time ever, I'll have to handle her alone.

My modelling agency has already forgotten who

I am.

I haven't heard a peep from my former agent, Wilbur, for weeks.

Nick hasn't called me.

And then my stomach twists uncomfortably.

Nat.

Because it doesn't matter how many schedules and lists I write to try and keep us together, things are about to change. As soon as term starts, Nat is going to make new college friends and she's going to start a new college life.

A life full of fashion people who know things about colour-coordination and handbag shapes; a grown-up life full of parties and shopping and *coffee or something.* A life where inventing codes and making choreographed dances in the living room just aren't on the plans any more.

A life without me.

Pretty soon, the pigeon and the monkey are going to start wanting to fly and climb without each other, and the gap between us is going to get bigger and bigger.

Until one of us falls straight through.

Right now, I have a strong feeling that person is going to be me.

Slowly, I take my pencil out of my mouth and spit out a few bits of yellow paint.

And then – painfully, carefully – I write:

<u>Reasons to Move to New York</u>

I don't want to get left behind.

15

"What are we going to do?" I hear Annabel say quietly as I slip back downstairs with Hugo chasing after me. "Did you *see* the way Harriet reacted?"

Dad sighs.

"She responded calmly, with thought and consideration. I've never been so frightened in my entire life."

You have got to be kidding me.

Just *once* in fifteen years I respond to unexpected news in a mature fashion, and all I've successfully achieved is terrifying my parents.

"Ahem," I say at the door. Maybe I should slam it a few times, just to reassure them.

They both look up.

"Wait," Dad says, looking me up and down. "Why isn't Harriet wearing an appropriately themed costume, Annabel? Where's the top hat and walking stick and monocle?"

"Go on then," Annabel says, nodding to the seat next to her. "Hit us with the Anti-American Powerpoint Presentation, Harriet. I've cleared a space on the table especially."

She's even got the extension lead out so I can plug in my laptop.

A little part of me wishes I'd given it a shot. Apparently twenty-seven per cent of Americans believe we never landed on the moon. That would have been a really excellent way to start.

I stand in the middle of the room with Hugo sitting quietly by my feet and clench and unclench my fists. I'm about to say goodbye to everything I know. Every person. Every brick.

Every piece of my life.

"Let's do it," I say. "Let's move to America."

"Oh," Annabel says, dropping her head into her hands. "Oh, thank *God.*"

"It's a trick," Dad says, squinting at me. "I want to know where my daughter is, Mature Stranger. I bet she's locked upstairs in a wardrobe. I demand you let her back out again in three or four hours' time once we've had a nice quiet cup of tea and some lunch."

I stick my tongue out at him.

"Oh, there she is," Dad grins. "Phew."

"Seriously?" Annabel says. "You're not just saying that, Harriet? You really want to come?"

"Yes," I say firmly. "I do."

My parents both assess me with blank, surprised expressions. Then – in one seamless movement – they jump simultaneously off the sofa and tackle me into a hug with Tabitha tucked carefully between us.

"YESSSS!!" Dad shouts, grabbing my sister's little hand and punching the air with it. "In your *face*, boring old England! The Manners are taking over *Ameeerrricaa*!"

I smile into my parents' shoulders.

I can change my plans. But I can't change my family.

And this way, I'll leave everything behind before it gets the chance to do the same to me.

16

Ways to Tell Your Friends You're Emigrating

1. "I've been given a secret FBI mission and it involves a meteor and there's nobody else who can save the world, so I'll be gone for six months..."
2. "I'm afraid I've accidentally consumed a potion that will render me invisible for the next six months..."
3. "I've found a portal to another universe and it's my duty to explore it, so I'll be back in six months..."

Instead, I opt for the truth.

The truth, and closing my eyes tightly.

When Nat is hurt, she gets angry, and when she gets angry she throws things. There's a pair of high heels in close proximity, and there's a good chance they are about to get wedged into me permanently.

Finally, I open one eye and peer cautiously through my eyelashes.

Nat's still sitting on her bedroom floor, surrounded by a heap of clothes. Her first words when I entered the room were: "According to *Elle* I need a capsule wardrobe, Harriet. Twelve items that can be mixed and matched to create a seamless and coordinated outfit choice for any occasion so as to achieve maximum sartorial efficiency."

There's an endangered language in Peru called Chamicuro, and I think I'd have had more chance of understanding this greeting if Nat had just opted for using that instead.

"Are you OK?" I ask, after the silence that follows my bombshell.

"What do you mean you're *emigrating*?"

Pink splodges are starting to climb up Nat's throat and on to her cheeks. She's gripping the sleeve of a jumper so tightly it looks like it's about to get ripped off. "Like a... *woodpecker*?"

I don't think Nat's been paying attention to any of the recent documentaries we've been watching.

"Woodpeckers tend to stay very much in the same place, Nat." I sit carefully on the floor next to her. "You're thinking of King Penguins."

"But... *forever*?"

"Well..." I may have slightly over-egged the pudding. "Not exactly *forever*. Six months, if we're being precise."

The pink flush climbs higher and higher until Nat's ears look totally separate from the rest of her face, like Mr Potato Head.

And then – in one sweeping motion – she jumps up and the entire pile of clothes falls over.

"Oh my *God*," she shouts, gripping her hands together. "Harriet, isn't this just the best news *ever*? You're *so lucky*!" Nat starts leaping around the room, picking things up and spinning dreamily around with them. "You'll have your own doorman. You can eat hot dogs *every day*. You can find the grate where Marilyn Monroe's dress blew up and copy her."

"You can go to the Museum of Modern Art and study *The Persistence of Memory* by Salvador Dali," a voice says from outside the bedroom. "I've heard it's disappointingly small."

I open Nat's door.

"Toby, how long have you been here?"

"Long enough," Toby says happily, wandering in. "Although this news *does* mean I'll have to reorganise my stalking plans. Would you consider wearing a tracking device? That way I can just follow you online from the comfort of my own room."

I stare at them in dismay.

Aren't there supposed to be tears? Recriminations? *How could you do this to me?* and *What is my life supposed to be like without you in it?*

"OOOH!" Nat shouts at the top of her voice. "You can see where Calvin Klein was born and Leo DiCaprio lives!"

"You can visit the Museum of Math in Brooklyn."

"You can stand outside shop windows wearing lots of costume jewellery and eat pastries," Nat sighs, her eyes lit up. "You can see celebrities buying sandwiches *every day*."

"Hopefully," Toby adds, "you will not be one of the 419 murders that happen per 100,000 people in the city. Statistically, the odds are in your favour."

I blink.

If I'd known the impact of me leaving the country would be so slight, I'd have started training to be an astronaut some time ago.

"I'm glad you're both so delighted."

"Harriet," Nat laughs, putting an arm round me. "Six months is nothing. Although it does suck that you're going before your birthday – maybe you can have second-round celebrations when you get back, like Kate Moss or the Queen. And you'll be having so much fun it will just whizz past."

"It's only 184 days," Toby agrees, nodding enthusiastically. "4,416 hours. 264,960 minutes. I can invest the time wisely and think up a *really* excellent plan for when you get back."

As mature and supportive as they're being, I can't help wishing I was having a shoe thrown at my head. Or an eyeshadow compact.

At least then I'd know they'd miss me.

"Exactly," I say in my fakest, sunniest voice. "It's all very exciting. Anyway, I've got some packing to do and…"

My phone starts ringing.

Oh, thank *goodness*. My parents have finally got their interruptive timing spot on.

"Oops," I say loudly as I grab my phone out of my pocket. "I should probably take this outs—"

There are five million hairs all over the human body, and suddenly every single one of mine is standing on end.

Because it's not my parents.

It's Nick.

17

July 8th

"Are you sure?" I said doubtfully. "I'm not really on the list."

Nick laughed.

"You're on my list," he said, putting his arm around me. "Admittedly it's a really short one and for the next few hours your name is –" he looked at the silver ticket in his hands – "*Isobel Marigolden*."

I stared at the enormous warehouse.

It looked like it was still under construction. There were dark grey bars lining the ceiling, and blotches of white paint on the floor. Dirty plastic sheets were hanging in grimly lit sections at the back. Down the middle was a wide, shabbily painted silver strip and hard metal seats neatly lined the two longest sides of the room.

I sat down nervously.

"Can I come backstage with you?" I asked. "Maybe

I can help you get ready."

Nick gently picked me up and moved me three seats along and two rows back.

"You can't just sit where you like at a Prada fashion show, Harriet," he laughed. "And backstage there are going to be thirty boys in dirty underpants and mismatched socks. I'm not entirely sure you'd want to see that, even if the designer allowed it."

The boy's PE changing room at school sounded eerily similar. "Good point."

"So can you wait here?"

"I have this," I said, waving *Anna Karenina*. "I can probably sit for three whole days happily."

"*If you look for perfection, you'll never be content*," Nick said in a bizarre voice.

My eyes widened. "OK, a) you've read *Anna Karenina*? and b) that was possibly the single worst attempt at a British accent I've ever heard."

"That's because it was Russian," Nick said, raising an eyebrow. "And yes, I've read it. Or, you know: looked at the pictures really hard. I am a model, after all."

He smiled and leant down to kiss my nose.

"I'll wait," I said, flushing and opening the book, which I suddenly liked a billion times more because it now had Nick in every single line.

"Thank you." My boyfriend gave me another quick kiss on the lips. "I'll see you later, my little geek."

Over the next two hours, the room filled with people; slowly at first, and then in great, noisy swarms.

People in shiny black, people in red lace, people in white shirts with pointy collars. People who knew exactly where they were supposed to sit and were doing it without complaining about the hardness of the seats.

Then the room got very quiet and very dark. Music started pumping and lights started flashing. The dirty plastic sheets parted.

And out walked the boys, one by one.

They slunk to the front of the room, stopped, stared, turned and slunk back out again like prowling, pointy-hipped wolves. Dozens of them: angular and floppy-haired and stern. In sharp silver shirts and grey suits; black jackets and blue ties.

As the music vibrated, I could feel my stomach clenching.

I miss this, I suddenly realised.

I missed the music I didn't recognise and the bright lights and the dark audience. I missed the bustle and panic and noise in a room somewhere behind us. I missed the excitement and the bright eyes and the rustle of papers as people made notes.

I missed Wilbur and his ridiculous outfits and his made-up language. I missed Rin and Kylie Minogue, the sock-wearing cat who hated going for walks. I missed Tokyo and being transformed by stylists. I even slightly missed the terrifying Yuka Ito.

But most of all I missed Nick.

Suddenly, the plastic sheets parted and out walked another boy. A dark-haired, olive-skinned boy in a sharp black jacket with a bright silver collar. His face was set, his dark eyes were narrowed, his mouth was clenched. He strode towards us with firm, straight steps: purposeful. Furious.

I blinked as this angry, tense stranger pounded down the catwalk. There wasn't a single twinkle or slouch. Not a jot of laughter or crinkle around his eyes.

Two hundred people watched keenly as my boyfriend got to the end of the catwalk, stopped and posed.

The blue whale has a heart big enough for a human to crawl through its ventricles. For just a few seconds, my heart felt so big, a blue whale could have swum through mine.

I waited for Nick to turn towards me. To notice me in the crowd.

Finally, just before he started back towards the curtains, he looked straight at me.

He winked.

And – just like that – I had my Lion Boy back.

18

I have never left a house as quickly as I leave Nat's.

Seriously.

If it had been on fire, I doubt I could have moved faster.

"Nick?" I say breathlessly as soon as I've shut the front door. "Nick? Are you there?"

Then I try to rephrase it so I sound a bit less desperate. "I mean, hi, whatever, how are you?"

"Hey," he laughs warmly. "And *whatever* to you too."

Apparently butterflies need an ideal body temperature of between eighty-five and one hundred degrees to fly. I must be exactly the right habitat, because my entire body is suddenly full of them. Red ones, blue ones, green ones, white ones. Fluttering like a rainbow inside me.

Then I remember the silence over the last few days.

"How's Africa?" I say, and the butterflies suddenly

go very still.

"Harriet, I'm so sorry. I've been out in the desert on a shoot, and there was zero reception. I even got the photographer to drive me to the nearest village, and there was *still* nothing. How did you do? I want to know *everything.*"

A wave of relief hits me so strongly that I have to temporarily lean against a statue that Nat's mum thinks is Andromeda but is actually Artemis just to get my breath back.

Roughly forty-three per cent of Africa is desert, and it hadn't occurred to me for a single second Nick might be stuck in *any* of it.

"It went kind of brilliantly," I say, giving him a brief update on my result.

"I'm so proud of you."

I beam at the phone, and then at the sky, and then at a random passing squirrel. I'm so warm the butterflies have given up flying and have started sunbathing instead.

"So," and this time it's a real, genuine question, "what *is* Africa like?"

"Hot. Lots of weird-looking tall creatures that can't run properly hanging around with long necks and eyelashes and horns coming out of their heads."

"Giraffes?"

"I was aiming for 'models'," Nick laughs. "But yeah, there's some of them wandering about too."

I giggle like an idiot.

Normally this would be the point where I'd break into an array of interesting facts. For instance, did you know that giraffes have four stomachs, and their spots are like fingerprints and no two giraffes have the same pattern?

Or that their necks are too short for their heads to reach the ground so they have to drink water by squatting?

Or that they are the only animal who moves two legs on one side of the body and then two on the other to walk?

Instead I clear my throat.

"Come on then," Nick says. He's smiling: the words are all stretched and snug. "Hit me with it."

"Hmm?"

"Whatever is preventing you from telling me multiple facts about giraffes right now."

Sugar cookies.

"I'm… umm." I cough. "I think that…"

Of *course*. I should be approaching my news about America from a totally different angle.

"Nick, did you know Admiral Horatio Nelson started dating Emma Hamilton in 1798, and then went away for two years to fight the Napoleonic Wars? They wrote a lot of letters, and their budding relationship wasn't affected in the slightest and remained strong and beautiful throughout."

"Is that so?"

"And OK, he was fatally wounded by a musket ball at the Battle of Trafalgar in 1805 and died before he could see her again, but that's not really the point." *Wrap it up, Harriet.* "So…"

"Harriet," Nick says. "Are you going away to fight the Napoleonic wars?"

"No."

"Are you at risk of getting hit by a stray musket ball fired from a French ship in suburban Hertfordshire?"

"No."

"Are you planning on dying next to a man named Hardy and then having your body preserved in a large barrel of brandy?"

My boyfriend knows a lot more about Admiral Nelson than I thought he would. "No."

"Then you probably don't need to sound so worried."

OK.

I need to pull this out all at once, before it gets all green and liquidy like the splinter in Year Two.

"I'm leaving England," I say quickly. "My family is moving to New York for six months and I'll be gone before you're home but I'll buy some pretty stationery and write you some poignant and heartbreaking letters and get novelty stamps and—"

"Harriet, that's *brilliant,*" Nick interrupts. It's a genuine, delighted *brilliant.*

I blink.

Right. It's bad enough that Toby and Nat are thrilled by my departure, but my *boyfriend*? He's supposed to be making impassioned speeches on the edge of bridges about the darkness of life without me. Not throwing a mini verbal celebration and cracking out the Harriet's Finally Leaving banners.

"Fine," I snap, "if that's the way you feel then you can just—" Nick's laughter stops me mid-rage.

"That's not what I meant, Harriet. New York Fashion Week starts soon, so I'm going to be there too. I get more modelling jobs in America than anywhere else. I'll be able to see you loads. This is really brilliant news."

I pull my phone away from my face while I get my emotions back under control.

"Harriet? You haven't been attacked by any other

kind of artillery, have you?"

"Really?" I say. "You'll really be in New York?"

"Of course," Nick laughs. "It'll take a bit more than a couple of miles and an inch of water to stop me seeing you."

I impulsively kiss my phone, even though Nick is seriously underestimating the size of the Atlantic Ocean.

"Harriet, did you just kiss your phone?"

"Umm. No. My cheek is just very... sucky."

"Ah," Nick laughs. "I've always had a weakness for girls with sucky cheeks..." There's a shout in the background. "Shoot. I have to go. Apparently the elephant I'm riding doesn't like my voice."

"You rang me from the back of an *elephant*?"

"Yeah. I suddenly got reception and I miss you."

"I miss you too."

We beam at each other in silence. I don't know how I know he's beaming, but I just do.

"Nick," I say, taking a deep breath. "I I—"

"Got to go. I'll see you in New York, Freckles."

And the phone goes dead.

19

<u>Harriet and Nick's Romantic New York Plans (HNRNYP)</u>

- *A horse-drawn carriage ride around Central Park.*
- *A kiss on top of the Empire State Building at sunset.*
- *A cruise around the Statue of Liberty.*
- *Kissing while ice-skating at the Rockefeller Center.*
- *A visit to the famous LOVE statue, with kissing.*

And yes, there's quite a lot of kissing, but I just quite like it, OK?

By the next morning I am desperate to leave.

In fact I'm so keen to get to New York I've asked my

parents if I can go ahead without them.

"Do you think we're *insane*?" Dad replies.

"Yes," I tell him promptly and focus on packing with renewed enthusiasm.

Everything is ready. The house is clean. The electrics are off. The last of our belongings are being lobbed into a large van by a man who is tutting about our 'ineffective boxing skills'.

A note has been left for Bunty saying DO NOT TRY TO DYE, BURN OR REUPHOLSTER ANYTHING. PLEASE FEED THE CAT ON A DAILY BASIS. Hugo has been sent to live temporarily with a delighted Toby while we get his American passport sorted.

And I've spent the evening putting together my own little box of home souvenirs to take with me. A 1,000-yen note with a picture of Mount Fuji on it. A T-shirt with a photo on the front of Rin and me riding a computer-generated unicorn. An American-English dictionary from Toby. An envelope containing a newspaper cutting of me sat with Fleur on the catwalk in Moscow, and a photo I took of Wilbur in Tokyo wearing wing-shaped sunglasses. A photo of me and Nat in cowboy hats and moustaches.

Finally, I get out a brand-new scrapbook, write HARRIET AND NICK'S AUTUMN (OR 'FALL') OF

LOVE on the front and decorate it with a lot of hearts.

There are going to be so many things to stick in it.

Museum tickets and love letters and pressed flowers picked on our moonlit strolls in Central Park. The wrapper from a chocolate he unexpectedly pulls out of his pocket. A photo of us, playing with perspective so it looks like the Statue of Liberty is in our hands.

I'm just contentedly tucking the toy lion he bought me into the corner when my phone beeps.

H, I can't make it to the airport! I forgot we have initiation day at college. I'M SO SORRY. Skype me when you get there! Love you so much. Nat xxx

I look blankly at the message, then text back:

No probs! Goodbyes are rubbish anyway, aren't they? Speak soon! Love you too! H xxx

"Ready?" Annabel says as I pop my little shoebox of memories into my backpack, zip it all up and sling it over my shoulders.

"Ready," I say quietly.

America, here I come.

20

All I'm going to say about the ensuing journey is: two-month-old babies and long-distance flights are not a relaxing combination.

I have a lot of things to do.

Documentaries about turbulence to watch, crosswords to complete, key landmarks to look for out of the window, a long and confusing list of American spellings to learn.

Unfortunately, Tabitha has other plans.

I'd never realised she liked England so much, but she's obviously quite attached. As soon as the air steward starts showing us the emergency exits, she starts yelling and doesn't draw breath for the rest of the journey.

Apparently women in Ancient Greece made blusher from a mixture of crushed mulberries and strawberries. By the time we land, seven hours later, Annabel is so flushed it looks like she's made a bath of it and jumped straight in.

"Tabitha," she says firmly as we collect our bags from the overhead lockers. She wipes her forehead with her jumper sleeve. "I love you more than life itself, but if you scream again like that on public transport I will leave you in the hold, OK?"

Tabby blinks at her with wide eyes, hissy-fit over.

"Don't give me that look, missy," Annabel sighs. "I've had eleven years of practice with your father."

Dad leans over Tabitha. "She's *nailing* it," he says approvingly, tickling her tummy. "That's my girl. Work that twinkle."

My sister squeaks and kicks her little legs like a frog attempting the high jump. An air steward stops by us in the aisle.

"Oh ma *Gahd,*" she says, putting a hand on her chest. "Your baby is *the cutest*. Isn't she *just adorable*? I could *eat her up.*"

We look at Tabitha with narrow, exhausted eyes.

Dad put her in a Union Jack onesie especially for the journey. Her red hair is all curly and fluffy, her cheeks are all pink, the toy rabbit I bought her is propped on her shoulder and she's blowing enthusiastic bubbles like a tiny goldfish.

Tabby does, indeed, look adorable.

They were obviously working in a different part of the plane twenty minutes ago. There was an entirely different word for her then.

"Please go for it," Annabel says drily. "She goes well with ketchup and a bit of oregano."

The air steward's eyes get very round. "Ha," she says awkwardly. "Hahaha. You Brits are *hilarious.*"

And then she hurries away as fast as possible.

This is *it*, I realise as we push ourselves through the enormous, shiny JFK airport.

It's like we've just hit the restart button.

It feels like London, except bigger. Glossier. Cleaner. The floors are sparkly and everything is ordered and in neat lines. There's a twang in the air, and the biggest American flag I have seen in my life is hanging from the ceiling.

We all stand and stare at it in silence.

"Well," Annabel says finally, "at least we don't need to check that we're in the right country."

"Unless it's a trick," Dad shrugs. "That would be pretty funny, right? *Welcome to Australia! Hahaha GOTCHA!*"

"You have a nice day, now!" a lady in an airport outfit says chirpily as she walks past.

"You too!" Dad shouts after her. "Thank you so much! How extremely thoughtful of you! Do you have anything fun planned?"

She looks in alarm at the airport security.

Dad signs a few bits of paper and then leads us in excitement outside into an enormous car park and towards a large silver car. It's so enormous it makes our car at home look like something a toy drives.

"A *Dodge Durango*?" Dad says. "They sent me a *Dodge Durango*?" He starts running his hands along it. "Front engine, rear-wheel drive. Harriet, this is built on the same platform as a Jeep Grand Cherokee!"

This is possibly the only fact in the world I've ever heard that I'm not even vaguely interested in.

"Are we prepared for an adventure?" Annabel says, popping Tabitha into the car seat and winking at me.

"Of course," I say with a deep breath.

And we start the drive into the bright lights of the Big Apple.

21

According to the internet, New York City has:

- *More than 20,000 restaurants and 1,700 bars.*
- *231 skyscrapers.*
- *Between 1,700 and 1,800 parks.*
- *3,492 clothing stores.*
- *11,871 traffic lights.*

I don't want to be rude, but frankly you'd think they'd be a bit more noticeable.

Fifty minutes into the journey I still can't see any of them. I've got my nose pressed against the window and three guidebooks on my lap, but the roads are getting wider and the buildings are getting smaller and the people fewer, rather than the other way round.

There's a dodgy-looking restaurant on the side of the road, and an enormous superstore with flashing lights on the other. There are some of the biggest trucks I have ever seen in my life, blowing their horns at each other.

So far, skyscrapers spotted: 0.

Parks: 0.

Little ladies with push-along shopping trolleys: 6.

The Empire State Building is 381 metres high. It really shouldn't be this difficult to see.

Another twenty minutes pass, and then another thirty, and I'm finally starting to lose my brand-new shiny patience. I know I'm supposed to be acting like an adult now, but clearly my parents don't know how to navigate America.

"Are we lost?" I say helpfully, leaning forward and sticking my head in between the seats. "Because if you need help reading a map, I have a Brownie badge that will confirm I'm quite good at it."

Silence.

I look back at the guidebook. "I think we should have gone over the Hudson River by now. Are you sure we're going in the right direction?"

Then I see my parents glance at each other.

"What's going on?" I say as the car starts pulling into a tiny little road surrounded by small, solitary houses made out of white, blue or grey slats and shutters around the windows and pointy roofs. There's a dog sitting on the porch, casually licking itself, and a ginger cat perched on the fence opposite, staring at it in total disgust.

One of the curtains twitches, and a small boy on a bike rides slowly past. Another silver SUV drives by with a family inside it.

At random intervals on this road there is a tiny hairdresser's called CURL UP AND DYE, a small mechanical shop called JONNO'S AUTOPARTS and somewhere that sells chicken called MANDYS.

On the corner is a tiny church the shape of a box, with an enormous blue sign that says GREENWAY CHURCH OF CHRIST.

And then, in small letters underneath:

TRY JESUS! IF YOU DON'T LIKE HIM, THE DEVIL WILL HAVE YOU BACK.

Dad pulls into a driveway and with a quick flick of his wrist turns the engine off.

"Are we visiting someone?" I say curiously, rolling down the window. "Or maybe picking up the keys to our super-cool Manhattan loft-with-a-view?"

There's another silence.

And then I can feel it: sticky alarm rising from

my feet upwards until my whole body feels full of something explosively panicky.

"This isn't New York," I say slowly as Annabel and Dad open their car doors. We're parked outside a small grey house with neat little hedges and a pointed window in the roof. "This isn't New York. We're nowhere near it."

"Umm." Annabel clears her throat. "Yes. About that..."

I can feel the panic starting to surge into my head until all I can hear is an incoherent, wordless roar.

"This is *our house*?"

Annabel inclines her head. Just slightly enough to mean *uh-huh*.

"But... you *said*." The roar is getting louder. "You *said* your job was in New York, Dad."

"My job *is* in New York," he says, turning around in the driver's seat. It's a token gesture, because he's not actually looking at me. He's staring at a bit of car seat to the side of my left ear. "But the house... kind of isn't."

As if half of it is here, and half of it is situated in Central Park with a magic tunnel between the two.

"We're not staying in a cool skyscraper New York loft apartment in the middle of Manhattan?"

"No."

"With a doorman who always forgets our names even though we've told him lots of times?"

"No."

"With our very own gold and glass elevator with a mahogany floor?"

"Umm." Dad and Annabel glance at each other. "That's not really how skyscrapers are, sweetheart."

I am never going to trust an adult again. This is exactly like when I was five and found them scoffing the mince pies I left out for Santa.

"So where are we?"

"Greenway," Annabel says quietly. "New York is only an hour and a half away by train."

Only an hour and a half away by train.

Nick is an hour and a half away.

The Empire State Building is an hour and a half away.

The ice rink is an hour and a half away, as is Central Park and romantic horse-drawn carriages and boat rides and the Statue of Liberty.

Marilyn Monroe's famous grate and the Museum of Modern Art are an hour and a half away.

The buildings, the lights, the museums, the galleries: everything I've got planned for the next six months.

My new *life* is an hour and a half away.

And I'm stuck in the middle of nowhere.

My parents tricked me into giving up everything I care about and everyone I love for this.

For *nothing*.

I try to take a deep breath. *Be calm, Harriet. Be mature. Be the adult you know you should be growing into and respond in an orderly and—*

"OH MY GOD!" I scream, opening the car door and jumping out of it. I'm so furious my hands are shaking as if they're resting on top of a road drill. "I HATE YOU! I HATE YOU, I HATE YOU, YOU'VE RUINED MY LIFE AND I NEVER WANT TO SPEAK TO EITHER OF YOU, EVER AGAIN!"

And I run straight into the garden behind the house and burst into tears.

22

On the upside, at least my parents have got the old Harriet they know and love back.

On the downside, they won't be able to enjoy it because I am never talking to them, ever again.

It's a good thing the American legal services are so comprehensive, because I am going to divorce them and there's not a single thing they can do about it. I'll start the procedure just as soon as I come out of the enormous bush I've crawled into.

I curl into a ball and cry silently into my knees.

Maybe I can go back.

Maybe Bunty will look after me.

How long does it take to book a new flight to England? How can I let school know that I need my place back immediately?

Everyone is going to laugh at me because I couldn't make it in America, like some kind of failed pop star.

"Harriet?" A blonde head pops into the bush, and

then a ginger head joins it. "Shuffle over."

I don't shuffle over, but somehow Annabel and Dad manage to squeeze into the bush next to me.

Tabitha has been propped up in her car-seat just outside the bush and is staring at us with a strangely wise, owl-like expression.

Maybe I should have screamed for the entire plane journey too.

"We know this probably isn't what you were hoping for, sweetheart," Dad says, putting an arm round me. "And we're sorry."

"No, you're not," I snuffle into my shorts. My nose is damp, and leaves a shiny trail. "You lied."

"We didn't *lie*," Annabel explains gently. "We just... didn't totally elucidate the facts accurately."

"Same thing."

"Not legally, it isn't." She sighs. "Sweetheart, I thought you understood that. We can't afford the rent in New York."

I *knew* there was no way a normal family could live in Manhattan. Somebody needs to sue every American sitcom ever made.

"But what am I supposed to do for six months in *Greenway*?"

"Harriet," Dad says, "Greenway has almost exactly

the same population as our hometown in England. We haven't moved you to Outer Mongolia."

"I wish you *had*. They have two-humped indigenous Bactrian camels there."

Dad and Annabel laugh, even though I'm being totally serious. A thirsty camel can drink thirty gallons of water in thirteen minutes. That would at least be something to watch.

"Give us a chance?" Dad says softly. "I'm sure there's a whole bunch of stuff to do here. I think I saw a bowling alley around the corner."

I scowl at him furiously.

"Please?" Annabel says. "For us?"

I glare at them, and quickly run through the alternatives in my head.

It doesn't look promising. There aren't a lot of options available for a penniless fifteen-year-old on the wrong side of the world, with nothing but a satchel and a guidebook to her name.

I'm resourceful but I'm not Pocahontas.

"Fine," I say in a small voice. "I'll try."

"Thank you," Annabel says, kissing the top of my head. "We really appreciate how mature you're being, sweetheart."

"There's a door on the front porch you can give a

good slam, if you want."

I glare at Dad.

"Too soon?" he adds.

"Yes," I confirm.

"You know what?" Annabel says as she starts clambering back out of the bush. "I think you're going to be surprised, Harriet. There's always something interesting to be found if you just look hard enough."

23

I spend the next five days looking very hard *indeed*.

Here's what I discover:

Interesting Facts About Greenway

- *President Bush Senior once passed through on his way to somewhere else.*
- *The local minimart used to sell a chocolate biscuit called Magic Middles.*
- *It doesn't any more.*
- *Somebody once saw someone who looked a bit like Tom Cruise far away, from the side.*
- *It wasn't him.*

That's it.

As Dad heads out at the crack of dawn to his new job in the city, Annabel slowly transfers all the mess and chaos of our old house into our new house. And I put Tabitha into her buggy (or 'stroller') and venture into the local neighbourhood, asking questions and looking for somebody to be New Best Friends with.

It's a lot harder than I thought it would be.

"Oh *my*," the ancient hairdresser says on the third day when I've desperately gone in for a 'wash and dry', even though I obviously know how to wash and dry my own hair. She bends down to peer into the buggy. "What a *cutie*. How old is she?"

"Eight weeks exactly."

The hairdresser prods one of Tabby's fat cheeks. "She is the *spitting image* of you, honey."

"I know," I say proudly. "Did you know that a baby has 10,000 taste buds all over its mouth, not just on its tongue?"

There's a pause, and then the hairdresser looks me up and down. "And how old are *you*, sugar?" she says. "If you don't mind me asking?"

"Fifteen," I say even more proudly. "Nearly sixteen, though. My birthday's this week."

"Oh *honey*," she says, and that's the conversation over.

On the fourth day, I venture into MANDYS.

"Hello," I say to the girl behind the counter. She looks

a tiny bit older than me, but I like her rabbit earrings. "Did you know you're missing an apostrophe?"

She stares at me blankly. "*What?*"

"An apostrophe." I point at the sign. "This shop belongs to Mandy, right? So it's possessive. It should be MANDY-apostrophe-S." I think about it. "Unless all of your chickens are called Mandy, in which case it's grammatically accurate."

"I don't know what the chickens are called," she says flatly. "Oh, I've got one of them," she adds, pointing at Tabitha as she hands me a greasy paper bag.

I beam at her.

"They're nice, aren't they?" I say, poking my head over so I can stare fondly at Tabitha's sleeping face.

"Meh," the girl says, shrugging. "Bit of a mistake, if you ask me. I'd rather be out partying."

I couldn't agree less, but I nod anyway.

"Absolutely," I say. "But you can always just leave them at home, right?"

Her eyes widen.

I leave my name and email address on a piece of paper and ask her to write to me, but she doesn't.

In five days, Tabitha and I leave no stone unturned.

We say hello to the man at the car-repair garage. We say hello to his dog. We say hello to the old man weeding his garden. We go to the supermarket five times and lurk in the cereal aisle, saying hello to shoppers and reading all the bright boxes that say things like FROOT LOOPZ and HONEY SMACKZ and SMORZ. None of which look like something Annabel is going to let me eat first thing in the morning.

We sit on the side of the road and wait for somebody to ride past on a bike, and then we wave at them. We even consider going into the church, and then change our minds because they've altered their sign to say:

DON'T LET WORRIES KILL YOU.
LET THE CHURCH HELP.

Frankly, that's a little too ambiguous for my liking.

Finally, on the fifth day, we walk past a tiny park with a roundabout, three swings and a large slide. I can hear laughter from around the corner.

"Oh no," somebody shouts. "*No!* She didn't!"

"She so did! She was *all over him*!"

"That's gross. Like, literally gross. I could be sick on the floor, that's how gross it is."

I poke my head around the bush hopefully, and

there are six girls sitting on the slide: squidged into the bottom.

They appear to be my age exactly.

So I take a deep, calm breath, straighten my shoulders and start pushing the buggy towards them.

"Right, Tabitha," I say, pausing to pull the blanket down so they can see her sweet face. "Get your cutest charms ready. It's time for your big sister to make some new friends."

24

After a short deliberation, I opt for, "Heya."

I've seen quite a few American films, and this seems to be the most international greeting available.

Then I wait.

"*Heya,*" I say a little more loudly as they continue talking, pushing the buggy a bit closer.

Still nothing.

"HEY!" I shout, and – one by one – the girls turn around and stare at me.

"Hey, yourself," one of them says. "Who the hell are you?"

I clear my throat.

'Who the hell are you' obviously means something totally different in America. I'm not going to let a little cultural barrier get between me and an entire group of ready-made non-kissing soulmates.

"I'm Harriet Manners," I say brightly. "This is Tabitha." I point downwards. "We've just moved here from England. It's very nice to meet you all."

"Do you go to Greenway High?"

"No-ooo," I admit. "I study at home."

"Right." The girl with the black hair turns back to the group. "So, what's he like? I mean, is he like *super* ugly, or just a *bit* ugly?"

"Dude, he's banged-up."

"Oh no," I say. "Who did that to him? Is he OK? Violence is so horrible, isn't it?"

There's another silence, and then they all turn to face me again.

"Do you want to tell her, or shall I?"

I lean forward hopefully. "Tell me what?"

"It's cool that you're new and everything, but we're TASKEB: Taylor, Amanda, Shelby, Kelly, Emma and Brittany. We don't have room for more."

"But..." I blink. "If you put an H in there you could be TASHKEB. That sounds even better."

One of them laughs, and I flinch.

I know that laugh. It's the only thing that translates perfectly around the world without the need for a dictionary.

"And no offence," one of them adds, "but we definitely don't need no teenage *baby mama*."

What?

"N-no," I stammer, face starting to flush furiously. "I think there's been some kind of mis—"

"Are you dumb or something, dork?" the biggest one snaps. "We said *go away.*"

I blink at them a few times while I struggle for a witty response. I'm 5,000 miles away from home. How do they know I'm an idiot already?

"Actually," I say, lifting my chin as high as I can get it. "Dumb people can hear perfectly well. I think you mean *deaf.*"

Yeah, I think, flushing even harder. *That'll do it.*

And I push my sister back out of the playground, with the girls still laughing behind me.

25

I had assumed my social inadequacies were quite localised, but apparently they are perfectly capable of crossing the Atlantic unscathed.

It would be quite impressive if it weren't so incredibly depressing. I've completely lost the will to translate anything into American ever again.

"Hello, girls," Annabel says as Tabitha and I struggle back into the house. "Did you have fun?"

I look at Tabitha, and her chin immediately crumples and starts wobbling.

We are *so* on the same page.

Sadly, only one of us is allowed to act like a baby.

"It was OK," I lie, handing Tabitha back and sitting on a kitchen chair next to her. "I ate a lot of chicken that may or may not have been called Mandy."

"What a horrible name for a chicken. I'd have gone with Gertrude, or maybe Clementine."

Then Annabel lifts Tabitha up and gives her a little

kiss on the cheek. "So," she adds with a grin, "I have good news, and I have bad news. Which one do you want first?"

"Bad news, please," I say, kicking the table leg gently. "Seventy-five per cent of people go for bad news first, because then you can end on a high note."

Annabel nods. "Eminently sensible. In which case, your tutor is about to arrive. I'm afraid it's time to get back to studying."

My eyes widen, and I jump out of my seat.

Does my stepmother know me at all? My Latin-speaking, singing and potentially magical governess – sorry, home tutor – is the sole ray of illumination in an otherwise lightless existence.

"Brilliant," I cry, relief flooding through me. "So how good is the good news? Button-pressing interactive exhibition good, or just normal-exhibition good?"

"Button pressing," Annabel says, thrusting a small envelope at me. "Here."

I stare at it, and then squeak so loudly that Tabitha lets out a small, surprised burp.

"A new American SIM card," Annabel confirms as I leap up and start kissing it frantically. "And the Wi-Fi's up and running."

26

FROM: Hugo Manners
TO: Harriet Manners

Re: My New Abode

Dear Harriet,

Can you believe how quickly I've learnt to type? I am obviously a dog of extraordinary abilities, although I also ate Toby's father's Sunday pork chop by dragging it off the kitchen counter so I am currently a genius in disgrace.

As for Toby, he is having a wonderful time preparing for sixth form. He is looking forward to learning all kinds of things about quarks and leptons. And will try not to correct Mr Kemp too much, as apparently he doesn't like it.

I like my new temporary owner very much, by the way, especially as he doesn't mind when I lick his face in the morning.

Barks,
Hugo Manners and Toby Pilgrim

FROM: Natalie Grey
TO: Harriet Manners

Re: OH MY GOD

College is AMAZING. I went to the pre-term opening day and they told us we're gonna make our own dresses! Mine's going to be a blue one with frills around the bottom, I think.

I met a few nice girls who will be in my class, and I think you'd really like Jessica. She has green eyes and freckles and hair exactly the same colour as yours. We're going for coffee tomorrow.

How's NEW YORK? I've attached a celebrity map so you can sit outside their houses. TAKE PHOTOS.

Love you.

NxOxOxOxOxOxOx

FROM: Nick Hidaka
TO: Harriet Manners

I'm here!! Where are you?
LBxx

I read Nat's email three times – who the sugar cookies is Jessica, and why is she drinking my coffee? – and I write:

FROM: Harriet Manners
TO: Natalie Grey

It's GREAT! Will update later! Sooooooo busy exploring New York right now!
xx

FROM: Harriet Manners
TO: Toby Pilgrim

WHAT IS A LEPTON?! AND WHAT IS A QUARK?!

FROM: Harriet Manners

TO: Nick Hidaka

Long story! Ring me ASAP!! xx

I have literally never used so many forced exclamation marks in such a short space of time in my entire life.

I'm exhausted just looking at them.

"Harriet?" Annabel calls up the stairs as I pop my American number at the bottom and press SEND. "Miss Hall would like to meet you."

27

Now, I know quite a lot about governesses.

Thanks to Victorian literature and films on TV at Christmas, I have deduced that they are either pretty, warm and exuberant – Mary Poppins, Maria from *The Sound of Music* and Anna from *The King and I* – or small, plain and unappreciated, like Jane Eyre or Agnes Grey.

I'm also aware that they tend to like running off with the man of the house, but once they've met Dad I don't think that'll be a problem.

I bounce down the stairs and then impulsively bounce outside and grab a wild yellow flower growing next to the front door. Then I bounce through the hallway and into the living room.

Where I promptly stop bouncing.

My new governess is neither pretty nor small, meek nor potentially magical, shy nor about to burst into song at any given moment. She doesn't have a lamp in her handbag, or the malnourished gaze of a grown-up orphan with trust issues.

The woman standing in front of me is about six-foot two, with enormous shoulders and calves wider than my thighs. She's wearing khaki shorts, a white T-shirt, and is standing bolt upright, staring at me with the steady, intense gaze of somebody who knows how to punch a hole through a door.

"Uh," I say, suddenly nervous. I thought we'd be holding hands and swinging in circles by now, reciting Latin verbs. "Hello. I'm Harriet Manners. This is for you. It's a *Rudbeckia Hirta*, otherwise known as a Black-Eyed Susan."

Let's just say I had a lot of time on my hands last night and somebody left a local fauna and flora book in my bedroom.

"How nice," she says, grabbing the flower in her enormous hand and totally crushing it.

"Miss Hall comes with glowing references and the most incredible CV I've ever seen," Annabel says. "Harvard, Cambridge, a stint in Switzerland, the whole works."

My eyes widen.

Clearly I judged her far too quickly, like a magazine cover. But – on the other hand – isn't that kind of what they're there for?

"*Oooh,*" I say in excitement. "Which Cambridge college did you go to? I can't decide whether I want to go to Magdalene, like CS Lewis, or Trinity Hall, like Stephen Hawking. But then St John's has the most beautiful library and—"

"Harry," Miss Hall interrupts. "I don't like discussing my background with students. It creates a false level of intimacy and impedes the absorption of knowledge."

I blink. *Harry?*

"It's Harriet," I say as assertively as I can.

"I shall call you Harry," Miss Hall says sharply. "It saves time. Now," she adds, "I think we should start straight away." She looks at Annabel. "I prefer not to have parents around for the education of my students. They can be a distracting influence."

"Right," Annabel says. "Can I get you a cup of tea, or a biscuit, or a—"

"That won't be necessary," my governess says, pulling a backpack on to both shoulders. "I prefer to keep the mind clear to work at full capacity."

I exchange a delighted glance with Annabel. At this rate, I'm going to pass my A levels before Christmas.

"Excellent," Annabel concurs. "In that case, I'll leave you to get on with it." She kisses Tabitha's head.

"*One* of us appears to have pooped ourselves again and it's not me." She winks at me and closes the living-room door quietly behind her.

28

They say that fiction is the closest we ever get to magic.

Forget top hats and rabbits: open a book, and an entire world will pop out. And it doesn't matter whether it's full of dragons or Victorian orphans or wizards, you are immediately somewhere else and someone else.

Transported.

It's not like that with textbooks.

Open a physics A-level book or a biology syllabus and nothing will really happen. Read the periodic table, and you'll stay very much you, and very much in the same place.

But if stories are like magical top hats, textbooks are the wands that change everything. Because the more you know and the more you learn, the more *real life* opens up.

Trees aren't just green any more: they're full of cells

that contain the pigment chlorophyll that only uses the blue and red wavelengths of light.

A strawberry isn't a berry, but bananas and watermelons are.

Chalk isn't just chalk, it's trillions of microscopic skeleton fossils of plankton.

Fact by fact, step by step, the world unfolds, like one of the little origami flowers Rin used to make me, except the other way round.

And you realise *everything* is magic.

Without a word, I run to the corner of the room and pull out my special cardboard box. In it are piles and piles of brand-new textbooks. Coated in plastic, with shiny and unbroken spines. Each with hundreds of bright white pages filled with countless diagrams and facts, begging to be absorbed and annotated.

I take a deep, contented breath. It's like seeing a field of clean, unmarked snow and knowing you're about to get your footprints all over it.

"What do you want to start with?" I say, pulling out a pale blue book with butterflies on the cover. "I'm really keen to find out what a *lepton* and a *quark* are. Do you know?"

"Education is an adventure," Miss Hall says abruptly,

sitting on the sofa. "I cannot make the journey for you."

I couldn't have put it better myself.

So I pore happily through a few books and say:

"This one says a quark is one of the hypothetical basic particles, having charges whose magnitudes are one-third or two-thirds of the charge of an electron."

"Exactly," my governess agrees.

"And a lepton is any of a family of elementary particles that participate in a weak interaction."

"There you go. And how do you feel now?"

"A bit confused," I admit.

"I was given the impression that you were a clever girl, Harry. Have I been misled?"

I flush. Up to this point, I thought I was too.

"N-no," I stammer, picking another textbook up. "I've got top grades, Miss Hall. Straight A*s."

I'm not going to include technology. Nobody cares about my ability to sand things properly.

"Good," she says. "Because I will be extremely disappointed if I have to hold your hand throughout this process. I am an *academic*, not a babysitter."

I flush a little more.

"I know," I say more indignantly than I mean to. "And I don't need a babysitter."

"Then we understand each other. Read chapter sixteen, and in ten minutes I will test you on it."

I flip the physics textbook back open. It's a chapter on something called 'Damping'.

"But..." There are a lot of complicated-looking graphs, and something about *oscillating equilibriums*. "Don't you think that's a little—"

Miss Hall lifts her eyebrows. "If you can't keep up, Harry, I suggest we put these textbooks away and start again with Year 11. If you're not intellectually ready to move on, then I see no other option but to treat you like a child."

I've been called many, many names in my life, but *intellectually deficient* is not one of them.

"I'm ready," I say, lifting my chin slightly and thinking of all my favourite facts that I'd lovingly listed in my diary.

"It seems to me that you seem to lack what here in America we call *character*. I'm hoping you simply make a weak first impression."

I put my chin back down. "Sorry."

"Nothing can hold you back but yourself, Harry. Remember that. Now get on with it."

29

Here are some of the highlights of the next four hours:

- *I try to find the discriminant of a quadratic polynomial.*
- *I have to Google polynomial.*
- *And discriminant.*
- *And – just to make sure – quadratic.*
- *Miss Hall tells me I have very little 'spark' about me.*
- *I have to Google polynomial again because I forgot what it said.*

By the time I've waded through an entire chapter on nuclear fusion my brain feels like it's been dissolved in sodium hydroxide and then popped in a blender.

I am nowhere *near* as smart as I thought I was.

Finally, Miss Hall tells me that's enough 'easing in', tightens her backpack straps and leaves in a stomping march.

"How did it go?" Annabel says as I stagger up the stairs and stand, rubbing my eye, in the middle of the hallway.

Every single cell of my brain aches. A brain which – I've just discovered – doesn't actually have any nerve endings and therefore can't feel physical pain.

Right now, I am seriously starting to question that fact.

"Great," I say, putting my hand on the doorframe so I can yawn without falling over.

Annabel's sitting on the bathroom floor, wrestling Tabitha into a clean onesie. It looks like she's trying to fit an octopus into a sock: there are arms and legs *everywhere*. "So did you like Miss Hall?"

"Very much," I say, crawling on to the floor next to Annabel and sleepily putting my face against Tabitha's warm, round cheek. Then I close my eyes and listen to the comforting dripping of the tap.

Drrrrrip. Drrrrrip. Drrrrrip.

"Harriet?" I open my eyes. Annabel is frowning at me. "Is it too hard? Because if it is, just tell me and I'll have a word with Miss Hall. I don't want her exhausting you."

Too hard? What is that supposed to mean? Does

my own stepmother think I can't keep up?

"Why would it be too hard?" I mumble. "Nothing can hold me back but myself."

Annabel's frown deepens. "OK."

"Our future selves are only as good as our past selves believe we can be."

"...right." Annabel frowns a bit harder. "That doesn't really make any sense, but as long as you're happy."

I close my eyes again. "I'm going to get spectacular results," I murmur sleepily, "and pass with flying colours, just... you... wait... and..."

Drrrrip. Drrrrip. Drrrrrip.

It's funny, in the moment just before you fall asleep, things start to sound different. The bathroom tap sounds like a spaceship.

Or a helicopter.

Or some kind of giant bee, with huge fluorescent rainbow wings, flying closer and closer, landing on my leg, vibrating and—

"Harriet? Are you going to answer your phone?"

My phone feels like it's about to take off in my pocket. I grab it out and hold it to my face without even looking at the screen.

"Hmmmm?" I say.

"Hmmmm to you too," a warm voice says on the other end. "And *brrrrrrr* and *baaaaaa* as well, if we're just making noises."

I jump up so quickly my hip smashes into the towel rail. "*Nnnneoowww,*" I squeak in pain.

"Another classic. How about *grrrrrr* or *pnnnnnnggg* or *dingowombatikan*?"

"*Dingowombatikan?*" I smile. "That sounds like some kind of tiny marsupial."

"I'm Australian," my boyfriend laughs. "I've got imaginary indigenous species on the brain. This particular one looks like a dog crossed with a kangaroo."

And suddenly my brain feels just fine.

30

July 15th

"I've got an idea."

Nick and I were lying against each other on the roundabout in the park near my house, watching the sky rotate above us and the sun flash in and out of the trees.

We hadn't spoken in more than thirty minutes, other than little kisses strewn throughout, and I was very nearly asleep.

"Mmmm," I mumbled into his shoulder. "We should make a note of it and bury it in the garden for posterity."

Nick laughed. "Do you want to hear it, or do you want to be a smart-arse?"

"I want to be a smart-arse," I said firmly, sitting up and holding my hand out. "Hi, I'm Harriet Manners. We obviously haven't met before."

"Nice to meet you," Nick grinned, swooping in

for another kiss and then leaning back and scruffing his hair up. "Harriet Manners, I'm about to give you six stamps. Then I'm going to write something on a piece of paper and put it in an envelope with your address on it."

"OK..."

"Then I'm going to put the envelope on the floor and spin us as fast as I can. As soon as either of us manage to stick a stamp on it, I'm going to race to the postbox and post it unless you can catch me first. If you win, you can read it."

I thought about it briefly.

Nick was obviously faster than me, but he didn't know where the nearest postbox was.

"Deal," I agreed, yawning and rubbing my eyes. "But why six stamps?"

"Just wait and see."

A few seconds later, I understood.

As we spun in circles with our hands stretched out, one of my stamps got stuck to the ground at least a metre away from the envelope. Another ended up on a daisy. A third somehow got stuck to the roundabout.

One of Nick's ended up on his nose.

And every time we both missed, we laughed harder and harder and our kisses got dizzier and dizzier until the whole world was a giggling, kissing, spinning blur.

Finally, when we both had one stamp left, I stopped giggling. I had to win this.

So I swallowed, wiped my eyes and took a few deep breaths.

Then I reached out my hand.

"Too late!" Nick yelled as I opened my eyes again. "Got it, Manners!" And he jumped off the still-spinning roundabout with the envelope held high over his head.

So I promptly leapt off too.

Straight into a bush.

Thanks to a destabilised vestibular system – which is the upper portion of the inner ear – the ground wasn't where it was supposed to be.

Nick, in the meantime, had ended up flat on his back on the grass next to me.

With a small shout I leant down and kissed him hard on the lips. "HA!" I shouted, grabbing the envelope off him and trying to rip it open.

"I don't think so," he grinned, jumping up and wrapping one arm round my waist while he retrieved it again. Then he started running in a zigzag towards the postbox.

A few seconds later, I wobbled after him.

And we stumbled wonkily down the road, giggling and pulling at each other's T-shirts and hanging on to tree trunks and kissing as we each fought for the prize.

Finally, he picked me up and, without any effort, popped me on top of a high wall.

Like Humpty Dumpty.

Or some kind of really unathletic cat.

"Hey!" I shouted as he whipped the envelope out of my hands and started sprinting towards the postbox at the bottom of the road. "That's not fair!"

"Course it is," he shouted back. "All's fair in love and war."

And Nick kissed the envelope then put it in the postbox with a flourish.

I had to wait three days.

Three days of lingering by the front door. Three days of lifting up the doormat, just in case it had accidentally slipped under there.

Finally, the letter arrived: crumpled and stained

with grass.

Ha. Told you I was faster.
LBxx

31

I tell Nick everything.

Well, not *everything*, obviously.

I'm not insane.

But I tell him a carefully edited version of events. Or – as Annabel would put it – I just don't *elucidate the facts accurately.*

I don't tell him, for instance, that my governess thinks I'm stupid and she might be right. Or that I haven't made any friends or that I'm so bored and lonely I'm tempted to draw eyes on my cupboard and just start talking to that instead.

I don't tell him Hugo seems to have let Toby supersede me in his affections already.

I don't tell him that it's taken Nat precisely five hours to find a new best friend called *Jessica* who looks exactly like me.

Or that they're already drinking coffee together.

No, I lock myself in my bedroom so Annabel can't

hear me, and I simply tell him that things aren't exactly going to plan.

And, as I talk, I can feel my voice getting higher and tighter and my breath getting faster until Nick says:

"Hang on, just how far away *are* you?"

"An hour and a half."

"That's not that far, Harriet. You haven't moved to the moon. I'll just come to you. No biggy."

Of all the things I love about Nick, this is what I love most. I love his calmness. I love the way my brain spirals out of control while next to it his moves in a straight and steady path. As if I'm a little tug boat in a storm, being thrown about by the waves and the currents, and he's the big ship I'm anchored to for safety.

My breathing starts to slow. "Really? You'll do that?"

"Of course I will."

"Will you come tomorrow?"

"What's tomorrow?"

My stomach sinks. "Nick, it's my b—"

He laughs. "Your birthday. I know. You've been reminding me for the last two months. I'm pretty sure you put it into my phone calendar. Three times."

And I set an alarm for him, just in case.

"I only turn sixteen once, Nick. Just because

your sixteenth birthday has slipped into the foggy mists of time doesn't mean that everybody else is so complacent."

"I'm only seventeen, Harriet. I can remember it quite clearly."

"Sure you can. You probably carved it into a rock with another rock."

We both start snorting with laughter.

"You know, I've worked out that if I lived on Mercury I'd be sixty-six years old tomorrow. I'd be twenty-six on Venus, and half a year old on Saturn. I'm only sixteen because I'm on *this* planet."

"Just," Nick says. "Sometimes with you it's debatable."

I stick my tongue out at the phone even though he can't see it. "So can you come?"

"Of course. I've got a show at Versace but I should be done by five so I can hop on a train and get to you by seven?"

"Then we can have a really romantic evening," I say hopefully, grabbing HNRNYP out of my pocket and staring at it. "*Ooooh*, can we have a picnic? Under an oak tree? With a field of corn blowing in the breeze and the sunlight falling just *so* against our faces and a dove with its wings spread and cooing and—"

"Sure," Nick grins. "Birthday oaks, corn, breeze, sunlight, faces, cooing wing-spread dove. Done."

"And cake? Will there be lots of cake?"

"Yes, Marie Antoinette. There will be cake."

I beam so hard I'm sure he can tell. Although this does mean that I've only got about twenty-four hours to find some kind of field. I'm not entirely sure there is one. We might have to make do with the supermarket car park and a slightly dazed-looking pigeon.

I jump up in excitement. Everything's starting to look perfect again. "So I'll meet you at Greenway Station at seven tomorrow then?" I squeak.

"Count on it."

And I settle down to write my new romantic American birthday plans in earnest.

32

My sixteenth birthday plans are now:

- Wake up in America with birds singing, sun shining, leaves rustling, etc.
- Read exuberant text messages from loved ones.
- Think about the fact that I am a legal adult,capable of driving a moped or an invalid carriage, joining a Trade Union and buying a lottery ticket.
- Do none of those things.
- Open the curtains jubilantly to face a world that feels entirely different.
- Bounce down the stairs, where my parents will pretend they have forgotten all about what day it is.
- Pretend to be surprised when they jump up and shout SURPRISE! and hand me an

enormous, expensive and very thoughtful gift.

- Do fun stuff with thoughtful gift all day.
- Have the World's Most Romantic Birthday Evening (WMRBE) with Nick.

It all starts perfectly.

I am up at the crack of dawn. The birds are singing. The sun is shining. The leaves are rustling. I beam, get my pen out and cross them off the list with a neat line.

On my phone are four texts already:

HAPPY BIRTHDAY FRECKLES! Can't wait for tonight. LB xxx

O tanjobi omedetogozaimasu!! Much loving of you on speciality day, Harry-chan! Rin. xxxx

IT'S YOUR BIRTTTTTHHHDDAY! Ring you later. LOVE YOU LOVE YOU YAAAAYYYY!! Nat oxoxoxo

Many happy sixteenth returns, Harriet Manners. We'd send a kiss but we don't want you to get the wrong idea again.
Hugo and Toby.

*

I stretch out happily, and then cross the next point off the list too. I think briefly about driving a moped and an invalid carriage, don't do it, and cross both these points off as well.

Then I pull open the curtains.

"Good *morning*!" I shout to a little girl outside. "Isn't it a *wonderful* day?"

She pauses from prodding a crisp packet stuck in a bush with the end of a stick. "Uh?"

"I hope you have a lovely morning!"

"Weirdo," she says, going back to prodding, and I beam at her anyway.

Then I jubilantly cross my fifth point off the list.

Finally I pull on my dressing gown and bounce downstairs, to where my parents are slumped, scowling at each other exactly as predicted.

I swing the door open with a joyful BANG.

My sister immediately starts crying. She's obviously in on it too.

"Harriet," Annabel says, picking Tabby up with a *sssshhhh*. "Was that totally necessary?"

I beam at everyone, and then take my seat at the kitchen table. "Probably not," I say nonchalantly. "It's such a *boring day*. Such a *nothing day.* Why did we even bother waking up in the first place?"

Then I mentally kick myself. *Pull it back, Harriet. You'll ruin everything.*

Dad gazes blearily at me whilst tightening his tie. "Have you been eating American breakfast cereal, Harriet? I'm not sure you're built to handle that many E numbers."

I look optimistically at Annabel. She's going to say something really grumpy now too. I can feel it.

"Don't leave your butter knife on the table like yesterday, Richard. Put it in the sink."

Ha.

"But I don't need a butter knife this morning, do I? There being no butter. Is there *anything* to eat in here?"

"There's a piece of pizza in the fridge."

"I'm off to work in the city and you want me to eat a piece of old pizza for breakfast?"

"There's a can of mini sausages in the cupboard."

"You want me to take *a can of mini sausages* on the commuter train?"

"Or a slice of plastic-looking cheese."

"You want me to take a piece of *plastic-looking cheese* to work?"

"No, Richard," Annabel says, putting her head in

her hands. "What I want is for you to stop repeating everything I say in italics and understand that I was up all night with the baby and haven't had time to shop. Can you do that?"

I blink a few times.

They're taking it a bit far, to be honest. There's no need to be *this* boring.

"So," I interrupt, spreading my hands out on the table in a present-welcoming kind of way. "I have *no idea* what I'm going to do today. *No idea*."

"Yes, you do," Annabel says as Tabitha spits up on to a bib. "Miss Hall is coming. You've got school."

"I'm going to be *late* for work," Dad says, grabbing his suit jacket. "Do we have coffee, or should I be getting that at the station too?"

"Station," Annabel says without looking at him.

"Amazeballs." He scowls at Annabel, and then kisses the top of my head. "Have a good day, sweetheart. I'll be back later, after the work drinks if I haven't *starved* to death and am lying in skeletal form in the middle of Manhattan being prodded by scientists."

And – before I can get a single word out – Dad's gone, slamming the front door loudly behind him.

I stare at Annabel.

"*Don't,*" she snaps softly. "Harriet, just *don't*. I'm not in the mood. There's a twenty-dollar bill in my handbag. Please grab something to eat from the shops."

"But—"

"Harriet, *please*."

"I thought—"

"Harriet."

"Annabel—"

"Now."

So I eat a solitary birthday muffin, sitting on the kerb outside the supermarket.

If they're prepared to put on that kind of show the gift must be *amazing*. I may need to keep a handkerchief ready for all the unexpected emotion.

Miss Hall appears to be in on it too.

"Right," she says when we're tucked away in my bedroom. "I went easy on you yesterday. I think it's time you showed me what you're made of with some complex algebra."

Of all my A level topics, algebra is at the bottom of my list. I was kind of hoping we could at least spend my birthday playing Scrabble. "You want me to do algebra *today*?" I say in dismay.

Miss Hall frowns. "Is there a problem?"

Annabel *must* have told her why today's special. Which means...

Ah.

Of course. My parents want to keep me out of the way in my bedroom because they're doing something *extraordinary* downstairs. Like building a massive tree house, or filling the house with thousands of tiny colour-coordinated cupcakes in order of the rainbow spectrum.

I bet Dad hasn't gone to work. I bet he's out, picking up my new yellow legally approved scooter as we speak.

Or – slightly less excitingly – my invalid carriage.

"OK..." I say, winking elaborately at Miss Hall and getting my air-quote fingers ready. "Let's *do algebra*."

There's a pause while she stares at my fingers.

"Harry, if you aren't going to treat education with the respect it deserves, I can take my extraordinary skills elsewhere."

"I'll show education respect," I agree, feeling slightly put out. "Of course I will."

"Good," Miss Hall barks. "Because I am not here to be told how to do my job by a teenager. Clear?"

"Yes," I agree meekly.

"We are only as strong as we allow ourselves

to be," she says firmly. "And, Harry, I suspect that you are nowhere near as remarkable as I have been led to believe."

I flinch.

This birthday present had better be *really* good.

Miss Hall settles back in her chair and closes her eyes. "Let's stop wasting time and get on to higher circle theorems, shall we?"

So I spend the next eight hours doing exactly that.

33

By the time Miss Hall finally leaves, my excitement levels are dangerously high.

It is clearly going to be the best birthday *ever*.

I lurk at the top of the stairs, but it's nigh on completely silent down there. If I listen really hard, though, I can almost hear my parents' fevered whispers. "I hope Harriet likes it", and "*Won't* she be blown away?" and "This box is too small to fit a brand-new scooter *and* a puppy!"

Judging by the quietness they're not quite ready for me, so I make the most of the time left and prepare myself for WMRBE.

First I have a shower and attempt to shave my legs with a few poorly balanced swipes. Then I clamber out and spray myself all over with Annabel's best perfume. I dry myself, realise the towel now stinks of Chanel, tie my hair carefully into a top-knot and hop cautiously into my favourite dress.

Admittedly, it's my *only* dress.

It's red with little white hearts on it, and Nat gave it to me this summer for 'all the sixth form and college parties we will be invited to'. She clearly forgot that I hate parties but I accepted it in the spirit of Best Friendship.

With a surge of *joie de vivre*, I raid Annabel's make-up box and apply a smear of red lipstick, a fluff of powder and a few strokes of mascara: some of which actually goes on my eyelashes.

Then I stand in front of a full-length mirror and stare at the stranger in front of me.

I still look like me, but somehow *different*. Gone is the girl in a Winnie-the-Pooh T-shirt and in its place is a sixteen-year-old in a dress.

Sophisticated. Glamorous.

I lean a bit closer. There's mascara in my eyebrows.

Well, I'm going in the right direction.

Nat would be so proud of me.

I do a swirly spin so that the white hearts on red fan out in a circle like a romantic bull-fighter's cape, and then skip down the stairs with joyful steps.

"Dad?" I say, swishing into the hallway. "Tabitha? Annabel? I'm ready for my big surp—"

The kitchen is exactly the same as it was when I left

it this morning. The empty tea mugs are still out, and the blinds are still half shut. The oven door is open, and there's a vague smell of burning. The chair is in the exact same position it was when Dad pushed it back in a huff.

I walk into the living room.

The curtains are closed, and Annabel is lying on the sofa with an arm sprawled out, fast asleep. Her mouth is open, her blonde hair is straggled across her face, her jumper has ridden up and Tabitha is lying on her stomach with her tiny hands bunched up by her face: also unconscious.

I glance around the room. There are no flowers. No cupcakes. No signs of any kind of tree house or chemistry kit. No scooter. No puppy. There isn't a single bit of wrapping paper anywhere. No Sellotape, no scissors.

Nothing.

Then I glance at the door. Dad's jacket is missing from its hook.

And it finally hits me.

I have to lean against the doorframe while I try to wrap my stupid, slow-moving brain around it. I'd have seen it before, if it hadn't been so totally unbelievable.

This isn't an elaborate subterfuge. This isn't the

world's most carefully planned, epic surprise.

It's half-past six on the evening of my sixteenth birthday, and my family aren't pretending to forget me.

They've actually *forgotten*.

34

Statistically, the chances of having a birthday on any particular day is 1/365.

With a world population of 7.046 billion, that means that approximately 19,304,109 people are having birthdays today. All over the world, they're celebrating.

In Russia and Hungary, they're having their ears pulled.

In North Germany, flour is being poured on top of their heads.

In Canada, they're having their noses greased with butter.

In Venezuela, faces are being plunged into cakes.

In Scotland, they're being repeatedly smacked on the bottom.

And I'd still choose *any* of those nineteen million vaguely violent birthdays over spending the day sitting in my bedroom with a governess who makes me feel like an idiot on the wrong side of the world.

Doing *algebra*.

As quietly as I can, I let myself out of the house and walk swiftly to the train station with my chest aching.

I can't think about it now. I only have five and a half hours of sixteenth birthday left.

I have to focus on making them special.

Greenway Station isn't what I was expecting. I'm used to a big brick building, lots of people in suits and a deep, electrocuted track you have to stand really far away from or somebody in a uniform shouts at you.

Here, there's a tiny wooden hut next to two single metal tracks you can walk across. There's just a bench, a ticket machine and a plastic timetable stuck to a pin-board.

And it's totally empty.

I sit down, breathe as slowly as I can and adjust my dress so my new adultness doesn't get all creased.

Then I wait.

And wait.

Finally, a tinny bell starts ringing and the wooden barriers start closing. A black car rolls to a stop behind them. An enormous silver double-decker train starts approaching from the distance, like something out of an old Western.

The average heart beats 100,000 times a day, and mine suddenly decides to get today's all out of the way at once. My chest is hammering so fast it feels like one really long beat.

With infinite slowness, the train stops and the doors open.

I stand up, clutching my hands tightly together.

A little old lady climbs off the train, adjusts her skirt and starts walking towards the exit.

Then the doors shut and the train starts moving off.

With a blank brain, I grab my phone out of my satchel. It says 7.02pm. Then it rings.

"Hello?"

"Where are you?" Nick says as I spin around looking for him. "Are you hiding? I've checked the stairs leading up to the shopping mall but you don't appear to be there."

"Stairs?" My ears suddenly go numb. "Shopping mall?"

"Yeah, I can see some kind of coffee place. Are you in there buying doughnuts? I told you I'd bring cake."

I look up and down the empty platform. The barriers are back up and the car is driving slowly away.

"Nick, there's no shopping mall in Greenway."

"What are you talking about?" he laughs. "It's right by the sign with the..." Then he stops. "Did you say Green*way*?"

My entire stomach flips over. "Greenway. Greenway Station."

"Green*way* Station?" There's a pause, and then Nick says: "Harriet, I'm at Green*ways* Station."

No.

No. No no no no ***NO***.

This can't be happening.

"There's no *s*," I say in a tiny voice that feels very far away.

"It really sounded like there was an *s*."

"But..." My brain is spinning silently, like a scratched CD. *Click. Click. Click*. "Nick, I don't understand. I emailed you a map. And directions. And a train timetable. I emailed you a detailed history of the entire local area. You had *everything* you needed to get here."

"I..." There's a long pause. "I didn't have time to look at them, Harriet. I was rushing in and out of jobs and I thought I knew where I was going. I'm so sorry."

I close my eyes and manage, "So where *are* you?"

"Hang on. Just checking the map." There's a

silence, and then he makes an *eeeeurgh* sound. "I'm two and a half hours in the wrong direction. I *thought* the train journey was taking too long."

Two and a half hours in the wrong direction. Which means four hours from me, not including transfer times.

I can feel myself starting to panic. "But..." I swallow. "Maybe you could get on another train? Maybe if you leave now, you can get here before midnight and then we can—"

"Harriet," Nick says gently. "The trains stop at eleven-thirty and I have another fitting at 7am tomorrow."

"But it's my birthday."

I know it sounds pathetic, but it's the only fact I have left to cling on to.

"I know." He sounds devastated. "I can't believe I screwed up this badly."

"It's my BIRTHDAY."

My voice is getting higher and louder. A stray dog at the other end of the platform turns to look at me anxiously before scampering off.

"Harriet, I *know*. I'm standing in the middle of nowhere, two and a half hours from New York, with sixteen purple balloons I blew up on the train and then could only just get out of the door, and sixteen cupcakes. Trust me, I want to be there. I'm one strong puff of wind from being blown away like Mary Poppins."

I look down at my stupid heart dress through my stupid mascara-d eyelashes. I look at my stupid hairless legs, and my stupid purple flip-flops. Then I put my hand up and touch my stupid hair, tied up in its stupid top-knot.

I should have just stayed as I was. Fluffy and wearing clothes intended for an eleven-year-old.

At least then I wouldn't be standing alone on a station platform on my birthday, feeling like a nobody.

I pull my birthday plan out of my pocket. I think it's safe to say there won't be any more crossing-off today.

"I have to go," I say quietly, ripping it in half and dropping it on the floor. The pieces lie there for a few seconds and then blow straight on to the track.

"No, Harriet. Listen, we can do something tomorrow, I'll get on the right train and—"

"I have to go," I say again.

And I hang up before Nick can say anything else.

35

One of my favourite ever facts is this:

Atoms never actually touch each other.

Because of the electromagnetic repulsion between their components, every atom floats an infinitely tiny distance away from the atoms around it.

Which doesn't sound like much, until you realise that atoms make up *everything*. Which means you're not really holding a pen: it's levitating very slightly in your hands. You're not really sitting in that chair: you're hovering just a fraction above it.

Frankly, I'm not sure I believe it any more.

As I walk home, my feet are very much touching the ground. I'm not electromagnetically hovering anywhere.

I start walking heavily up the stairs.

"Harriet?" Annabel is standing in the doorway. "Are you OK?"

I turn around slowly.

Dad appears next to her, grinning. "I'm sorry I was such a terrible grump this morning, chickpea. Work is a bit harder than I expected – even for a genius like me. But I went shopping on the way home. *Look*."

He points proudly at five plastic carrier bags, stuffed with the sort of things dads buy when they go shopping. Multi-packs of biscuits, enormous bottles of cola, unnecessarily large packs of toilet rolls. All Man Size, as if to prove that only girls need things in reasonable quantities.

I look at them, then at him.

"And *look*," he says, bouncing towards me. "Look what work gave me as a belated welcome gift!" He holds out his wrist. There's a thick black rubber band circled around it. "It's a *PowerBand*." I glance at it. "It shows me how much Power I'm using!" Then he clicks a button on the side. Numbers shine in green. "I've used 2,354 Powers today!"

"A Power is not a universally recognised measurement of energy, Richard," says Annabel. "Unless you're He-Man."

"Maybe I am, Bel," Dad says, wiggling his eyebrows

and then kissing his bicep. He waves his arm frantically above his head and then presses the button again. "I've used five Powers just waving!"

"Have you, indeed," Annabel says, rolling her eyes.

"Annabel, are there any household chores I can help with? Ironing?" He makes large ironing motions with his right hand. "Painting fences? Any orchestras you need conducting?"

Annabel sighs. "You could rock Tabitha to sleep. How's that for hand-based Power consumption?"

"Perfect," Dad says, starting to push Tabby's cot so energetically that she immediately starts crying.

I start walking back up the stairs.

"Harriet, what is *wrong* with you?" Annabel says, holding on to the banister. "Did something happen with Miss Hall?"

Slowly, I turn around.

"Dad?" I say. "What else does that thing do?"

"*Well*," he says, looking at it proudly, "if you click it three times, it'll tell you how many Hours you've Won. Then calories and distance. If you click it five times, it'll show you the time. Like a proper watch."

He clicks it five times and holds it out to me.

"Does it show you the date?"

Dad frowns. "I think if you hold the button down...

Yup. There you go. It's the 31st of Aug—"

He goes very quiet.

I look at Annabel. Her entire face has drained of colour.

"*No.*" She steps over to Dad and grabs his wrist hard. "NO."

"Annabel," Dad says. "I know you keep the diary around here, but isn't the 31st Harriet's..."

"Yes, but it's the 30th today. Press it again, Richard. *Press it again.*"

"I'm *pressing* it," Dad says urgently. "Annabel, it's *still the 31st* of August."

They both stare at the stupid green digits on the stupid black rubber band and then back at me.

"What a useful gift," I snap, starting up the stairs again. "I'm glad somebody got one."

"Oh my God." Annabel's hand is over her mouth and she sounds like she's going to cry. "Harriet. It's your birthday."

Dad says a loud word that a tiny baby probably shouldn't hear.

"Yup," I snap. "Happy sixteenth birthday to me. Many felicitations, etc., etc. May my day be full of joy and so on. Except it wasn't."

"Harriet, listen—"

"*No*," I say sharply, reaching the top of the stairs and spinning round to face them. My parents are staring up at me from the dark hallway, like two round white pebbles at the bottom of a pond. "You brought me here. You took me away from my entire life, and now I have nothing and nobody. I'm sixteen years old and I don't have to listen to either of you. Ever again."

With a final heavy step I walk into my bedroom and slam the door behind me.

And then I lock it.

36

That's one good thing about our new house.

The doors have locks on them.

My parents sit outside my bedroom, pleading, apologising and making really bad jokes. Dad pushes a biscuit and a little envelope under the door that says:

> WE'RE THE WORST PARENTS EVER.
> But WE love you to infinity AND beyond.
> DOES that help? :(
> XXXXXX

Inside it is $100 in cash.

I scrawl *NO THAT'S NOT EVEN PHYSICALLY OR LOGISTICALLY POSSIBLE* across the envelope in enormous letters, take the money out and push it back under the door. Then I turn the BBC World Service up so loudly that the floors start rattling.

Finally – when every biscuit in the house has been pushed under my door and then thrown out of the window – my parents eventually get the message and leave me alone.

I lie face down on my bed in my Mickey Mouse T-shirt and turn my phone on. It immediately beeps five times.

H, sorry I didn't call earlier – stuck in college. Can we Skype tmrw? So sorry. :(Bet you had the best birthday in NY EVER. Miss you so much. Nat xoxoxoxo

I'm SO SORRY. I screwed up. Please talk to me. LBxx

PS I'm sorry I'm sorry xxx

PPS You can have ALL the postscripts

PPPPPPPPPPPS? x

With my nose pressed into my duvet I delete everything, and then click on my email. Among offers to enlarge various parts of my body which I don't actually own, there's just one waiting in my inbox.

Just one email from somebody I recognise.

FROM: Alexa Roberts
TO: Harriet Manners

I thought Twilight was boring but your delusional fantasies are even worse.

I'd stay in New York if I were you.

A

The only person without an apology on my birthday is the person currently wading through my most precious memories for something to hurt me.

That's nice.

I stare blankly at the empty walls of my new bedroom.

Not a single thing in this house has a memory wrapped around it. I don't know what has been accidentally dropped between the floorboards or what's been secretly stored at the back of these cupboards. I don't know what the stains on the carpets are, or what angle the sunshine hits my bed in springtime.

I can't climb down the stairs in the middle of the night without turning a light on. There's nobody waiting for me in the bush outside. Nobody sitting on the bench on the corner of my road with her legs on the armrest.

It's just a house. With floorboards and cupboards and carpets and unrecognisable sunshine and empty bushes and benches.

It's not my home.

For the first time in my life, I am totally on my own.

I sulk for the next three days non-stop. I refuse all offers of belated birthday weekend fun from my parents. I don't even bother switching my phone on again. I think about Skyping Nat but decide she'll be too busy drinking coffee with Jessica to answer. And Toby will be too busy stealing the affections of my dog to have time for me either.

So on Sunday evening when I finally switch my phone back on and it immediately starts ringing, I reach down to cancel the call. I don't want to talk to anyone. Not Nick, not Nat, not my parents who are probably ringing me from downstairs like obsessive weirdos.

It rings again, and I cancel it.

Then again, and I cancel it again.

Finally – on the fourth call from an unknown number – curiosity gets the better of me. "*What?*"

"My little Bacon-chops," a voice says. "Let's try for something a little more welcoming than that. *Hello* is a traditional way to start a conversation. Go again."

I stare at the phone and then put it back to my face. "*Wilbur?*"

"Trunkle-bum, I like that even better. Answer *every* phone call like that forever. We could start a trend."

"Wilbur, is that really you?"

"Why of course it is, my little Storm in a Teacup." Wilbur tinkles with laughter. "Who in diddle-cats else was it going to be?"

37

For a few seconds, I don't say anything.

Luckily I don't have to, Wilbur continues talking regardless.

"Possum-feet. Isn't this fun? It's just the same as normal, except we're in a different country again. At least, I assume we both are, Kitten-munch, or this is a very strange number for you to have."

"Where *are* you?"

"New York, Bunny-buttons. Where else?"

"But..." I don't even know where to start. "How did you get this number?"

"I have my sources," he says. "I'm like Tom Cruise except with a better physique and swishier hair. And I don't move my arms so much when I run."

"I didn't think I'd ever hear from you again."

"Don't be such a silly Sausage-cake. I was just biding my time. Gaining infinite power, like an iPod plugged into the mains."

As usual, I have no idea what he's talking about. It's so comforting. "OK."

"And now we must reunite for the benefit of mankind, like Take That. So where *precisement* are you? A tiny birdy tells me you're in NYC too. Is this true, or is it like the time somebody told me Oprah was in the bagel shop and she wasn't and I was *devastated*?"

"I'm an hour and a half away."

"Close enough. You'll just have to get up at super-dawn, like an early worm so the birds can catch you. I need you here first thing tomorrow morning. There's a magazine job I want to put you forward for."

"But..." How do I put this nicely? "I'm not actually a model any more, Wilbur. Infinity Models dumped me."

There is literally no way to put that nicely.

"Nobody here knows that, so potato potato." He says them both the same. *Potato potato*. "Just meet me in Manhattan and we can take it from there. *Don't* eat any chocolate between now and then. We can't have any more skin explosions, Baby-baby Panda. They're a lot less forgiving about that in America."

I blink a few times. *Baby-baby Panda. Manhattan. A job.* A familiar, excited wriggling starts at the bottom of my stomach.

"But—" I object, about to sensibly tell Wilbur it's Monday tomorrow, I have to study, my parents will never allow it and then I stop.

I'm sixteen and I'm not a child any more.

Miss Hall clearly thinks I'm useless anyway and I appear to be learning nothing so it's not as if I'm missing anything here and…

I'll finally get to see New York.

I can model again.

And I can live the dream, just like Nat.

What other options do I have? Sitting here, waiting for everybody to get on with their lives without me?

I close my eyes.

I can either stay here, ignored and alone. Failing and being forgotten about.

Or I can run away and have the life I choose.

Scientists say that if you went into space without a spacesuit, you would explode before you suffocated because there is no air pressure. I may not be in space, but that's precisely how I feel now. As if – if I don't do *something* – that's exactly what's going to happen to me.

"I'll do it," I say defiantly, opening my eyes.

"Of course you'll do it, Bunny-face," Wilbur laughs. "It's fashion. New York. What else is there?"

38

The next morning, I simply get up and leave.

That's it.

I consider other, more elaborate options. I think of carefully planned strategies: pretending I need library books from New York, or that I'm sick and in need of a doctor with city expertise. I consider tying my bed sheets into a rope and climbing subtly out of the window, like a heroine from a *Famous Five* novel.

Then I realise that my poor knotting and rope-climbing skills might probably result in a much more permanent departure than I'm aiming for.

So at 6am on the dot, I jump out of bed and stand in front of my wardrobe, trying to decide what a sixteen-year-old would wear to a model casting in New York City.

I experiment with a few options.

I try my Eeyore jumper and jeans, followed by my spotty vest and shorts, then I take them off and try a yellow T-shirt and zigzag leggings. In a moment of desperation, I even consider the conjoined white trousers and red jumper I wore trick-or-treating a few years ago when I was dressed as a can of Campbell's soup. But then I realise you can still see the vague outline of the word TOMATO painted across the middle.

And I'm not sure that a fruit pretending to be a vegetable is the style icon I should be channelling.

Finally, I chuck my childhood back into the wardrobe and crush it down as hard as I can. Then, slightly cautiously, I walk over to the corner of the room where the red and white heart dress is lying in a crumpled heap, from me throwing it there four days ago.

I don't think this is scientifically possible, but somehow it looks sad. Flat. A bit resentful.

I *did* stamp on it quite a few times.

"Sorry," I whisper, picking it up and trying to straighten it back out. Somehow, it feels like Nat might mystically know. "Can we try again?"

The dress doesn't say anything so I wave it around a few times to try and get some creases out, and then carefully climb back in and zip it up. I wash my face, apply some more of Annabel's mascara and stick some lip balm on my lips.

Then I stick a blue stripy hoody on over the top and put my New York guidebook and my birthday money in my satchel.

There's a jam jar on the windowsill, stuffed with a messy bundle of 'emergency kitty': several twenty-dollar bills, crumpled up together.

After a few seconds of guilty deliberation, I grab that too.

Then I run down the stairs.

"This is very early for you, sweetheart," Annabel observes, coming out of the living room still blinking in the morning sunshine. "Where are you going?"

"Out," I say, opening the front door.

And I close it firmly behind me.

Greenway train station is no longer empty. There are people quietly lining the edges of the platform like a sleepy army. Men in suits, women in smart dresses and heels. A couple of young girls in jeans, talking on their mobile phones. A lady and her little dog. A man with a suitcase.

I look up and down for Dad with another pang of guilt, and then lift my chin defiantly and take my place in the line.

This is it, I realise as the bell rings, the barriers lower and the silver train starts slowly approaching. *From this point, everything changes.*

The train stops, the doors open and I climb up on to the top deck and take a seat, accidentally spreading my dress out on to the lap of the girl next to me. For the first time in weeks, there's no weight in my stomach. No ripples of panic.

Nothing.

And as Greenway and everything in it retreats behind me, I don't feel sad or invisible.

If things won't be perfect for me, I'll have to make them perfect myself.

And there's no going back.

39

Here are some interesting facts about Grand Central station in New York:

- *It is more than a hundred years old.*
- *It has sixty-seven tracks and forty-four platforms; more than any other train station in the entire world.*
- *It gets an average of 750,000 visitors a day.*
- *Its clock has four faces, is made of opal and is worth twenty million dollars.*

But none of these are my favourite facts.

The best one is this: if you look up there is a vast, bright turquoise ceiling, and on this ceiling are painted 2,500 individual stars depicting the zodiac of the Mediterranean winter sky.

Even better, the stars are *backwards* because they were inspired by a medieval manuscript that shows the constellations as they would have been seen from the *other direction*.

In other words, when you look at the sky of Grand Central station, you are viewing it as God.

Which means that where you're standing is supposed to be heaven.

I can kind of believe it.

The second I step off the train, the sleepiness of Greenway instantly evaporates.

As I stand in the middle of the station, staring at the ceiling and clutching my satchel, it feels like the whole world has opened up to its proper size and I can finally breathe again.

There are hundreds of people everywhere.

Taking photos, eating cheesecake with little plastic forks, checking the train timetables. According to my guidebook, there are 4,000 bulbs in this station, and every single one of them is on and shining: the room is full of warm light and noise. Dozens of conversations and questions and accents blur into each other until they form a comforting, drone-like hum. It's like being in a warm, friendly beehive, if a beehive cost two billion dollars to build.

I stare at the star-filled sky until my neck starts aching, and then open my map and wander slowly into the street.

At which point the world opens up even further. And further and further.

And then it just keeps opening.

Giraffes have the same amount of vertebrae as humans, and I'm genuinely concerned that mine are going to stay stretched out permanently as I try to take it all in.

New York City is *enormous*.

It shoots into the sky and just keeps going: like a normal city that's been sprayed with fertiliser and has suddenly grown in every possible direction. Upwards, outwards, across. Sprouting everywhere simultaneously, like a jungle made of concrete and glass and marble.

The buildings are huge. The roads are huge. The buses seem bigger and brighter; the crowds faster and louder. Everything seems *more*, except for the sky, which suddenly feels smaller and much, much further away.

In the corner next to the station a man in a bright blue T-shirt is playing a golden saxophone next to a yellow cap on the floor. Opposite him a man in a tracksuit is smashing at a makeshift drum kit made out of pots and pans.

A woman in shiny black leather boots with a tiny dog tucked under her arm pushes past, and a small girl wheels a ladybird suitcase over my toes.

A stand selling pretzels and doughnuts is next to a stand selling fried noodles, and the air is sweet and smoky and salty.

Everywhere is noise and colour. A couple are yelling at each other: "*Don't* talk to me like that, yo," "Don't *you* talk to *me* like that, yo," and another girl is crying hysterically into her friend's shoulder. A bright yellow taxi pulls to an abrupt stop in front of a group of tourists looking at a map.

"Are you trying to get yourself *killed*?" the driver shouts in a heavy accent out of the window, beeping four times.

They stare at him, eyes wide.

"*Move it*," he yells, and they do: stumbling backwards on to the feet of more pedestrians who look equally annoyed. The entire city seems to be divided into two sets of people: people who belong here, and people who do not.

Of which I am definitely the latter.

It's all strangely familiar, yet also unfamiliar. Like when you meet an old great-aunt you haven't seen in ten years and you recognise her face and smell and the way she leaves a wet mark on your cheek but at the same time you don't really know her. I've known this city all my life, but after sixteen years and hundreds of films and TV shows and four guidebooks, I'm finally here.

I'm in New York.

Happiness bubbles into my chest and up my throat until I can't help it: I squeak a couple of times and jump up and down on the spot, hugging my guidebook to my chest.

The saxophone player is watching me, so I stop jumping, put a dollar bill into his yellow cap and beam at him.

"You have a nice day," I say experimentally.

He winks and keeps playing.

I wink back.

And, slowly but surely, I start pushing my way through New York City.

40

Now, I know some basic facts about navigating New York. In fact, through personal research and also a lifetime of growing up with America as a cultural backdrop, I know quite a lot.

I know that the roads run parallel to each other in a grid shape based on an Ancient Roman system called *centuriation.*

I know that the distance between one road and another is a *block.* I know *streets* run east and west, and *avenues* run north and south, and that they're all numbered sequentially: *39th, 40th, 41st,* and so on.

I know that one direction is *uptown* and the other is *downtown.*

And I know I like it, because it's incredibly *logical*. Unlike in England, where landmarks and etymology and history and destination and famous individuals are all welded together in a hotchpotch that makes no sense unless you're a road historian. Which almost nobody is.

So I start out optimistically.

The address Wilbur has given me is only six blocks away from Grand Central station, and according to Google it should take eight minutes to walk there.

I walk down 42nd Street humming a tune, staring at the tops of the buildings and the glitzy shops and the food stands and the inexplicably gold fire hydrants.

I pat a dog on the end of an orange rope, buy a pen that says 'I HEART NY', a pencil that says 'You have NY heart' and a triangular slice of extremely hot pizza.

I say hello to somebody dressed up as a Mario Brother.

I watch an enormous red truck drive past with slabs of pavement attached by ropes to the back.

I take an arty photo of myself in a shop window reflection and then send it to Nat with a carefully constructed, breezy message:

Wearing the red dress! New York is AMAZING. Such a shame you can't be here! Hxx

Then I hit the river.

Which means I've gone the wrong way.

So I start walking back: past the shop window and

the food stands and the hydrants and Mario.

Except at some point I must have turned off 42nd Street, because now I'm standing outside a shop I don't recognise.

It turns out that if you don't actually know New York, there is no way of telling which direction you're heading in. Uptown or downtown. East or west. North or south.

It's like being Alice, falling through the rabbit hole. Except when you come out the other end, it's not even properly signposted.

"Excuse me," I say politely to a woman walking past with bright lilac hair and a fur collar.

She blinks a few times.

"Umm. Could you tell me which way is *up*, please?"

"*What?*"

"Which way is up and which way is down?"

She leans close and squints. "What *language* are you speaking?"

"Umm. English?"

"*English?* Where are you *from*?"

"England."

I've been to two non-English-speaking countries in the last six months, and at no stage has anyone queried whether I speak my own language. "I promise

I am," I add, because she still looks doubtful.

"Right. Well, *that* way is up." She points to the sky. "And *that* way is down."

She points to the pavement.

I flush so hard I can actually see the tip of my nose turning purple. I obviously look like the kind of person who doesn't understand three dimensions.

"Errr," I say, bobbing a little curtsey. "That's very helpful. Thank you very much."

"You're welcome," she says, sniffing slightly.

And I'm forced to walk slowly away, pretending to be inordinately interested in a passing cloud until she's gone.

At which point I turn my map around and try again.

Forty minutes.

It takes *forty minutes* to get to what Google says is an eight-minute walk away. On the bright side, I manage to find the Rockefeller Center which is:

a) nowhere near where I'm supposed to be
b) even bigger than everything else
c) nowhere near an ice rink
d) on my To Do List, which is handy.

I also go past a nice green park with lots of people playing chess and draughts, a carousel with pink and white horses, an enormous H&M, the headquarters of Facebook, a theatre showing *The Lion King* and a Lego shop with an enormous Lego dragon bursting out of the ceiling.

Getting lost is actually quite an educational experience. Which is good, because if this morning is anything to go by, it looks like it's going to happen quite a lot.

Finally I arrive outside a huge, shiny skyscraper with enormous windows and a big, revolving glass door. LA MODE it says in big silver letters on a plaque next to the door.

I take a deep breath.

Then I wipe my clammy hands on my dress and push through the revolving doors.

Back into the world of fashion.

41

As we know, I've been a model – on and off – ever since Nick found me under that table at The Clothes Show Live. But as I walk into the vast, glittering reception of one of the biggest fashion magazines in the world, it suddenly hits me that I haven't been.

Not really.

Two months ago, Yuka Ito told me that I didn't understand the fashion world because I'd never actually been part of it. That she and Wilbur had held my hand throughout the entire journey: from the moment I was spotted in a pile of broken hats in Birmingham to the second I ended my contract with her.

For the first time, I truly understand what she was talking about.

This is my first time in a magazine reception. I've never been on a normal casting or a go-see. I've never competed for a job or been rejected. I've never had a portfolio to carry around or a card with my photo on it.

I've never had to prove myself.

I've just stumbled through modelling as I stumble through everything: from one catastrophe to the next, optimistic that things will turn out all right in the end.

A schoolgirl with absolutely no idea how lucky she was or how much of a fairy tale she'd been handed.

This time, everything is different.

I'm going to be treated like everyone else, and I have to prove I can do it. This is *New York*. I'm just one of ten thousand girls who want the same thing.

I can suddenly hear Yuka's voice: *Fashion is hard work, fickle and unforgiving. It eats girls like you for breakfast.*

And I know I should be scared.

But I'm not.

This is what I want: to carve my own adventure, instead of being handed it ready-made and wrapped in a big pink bow.

"Yes." The man at reception doesn't look up: he keeps tapping away at his computer.

"Umm." I straighten out my dress and then realise one of the straps has snapped and is hanging down my back. I quickly grab it and start unsuccessfully attempting to tie it on to the front. "I'm here to see Wilbur?"

"Wilbur?"

"Wilbur..." I pause, and then flush. I've just realised I don't actually know Wilbur's last name. He's like Madonna, or Jesus. "He's about this high." I hold my hand just above my head. "A little bit..." I don't want to be unkind, so I stop. "He's probably wearing sequins. Or feathers. Or both. And wellies."

The man finally looks up and stares at me coldly. "I know who Wilbur is."

"Oh. Sorry."

"Take a seat," he says, pointing to one of the enormous white sofas. "He'll be down in a minute."

I nod in the most sophisticated way I possibly can while holding my dress together with my hands, and do exactly that.

I'd forgotten this world even exists.

Everyone and everything inside looks like it's been buffed and polished. Every time the glass doors revolve, somebody exciting enters the building. A woman in an unseasonably heavy fur coat. A man in tight trousers and pointed shoes. Three young models: beautiful, thin, wearing black from head to toe with enormous handbags.

There's a stupidly good-looking blond boy roughly my age sitting on the sofa opposite me. After fifteen minutes the silence is starting to get awkward, so I shuffle forward on my bottom and smile at him as brightly as I can.

"Hello," I say cheerfully. "How are you?"

He glances up, looks at me with piercing blue eyes and then goes back to texting on his phone.

"Did you know," I say in my most casual voice, "that the word 'skyscraper' was originally a nautical term referring to a small triangular sail set above the skysail on a sailing ship? We only adopted it for buildings quite recently."

The boy grunts slightly and presses a few more buttons.

I'm just trying to work out if I know any more relevant facts about New York landmarks when the doors of the lift open and somebody I know walks out.

Except it's not Wilbur.

It's a girl. She's tall and has long brown curly hair and an incredibly pretty face: heart-shaped, with a tiny pointed chin and wide brown eyes. She's wearing a pale blue dress, and her white platform heels are so chunky she looks like a baby horse. As if they're the only things anchoring her to the ground.

She adjusts the straps of her handbag on to her shoulder and starts clomping through the reception, towards the entrance.

Then she sees me and stops.

"Harriet?"

I stand up, blinking. The last time I saw this beautiful girl I was holding her hand. A few minutes before that, I was knocking her on to the floor of a catwalk in front of a room full of people in Moscow.

I didn't think I'd see her ever again. Except apparently when the world gets bigger, it also gets a whole lot smaller at the same time.

"Fleur?"

And I don't even think about it.

I run across the reception and throw myself around her neck.

"You have no idea how happy I am to see you," I squeak happily, kissing her cheek. "No idea at all."

42

Fleur and I talk about *everything.*

We talk about what we've been doing, and my Japanese job with Yuka, and how I'm now in America with my parents and my baby sister. We talk about how far away England is, and about how bad the turbulence can be on the flight over. We talk about the stars on the ceiling of Grand Central station, and the layout of American roads, and how weird it is that the fire hydrants are painted gold.

At least, I do.

Because as the conversation progresses, I realise Fleur's not really saying much.

Or anything, in fact.

Her eyes are flicking around the reception, and she's getting pinker and pinker.

Slowly, I grind to a confused halt.

Finally, she says, "I'm sorry, Harriet, but I have to go. I have a casting to get to."

She gives me a swift hug.

"Oh," I say, because suddenly grabbing on to her ankles and screaming *Please be my friend I don't have any left* doesn't seem a very dignified option. "OK."

"Let's do lunch sometime?" she says, starting to head towards the door.

I beam at her.

I *knew* I would find a friend in New York City, and I've only been here an hour. This is *so* much better than Greenway.

"Yes, *please*. I really want to try a slider, which is apparently an American miniature beefburger. Could you do today? Or maybe tomorrow? We could take some to Central Park and have a picnic?"

"Sure," Fleur says, adjusting her handbag and looking at the door again.

"So should we swap numbers?" I say, quickly scribbling mine down on a piece of paper. "I'm quite far away but just give me a bit of warning and I can get the train."

I hand her the piece of paper and she puts it in her handbag without looking at it. "Thanks."

"No problem," I say, as Fleur starts pushing the door with her hand and then nods.

"Catch you later."

And she disappears into the street, leaving me – totally numberless – behind her.

43

Apparently the centre of the sun is fifteen million degrees centigrade, but I think right now my cheeks can probably give it a run for its money. Maybe I should stop telling people about the colour of fire hydrants.

In fairness, I've got better conversation openers.

I walk back to my seat, just as the lift doors open again with a little *ping*.

"Thanks for coming in," a pretty blonde woman says to an incredibly tall, dark-skinned bald girl wearing an orange lycra catsuit. "We'll be in touch."

"Of course you will, babe," the girl says, kissing the air a metre from her left ear. "I have no doubt. Call my agent."

Then she stalks through the reception on enormous orange heels. "Come on then, you," she adds to the blonde boy still sitting opposite me, clicking her fingers. "We haven't got all day – I need to get my cards done."

The blond boy raises his eyebrows, puts his phone back in his pocket and, scowling slightly, follows the tall girl out of the swinging doors.

I look back to see Wilbur, who was obviously hidden behind her.

"Lord," the blonde woman says to him. "She's so... *aggressive.*"

"My hot potato-wedge," Wilbur says with a disinterested hand-wave. "That is, as they say, *irreleventia*. The girl has got cheekbones I could spread houmous all over my low-fat bagel with."

"Mmm," the blonde woman says. "I'm not entirely sure she'd let you do that. And I *do* wish she'd stop turning up to castings uninvited. So, where were we?"

"I believe I was refusing to allow you to pair a Versace jacket with that Prada pantsuit for the shoot next week. I'll eat them both before I let you do that. And the Gucci shoes. Heel first."

"Wilbur," the woman sighs. "Nobody is going to make you eat shoes, Gucci or otherwise. That would be insane."

"*Au contraire,*" my old agent says defiantly. "Insanity is thinking lime green goes with navy. That is the *very definition* of insanity."

Actually, according to Einstein, the definition of

insanity is doing the same thing over and over again and expecting different results.

In which case, I may have a problem.

I finally find my voice.

"Hello, W—" I start, but he keeps walking past me: purple-sequined jacket shimmering in the sunlight.

"Are you sure?" the woman continues in a tentative voice. She's wearing a very soft camel-coloured pashmina and her hair is bleached white and hangs in soft waves. "I can't help feeling you're wrong."

"Fine, Nancy, have it your way but don't say I didn't warn you," Wilbur replies. I make sure my broken dress strap is tucked under my armpit and try again.

"Hi, Wi—"

"So what about the shoot tomorrow, Darling-pie?" he continues. "Have you decided yet?"

"No," Nancy sighs. "I'm still not totally convinced by the girls, to be honest."

"As I keep telling you, darling, you need a statuesque one. Dark-skinned. Exotic. Cheekbones. Like lovely Kenderall back there with the attitude problem. But maybe with Beyonce hair."

I clear my throat. "Hi—"

The lady grimaces. "Maybe... But I kind of like the baldness."

Wibur nods. "Try a similar, less strident girl without hair then." He looks around and finally makes direct eye contact with me.

Thank goodness.

I was starting to wonder if I'd been rendered invisible during the last three minutes, or at the very least mute like Man Friday in *Robinson Crusoe*.

"*That,*" Wilbur adds, pointing at me as if he's never seen me before in his life. "Like her, except the absolute opposite."

I flush. *What?*

Nancy slowly turns and looks at me. She looks at my purple rubber flip-flops, at my broken heart dress and hoody, and then at the red hair escaping in little sweaty strands around my face.

I wipe under my eye and my finger comes away slightly black. Several of my eyelashes appear to be glued together.

"Who is she?"

"Just some nobody." Wilbur rolls his eyes. "As I said, we want the *opposite,* Sugar-plum. Use her as inspiration and go the *other* way. We don't want ginger and alien duck-face. It's not fresh. It's *so* over it's rolling down a hill, you know what I mean?"

Excuse me? Some *nobody*?

Ginger and alien duck-face, however, are pretty standard.

"No," Nancy says, walking towards me. "I have no idea what you mean, Wilbur." She puts a few fingers under my chin, and lifts it into the sunshine.

"*Yawn-o-rama*," Wilbur says tiredly. "This girl is a mess. Have you seen those freckles? That pointy nose? That chin? Those glassy, vacant, staring eyes? I'm falling asleep just looking at her. *Bor-ing.* She is totally and utterly forgettable."

I blink. Ouch.

"I like her," Nancy says decisively. "What's your name?"

"Harriet Manners," I say as politely as I can.

"Are you a model?"

"Well, not real—" I start and Wilbur clears his throat. "Umm... yes?"

"Mis-take," Wilbur starts singing. "Big mis-take. HUGE *faux pas*. Catastrophic and megalithic and—"

"Wilbur Evans," Nancy finally snaps. "You may be Creative Advisor at LA MODE but I am the new Fashion Editor so will you be quiet and let me choose the model I want for my shoot, please?"

Wilbur lets out an enormous sigh.

"*Fine*," he says dramatically. "If you will *insist* upon

going down this *disastrous* path then I suppose it is my *job* to support you." He throws his arm across his face. "Even if this strange and badly dressed girl is totally last year."

What's wrong with my dress?

"Thank you, Wilbur. Get her portfolio biked over ASAP and book her for 8am tomorrow." Nancy looks at me again, nods happily and adds, "Perfect."

Then she picks up some files from reception and heads back towards the elevator.

As soon as the doors shut, I turn to Wilbur with my mouth still hanging open.

"My little egg on toast," he says, giving me a hug and kissing my cheek. "Gosh, but you're as delicious as ever, I'm happy to see. Have you been taking multi-vitamins? Your spots are nowhere *near* as pulsating as they normally are."

I stare at Wilbur in silence, and then manage: "What the *sugar cookies* just happened?"

"A little bit of Creative Advisory magic," Wilbur says, putting on his sunglasses and winking at me. "And *that,* Harriet Manners, is how it's done."

44

That is not how it's done by the way.

Just to make that clear.

So much for being a proper, grown-up model, pursuing a fashion career through the traditional, linear methods. It looks like Wilbur has just psychologically manipulated an insecure fashion editor into giving me a job.

That is not what I intended *at all*.

"Nancy just needed a little nudge in the right direction, Bunny-crumble," Wilbur confirms. "With some people that involves shoving them very hard the opposite way."

Which doesn't make me feel any better.

"What's the job for?"

"It's a seven-page spread in LA MODE magazine, which the infinitely glorious *moi* shall be styling." He looks at me and lifts an eyebrow. "Don't look so guilty, Bacon-chops. If you weren't right for the job,

I wouldn't have rung you in the first place. I am a *professional.*"

I nod nervously. "OK."

I still feel like I've queue-jumped. Like the time I accidentally shoved in front of Alexa at lunch and had my ponytail dipped in gravy as retribution.

I glance quickly around, just in case anyone is planning on doing it again.

"So what's the inspiration this time, Monkey-moo?" Wilbur waves at my dress and flip-flops.

"I thought it was quite pretty."

"I Thought It Was Quite Pretty," he says in delight, clapping. "Is it made out of dolls' house curtains? *Amazement.* You light up my life, Petal-cheeks. You really do."

Right. I am never wearing this dress again.

"So you're not an agent any more?"

"Yuka Ito pulled a few strings as an amicable parting gesture," he says, wiggling his eyebrows at me. "It turns out genius is much easier to recognise in the States than back home, especially when your CV is somewhat – how do we put it? – *embellished.*" He drags a large black book out of his bag and hands it to me.

"You're going to need this," he adds. "So keep it

safe. I've already made a copy for Nancy."

I open it curiously.

Stuck in the front is an extremely close-up photo of a girl with snowflakes stuck to her eyelashes. You can see every single one of her billion freckles, and her eyes are wide and distracted and lit up from the inside.

I flip the page, and there's a photo of a ginger girl crouched on the floor in a tutu, covered in gold paint. Then another where she's holding a giant silver fish, dripping in octopus ink, and one standing in a sumo ring with a shadowy figure in the background.

There's one where the girl is stuck in a glass box, curled up in a pink wig with hundreds of identical dolls.

There's a picture of her floating in a lake in a lit-up dress, with Mount Fuji behind her and a thousand stars glimmering in the water.

And then I get to the final page and pause.

It's a photo of the same girl again, jumping in the air with a boy. A gorgeous boy with dark curly hair, sharp cheekbones, a big navy jacket and narrow, glowing eyes. The girl's feet are bare, her cheeks are flushed, her eyes are bright and she looks the happiest any girl has ever looked, ever.

No biggy.

My chest suddenly pings so badly I'm slightly worried the wire on my tiny bra may have poked through and stabbed me.

This is my portfolio. I hadn't even seen most of these photos before.

"You're not bad at this old modelling lark, Possum," Wilbur says, raising an eyebrow. "So don't think I'm doing you any favours, because I'm not. If anything, it's the other way round."

And then he pulls up his sunglasses and gives me a look.

A human can make more than 10,000 facial expressions, and I'm suddenly so embarrassed, so pleased, so grateful, I'm not entirely sure which one to pick.

So instead I flush and pull my phone out of my satchel.

Then I pause. "Why, Wilbur?"

"Why what, my little Carrot-cake? Did I fall asleep and miss a chunk of dialogue? I'm always doing that."

"Why do you always rescue me?"

Wilbur laughs. "Every Cinderella needs a fairy godmother, Baby-baby Panda," he says, shrugging and putting his sunglasses on. "But sometimes your fairy godmother needs you right back."

45

According to statistics, three billion phone calls are made every day in America.

This is the only one I care about.

"I'm sorry," I say the second Nick answers. "Before you say anything, I'm sorry."

"Don't apologise, Harriet. It was an important day and I screwed up badly."

"But you didn't do it on purpose."

"But I did screw up."

"But not on purpose."

My boyfriend laughs. "Do you want to fight? It's not your birthday any more, Manners, and I'll take you down. Verbally, with my sharp wit and free internet calls."

I smile. "Where are you?"

"The middle of Manhattan, between fittings. But I was thinking I could try to get to Greenway this evening? Although I probably won't blow the balloons up until I get *off* the train this time. Electronic doors are surprisingly difficult to negotiate."

"You could," I say, smiling a bit harder. "Or you could stay here."

"Here?" There's a pause and then, "As in America?"

"As in *here*." I hold my phone into the air so he can hear a fire engine screeching past and the blare of a thousand taxi horns.

"You're in *New York*?"

When I put my phone back to my ear I can hear the faint echo of a siren getting louder. If it's the same one, judging by the speed it was moving and the direction it was going in, Nick's probably less than half a mile away.

My entire stomach feels suddenly full of electricity.

My internal octopus is about to get fried.

"Uh-huh," I grin. "I want to talk to you about something."

"About what?"

"Anything," I say, beaming at the tiny, far away sky. "I just want to talk to you, Nick. About anything at all."

46

I think it's safe to say that plans matter to me.

Lists, schedules and itineraries: they're the cement that holds me together. Without them, I'm scared that I'll just dissolve into an illogical mess that makes no sense.

That I won't be *me.*

But as I turn the corner and see Nick, I suddenly couldn't care less about any of them.

His curly black hair is huge and sticking up everywhere. His grey T-shirt is crumpled, and his hands are slung into the pockets of grass-stained jeans. He's leaning against a wall – head cocked to the side – and as I approach his smile gets bigger and bigger until it breaks his entire face in half.

"Hi," he says as I get close.

"Hi." I put my arms around his waist and lean up. He smells of cinnamon for once. "Did you know," I say as I touch my nose against his, "that the energy Americans expend every day when chewing bubblegum would light a city of ten million people for a day?"

Nick laughs, takes out his cinnamon gum and neatly lobs it into a nearby bin. "In that case, for the sake of the environment, I should look into getting a bigger mouth."

I had so many plans for us.

We're supposed to be at the top of the Empire State Building. We're supposed to be on a boat, in the middle of a lake in Central Park. We're supposed to be holding hands on an ice-skating rink outside the Rockefeller Center (despite it not actually being built yet, which I admit was a massive oversight in my itinerary).

We're supposed to be in a field with a tree and blowing corn and sunshine and a random dove or at least a clean-looking pigeon.

There's supposed to be a sunset or a sunrise.

But there's none of that.

Instead, any sunshine is blocked out by an enormous cement skyscraper, and it's cold and weirdly dark.

When I look down, I see we're on top of a grate blowing warm, stale-smelling air into the street and up my dress, making it flutter around my knees.

We've stopped next to the back of a restaurant:

dubious-looking water is running down the pavement, and there's a bit of mushy bread stuck to the edge of my flip-flop. A truck pulls up and starts yelling at the truck next to it for blocking the road, and a man walks past with his finger up his nose.

I can smell cooked cheese, cabbage, detergent and something that may or may not be a blocked toilet.

I feel nothing like Marilyn Monroe.

But – as Nick leans down and kisses me – all of my romantic lists, schedules and itineraries disappear.

My plans evaporate, and I don't care.

47

We wander around New York for the rest of the day.

We walk down Fifth Avenue, past Cartier and Saks and Trump Tower and all the tourists wearing trainers and not buying jewellery in Tiffany & Co.

We walk through Times Square and see the flashing neon lights, with the enormous ticker showing the news and Madame Tussauds and red stairs that lead nowhere.

We walk past the Grecian-looking New York Library, and pop in to see the original *Winnie the Pooh*, which apparently has been taken out of England and not given back again.

At which point we discuss notifying the British Embassy.

We walk past the white, ship-like Guggenheim Museum and the Rubin Museum of Art and Theodore Roosevelt's birthplace, with its brownstone walls and tourists and American flag.

We keep going past Macy's and Bloomingdale's and Joe's and Lombardi's and Katz's and Scott's and I point out just how fond Americans seem to be of places that belong to people, and how nice it is to see apostrophes in all the right places.

We walk through Little Italy and the buildings painted green and white and red, and Chinatown with its bright reds and turquoises, and the shiny roasted ducks hanging upside down in the windows.

We spin round every few minutes so Nick can make observations about the Empire State Building getting smaller behind us: looming from behind the skyline like tall, pointed royalty.

And I barely see any of it.

I might as well be in the local park behind my house for all the attention I give to New York.

I see the little black curl at the back of Nick's head, and the tangle of his eyelashes. I see the points of his sharp teeth and the little line next to the right side of his mouth. I smell the warmth of his cheek and the greenness where his forehead meets his hair. I feel the dip in his shoulder where my head fits, and the way he beats a tune on my thumb as we walk.

And New York slides past behind him like an enormous, expensive backdrop. As if it's been put there, just to give us something to walk through.

We hold hands a lot. We kiss a lot.

A *lot*.

And we talk.

We talk about the blacked-out windows of his car in Africa and the hairdresser in Greenway and how if two rats were left alone for eighteen months they would have a million descendants and about the first time Nick learnt to surf and how the man who had the longest beard in the world stepped on it and broke his own neck and isn't that the saddest thing you've ever heard?

We talk so fast and for so long that I barely notice that it's dark, or that we've walked right through the city.

Finally, we look at the wooden slats under our feet and the enormous river running beneath us.

"Where are we?" I ask.

"This is Brooklyn Bridge."

I look through the silver webbing of wires holding it together, as if it's been built by a giant spider. To either side of us are millions of lights: Brooklyn on one side, and Manhattan on the other.

It's a glittering, hovering mass of white, yellow, green, red, blue: all shooting into the sky and mixing into the water. There are lights above us, linking the two sides: at the top of the Empire State Building, in the curves of the Chrysler.

It's like looking at the world's biggest Christmas decoration.

I take a deep breath and hold it for a few seconds.

"Nice, huh," Nick grins.

"It's..." I search my internal thesaurus. *Beguiling. Resplendent. Pulchritudinous.* "Perfect."

Nick stands behind me, puts his arms around my waist and tucks his chin into my neck.

"This is my favourite bit of New York. You can be part of the city but not part of it at the same time. It kind of gives everything perspective."

I nod. "I read that in 1884 a circus entertainer walked twenty-one elephants across Brooklyn Bridge to prove how strong it was."

Nick laughs, kisses my neck and looks up. "See up there?"

I follow his gaze to the top of the stone arches and nod.

"Peregrine falcons nest in the eaves. They fly all over the world, but they always come back here."

"The word *peregrine* actually comes from the Latin *peregrinus* which means *wanderer*, you know."

Nick suddenly goes very quiet so I lean my head backwards until it's resting on his collarbone.

We stand like that for a few minutes. And I appreciate the unspoken moment that hangs between us.

"Nick," I say tentatively: "I lo—"

"Shoot," Nick sighs.

OK, maybe not.

"Harriet, I left your birthday present at the model flat. I didn't know I was seeing you."

I shrug. "It's OK. You can give it to me some other time."

"Sorry." Nick squeezes my shoulder and grazes his nose against my ear. "It's getting late. Text Annabel and tell her I'll walk you to the station."

"Mmmm," I say, turning so he can't see my face as I stare out at the water. "Did you know that the Statue of Liberty wears a size 879 shoe?"

There's a long pause, and then Nick says, "Did you catch the train this morning with your dad?"

I clear my throat and squint at a tiny light in the distance. "Did you know there are seven spikes on the crown of the Statue of Liberty, representing the seven oceans and seven continents of the world?"

Then I hold on to Nick's arms really tightly and

pretend to really *invest* in the importance of this hug.

"Harriet," he says calmly, prising himself away from me. "Tell me your parents know where you are."

I sniff. "They've probably worked it out by now, yes."

"*What?*"

"Well, telling them where I am kind of defeats the point of running away, doesn't it?"

Nick's eyes widen, and then he takes a few steps back.

"What the *hell*, Harriet? You can't just run away to New York without telling anyone!"

"You're only a year older than me," I point out. "And you're here alone too."

"That's totally different," he snaps. "My parents know where I am, for starters. You're in a foreign country. It's dark. You've been missing all day. Your parents are going to be *out of their minds*."

"Well," I shrug, "that's what they get for—"

"No. That's not what they get for anything. I'm taking you home. Now." Nick turns round and starts marching back across the bridge.

I blink, and then run after him. "Wait..."

"Give me your phone."

He's so angry I hand it to him without another

word. He presses a few buttons and then starts talking almost immediately. "Annabel? It's Nick. Harriet's in New York, but she's on her way home."

There are a few high mouse squeaks on the other end and then Nick puts his hand over his face and adds, "I know. I'm so sorry."

There are a few more squeaks and then silence.

I can feel myself starting to get angry.

"You had no right to do that," I say when he hangs up. My cheeks are burning and I feel about five years old. How *dare* he? "This is between me and my parents. It has nothing to do with you."

"When you spend the day with me, it absolutely does."

Without another word Nick turns around.

And marches me all the way back to Grand Central station in total silence.

48

I am forced to sit with the ticket inspector the whole way home.

Nick tells her that I'm foreign and lost, and I have to sit right next to her and then follow her up and down the carriage while she checks people's tickets.

It is totally humiliating.

And also a little bit fun: she lets me punch holes into them with a tiny metal clipper.

Now, I know a lot of things:

I know an ant can lift fifty times its own weight, which is like a human lifting a really big car. I know that snails can sleep for three years, and sharks lose 30,000 teeth in a lifetime. I know an iPhone has 240,000 times the power and memory of the Voyager spacecraft and that a gorilla once ripped a sink out of a wall and blamed it on its pet kitten.

I know in Wyoming it is illegal to take a photo of

a rabbit in the month of June, and Disneyland uses 5,000 gallons of paint every year to keep it looking new.

And I know very little about being a girlfriend.

But there are some basic *rules* for us all to stick to.

I've read the books and seen the films and heard the songs, and the conclusion is always that a boyfriend is supposed to be on your side. Fighting for you, protecting you, defending you, against all odds. No matter what you've done.

Laughing at your foibles and eccentricities and finding your weird bits adorable, whatever happens.

They're supposed to be on your *team.*

I don't remember Romeo yelling at Juliet. I don't recall any chapter where Darcy rang Mrs Bennett and dropped Lizzie in it. Rochester didn't march Jane Eyre all the way through New York without even pausing or turning around to talk to her. Heathcliff never put Cathy on a train and told her to stop being such a brat.

Frankly, I don't think Nick is reading the right books. When he's talking to me again I shall have to give him a list.

I grumble all the way to Greenway, then stomp and grumble all the way down the road, and then all the way up the garden path. Then – just for good measure

– I add under my breath: What kind of boyfriend *does* that? Whose side is he on? How *dare* he?

Who does Nick think he is: *my parents*?

At which point I open the front door and am forced to reassess that last question.

Because Annabel and Dad are both standing silently in the hallway: feet apart, arms crossed, jaws set. Their faces are white, their lips are thin, and there isn't a smidgen of humour on their faces.

If I thought Nick was angry, I might have to think again.

My parents aren't cross.

They are *livid.*

49

I'm not going to detail the following conversation in full.

This is because:

a) it is not a conversation
b) it's so loud everyone in a four-million-mile radius heard it anyway
c) you already know exactly what was said.

As soon as the door shuts behind me, my parents go absolutely berserk.

They didn't know where I was. Miss Hall had to be sent home. They nearly called the police. *New York?* Dad had to leave work early. They spent hours wandering the streets, trying to find me. *It's midnight.* Do I have no consideration for anyone else? *NEW YORK?* I could have been murdered, or mugged or kidnapped.

Anything could have happened.

"Except it didn't," I point out when Annabel finally draws a breath and Dad sits down on the bottom stair because he's worn himself out. "I'm OK."

A little wave of guilt is rolling around the bottom of my stomach. I knew they'd be worried, but I had no idea they'd be *this* upset.

"That is *not the point,*" Annabel shouts, and Tabitha starts crying via the baby monitor.

"Well," Dad says more cautiously. "It is *kind* of the point, isn't it?"

Annabel opens her mouth in fury, and then pinches the bridge of her nose tightly.

"Look, I understand you're angry with us, Harriet," she says more gently. "But this is *not* the mature way to deal with it. You can't just *go.* It's *dangerous.*"

I kick the edge of a stair a few times with my toe. "I just wanted to see New York and..."

Some basic survival instinct kicks in just in time to stop me mentioning Wilbur, magazines or modelling. The pulsing of the vein in Annabel's forehead has just started slowing down: I don't want it to explode and kill us all.

"Nick," I finish.

"Then just *tell* us that. Your dad could at least have gone with you." Annabel sighs and sits down on the stairs.

"So what did you do?" Dad asks. "Because I walked up and down Fifth Avenue about six times, asking anyone if they'd seen you, and frankly I'm keen to see how I should have spent that three hours."

I open my mouth, and then shut it again. *Agreed to a modelling job and kissed my boyfriend a lot.* "Oh, you know," I say as sensibly as I can. "Museums. Galleries. Interactive exhibitions."

"Yes?" Annabel narrows her eyes. "Like what?"

"Umm, well." I swallow. "I went to the Metropolitan Museum of Art, which spans 5,000 years of culture, and the Guggenheim Museum, which is housed in the Frank Lloyd Wright building and is a work of art in itself, and the Museum of Modern Art, which has one of the world's most comprehensive collections including Picasso and Warhol."

Then I clear my throat.

I memorised that speech from my guidebook on the train on the way home, just in case anybody asked. It's a good thing I know my family so well.

"Give me your guidebook, Harriet."

Unfortunately, they appear to know me even better.

I reach into my satchel and hand it over. Annabel

flicks through it and then stops. I really wish I hadn't underlined those exact sentences in green highlighter.

"Right," she says slowly. "Well, I'm glad you've taken the study of New York so seriously. That should come in handy over the next few days."

She hands me back the guidebook.

"Why?" I frown. "What do you mean?"

"You're grounded, Harriet."

I stare at her, and then at Dad. "Do you mean *well balanced and sensible*?" I ask. "Or... prevented from flying, like an aeroplane?"

"I mean you're grounded. Verb, informal. You will stay in your room for the next five days."

OK: I've never been *grounded*. Ever.

"But..." I can feel alarm creeping up my throat. The shoot's tomorrow. I *have* to go. If I don't, I'm going to let Wilbur and Nancy down. My fashion career will be over for the second time. I'll be back to being nobody all over again.

"No buts," Annabel says, recrossing her arms. "Go to your room."

"*Dad—*"

"Nope," he says. "Beneath this deceptively charming and handsome exterior, I am genuinely quite angry." He clears his throat. "So do what

Annabel said. Go to your room, etcetera."

Then they both shuffle slightly and look at each other.

I think they're even more surprised about this than I am. It looks like they're rehearsing a scene from a play called *How to Deal With Naughty Children* and they haven't quite learnt their lines properly.

"Do I get to leave my room to go to the toilet? Or do you want me to use a houseplant?"

They glance at each other. "You can use the toilet," they decide unanimously.

"And the kitchen, or do you want me to starve?"

Silence. "We'll leave food outside your door."

"And the garden or do I have to take deep breaths through the floorboards?"

"*Harriet*," Annabel snaps. "Go to your bedroom. We will work out the oxygen requirements of this grounding later."

"*FINE*," I shout, stomping up the stairs and slamming yet another door behind me. "*WHATEVER*."

Except nothing is fine at all.

So I get up the next morning at 5am, when the entire house and everyone in it is still fast asleep.

I turn off my phone.

And I run away again.

50

New York is a different place this early in the morning.

Gone are the tourists, the cameras, the breathable trainers and the waterproof backpacks. Gone are the giant maps and the confused conversations and the buzzy, impatient queues next to the information booths.

At 7am, New Yorkers take their city back.

I stand quietly in Grand Central station, watching their neat suits, tailored dresses and silk scarves: moving with the deliberate poise and grace of people who know exactly where they're going.

And even though I know my dad should still be in bed, every time I see a man with red hair, I have to duck behind one of them.

Running away is a lot harder than it looks.

Especially when everybody in the entire world suddenly seems to have morphed overnight into my dad.

"My little Pease-blossom," Wilbur says as yet another man in a suit and unnecessarily colourful tie walks down the stairs and I abruptly bolt behind a nearby column. "Are we playing hide-and-seek? Are you under some impression that you look exactly like an enormous piece of marble and therefore blend in perfectly?"

I peek out from behind it and glance at the enormous, lit-up, multi-faceted clock hanging above us. 6.34am. According to their usual schedule, Dad and Annabel *should* just be waking up now.

I shiver slightly.

It's starting to look like the clock isn't the only thing in this building with more than one face.

"Actually," I say, patting the column, "I think this is Indiana limestone, which is sedimentary rock, while marble is metamorphic. They're really quite different."

Wilbur rubs his eye tiredly with the sleeve of his gold lamé jacket. "Bunny-ears, they could both be made from the compressed souls of angels and kittens at this time of the morning and I wouldn't give a squirrel's bottom."

He starts wobbling off across the concourse so I quickly scan the room once more for angry redheads in their mid-forties and then follow him.

"So, where's the shoot?" I studied my guidebook on the train this morning for an hour and a half, trying to distract myself from the guilt by guessing where the location could be. "The Empire State Building? Central Park? The Rockefeller Center? Inside a diner, leaning against the metal counters and eating hamburgers?"

"Chunky-monkey," Wilbur laughs. "This is *high art*. We want *subversive. Insightful. Explosive.* We're not shooting the front cover for *New York for Tourists.*"

This is probably why models aren't really asked for their creative input.

Somebody shouts *Harriet* and I spin round with a dry mouth. "Hurry *up,*" a woman sighs again at a little girl, dragging her doll along the floor. "Why are you always so slow?"

I swallow noisily as Wilbur starts pulling a huge suitcase towards the stairs that lead down to the subway.

"Harriet?"

I flinch and turn to the side. "*Hawt,*" a man says, flapping himself with his hand. "It's so *hawt*, isn't it?"

And then the crowd dissolves into a hum of *Harriet Harriet Harriet Harriet...*

Oh my God. I'm going mad.

I ran away less than two hours ago and guilt is

already turning me into Lady Macbeth. Any minute now I'll be scrubbing imaginary blood off my hands, or – in this instance – the tears of my worried parents.

I pause on the stairs and look into the darkness. The handrail is sticky, there's a rush of hot, damp air, and it smells of sweat and oil and metal. A thundering sound starts rumbling and gets louder until the floor shakes.

I want to go back to Greenway.

"Umm," I say, turning around. "Wilbur, I've made a horrible mistake."

"Mistake?" Wilbur looks at my striped trousers and green gym shirt with pursed lips, and then shakes his head. "No, Sugar-lump. This look is divine. Although maybe try pool sliders instead of flip-flops next time."

"I mean –" I cough – "today. The shoot. Can they replace me?"

Wilbur starts laughing.

"Can they *replace* you? Bless my baby cabbages, you're not a salad with the wrong dressing, Munchkin. The shoot's in an hour. I can't magic models out of thin air like genies, as handy as that would be." Then he pats my shoulder. "What's up, Poppet? Don't you want a day at the seaside?"

And – just like that – my day splits down the middle.

I can go back to Greenway: to the loneliest bedroom, the angriest parents and the longest extended grounding in the known history of man, ever. I can sit in my bedroom and wonder what page of my diary Alexa is currently laughing at and which *amazing* new cafés Jessica has taken Nat to. I can wonder whether my dog even remembers what I look like.

Or I can go to the beach.

Sunshine. Sand. Sea. Hot dogs. Deckchairs. Dolphins, jumping in perfectly timed sequence through sparkling water. Apparently there are 7.5 billion billion grains of sand in the world, and it's been at least two years since I saw *any* of them.

I'm in huge trouble anyway. I may as well earn my punishment properly. That's just basic logic.

"A *seaside*? In New York? Really?"

"*Absolutement*. I'll even buy you an ice cream, which I will then not allow you to eat because you're a *model* and cold whipped fat is not one of the dietary requirements."

I think about it. The seaside sounds *very* far from Dad's New York City office, which might mean I can stop hearing my name every couple of seconds.

"Harriet?"

A woman walks past. "I just hate having to get up

this early," she says into her phone. "Don't you just hate it?"

I don't really have a choice. Plus I'm still wearing my favourite flip-flops this morning so at least I look marginally appropriate.

I nod and wait until Wilbur's plinking down the stairs again: one hand held loosely in the air, another dragging the suitcase in loud crashes behind him.

And I pull out the box in my head: the box I haven't touched in months. Tentatively, I open it. Then – gently, softly – I put in Annabel. I put in Dad. I put in Tabitha. I put in Nat and Toby and Hugo. I lob in Alexa, still clutching my purple diary.

Finally, with a guilty wince, I put in Nick.

And then I gently close it.

It's just for the morning, that's all.

Just one tiny morning while I have a bit of fun. And then, when I've had my morning of adventure, I'll get everyone back out again and deal with the consequences.

Whatever they may be.

51

Here are some fascinating facts about the New York subway:

- *It has more stations than any other public transportation system in the world (277).*
- *There are 656 miles of track.*
- *In an average year, 1.7 billion trips will be made on it.*
- *There are 31,180 turnstiles, 734 token booths and 161 escalators.*

And here are some things the guidebooks *didn't* mention.

They didn't say, for instance, that the New York subway makes the London Underground look like an enormous toy constructed for children.

They didn't say that everything is gun-metal grey: the floors, the lights, the outsides of the trains, the insides of the trains, the handrails and the seats.

They didn't say that the map isn't littered with chirpy names like Piccadilly Circus or Green Park, but has strict, angry-looking numbers and letters instead.

They didn't say how huge it is, or how busy, or how incredibly hot and bright.

But probably the single most defining fact that *none* of the guidebooks mention is that the New York subway map makes no sense.

Literally none.

Wilbur and I stand by a large map for at least ten minutes, tilting our heads to the side in the hope that one way or another will make everything clearer.

It doesn't.

"So..." I say after a long silence. "The red line is 1, 2 *and* 3?"

"Apparently," Wilbur sighs. "And the orange one is B, D, F *and* M."

I get a bit closer to it. "And this one is called 14th Street, and *this* one is called 14th Street? And *all* of these are called 34th Street?"

"Apparently so." Wilbur sighs as he starts scrolling through his iPhone. "Honey-puff, New York is the most magical place on earth, but the subway can kiss my cat's pyjamas. Next time, we're *so* getting a taxi."

*

I spend the rest of the journey tucked into a steel seat, staring surreptitiously at everyone getting on and off the train.

There's an old lady, dressed head to toe in fluorescent green with an enormous scarlet flower tied around her head. There's a girl with dreadlocks and enormous high heels and a pair of fluffy headphones. There's an old man, muttering to himself, and a woman in an expensive-looking suit, quietly crying into her handbag.

Every age, every nationality, every dress sense clambers on and off the F train as we rush through the city; through Manhattan over the river into Brooklyn, popping in and out of the ground like a little mole coming up for air.

And slowly the city starts to shrink: from enormous skyscrapers to smaller buildings with colourful graffiti and stars and words and paintings etched bravely across them.

Sunshine begins to pour in, and the sky opens out again. From tiny, far-away patches it gets closer and brighter and bluer and lighter until it's back to its normal size.

"Are we there?" I say as Wilbur starts packing up his sketchbook. He's been doodling in earnest ever since we left Manhattan, but every time I try to see what it is he bops me on the nose with the end of a pencil. "Are we at the seaside?"

"Uh-huh, my *petite grenouille.* As close as we can get without driving straight into it, anyway."

As if to prove his point, my stomach does an excited little frog-like hop. The windows of the train are open, and I can smell saltiness and sweetness and candy floss and hot dogs.

Maybe Wilbur will let me go for a quick swim with the dolphins. Ooh, maybe the shoot will be under water.

I'll just have to hope fervently that nobody ever finds out about the octopus in Tokyo or they will never let me near any kind of sea life.

"Where are we meeting Nancy?" I ask as we both climb off the train on to a platform that's much smaller, quieter and less cavernous than the last one.

"Right here," a clear-cut American voice says.

And I turn around and immediately begin to flush.

Nancy is standing behind us, glowing. She's in a large white shirt and white trousers; she's holding a bright white handbag and wearing bright white sunglasses. She looks like something out of *The Lord of The Rings*.

But that's not why I'm slowly changing colour.

Standing next to her is a boy. He's tall and deeply tanned. His hair is blond and swept in messy, sandy tufts across his forehead. There are little white strands around the front where the sun has bleached it, and his eyes are bright piercing blue.

He looks like a wolf, except one with a little scar across his cheek that somehow makes him even more handsome.

But none of this is why I'm blushing either.

The reason I'm getting steadily hotter and redder and more uncomfortable is that I already know him.

It's the boy from the reception at LA MODE.

Except he's not studying his phone now.

This time, he's staring directly at me.

52

Over the last year I have learnt quite a lot about boys.

I've learnt that some of them are frightened of seagulls, particularly large ones. I've learnt that some had a hamster called Strategic when they were six, and it met an untimely end when a door blew shut during an impulsive bid for freedom.

I have learnt that some enjoy playing retro Pac-man and hate passion fruit because they think it's slimy like tiny eyeballs and that badgers are brilliant because they walk like old men. I've learnt some have a favourite beach on the south coast of Australia and like the smell of lime because it reminds them of a pancake recipe their mum used to make when they were little.

I've learnt that some take stairs two at a time and throw their head back when they're laughing so you can see the secret mole at the base of their throat.

I've learnt that in the second before they lean down to kiss you, their bottom lip twitches slightly.

In other words: I've learnt a lot about *one* boy.

The rest are still a great, unsolved mystery to me.

As the blond boy stares at me, I can feel myself getting more and more confused.

I quickly wipe my face and look down, just in case I've got blueberry muffin all over my T-shirt or something.

When I look up, he's still staring.

So I decide to confront the situation the only way I know how.

"Hello again," I say, holding out my hand as Nancy draws Wilbur aside and starts talking quietly. "My name is Harriet Manners. It's nice to meet you properly."

He frowns as he takes my hand. "Have we met before?"

I flush a bit harder.

"I'm the skyscraper-facts girl," I say, clearing my throat. "From the LA MODE sofa?"

As if LA MODE Sofa is a distant country, like Spare Oom in Narnia, or Argentina.

"Are you sure? Because I don't think I'd forget a face like yours."

He must be gripping quite tightly, because it feels like every drop of blood is being squeezed into my cheeks. I suddenly wish I'd eschewed the traditional Western handshake in favour of a Nepalese head-butt.

"You'd be surprised," I say, trying to tug my hand back as politely as I can.

He finally releases it with a devastating smile. His teeth are blindingly white.

"Sorry," he says. "Beautiful British girls always make me forget myself. I'm Caleb Davis, but everybody calls me Cal."

My stomach lurches. *Beautiful?*

"I don't think that's what everybody calls you, Caleb," a loud voice says from behind me.

I turn around.

The really tall, bald girl from the LA MODE reception kisses the air a metre from his ear with a loud *mwah*.

"Be nice, K," Cal says with a frown.

"I'm never nice, babe," she says, straightening her orange maxi dress. "It's one of my striking characteristics. Kenderall," she adds, turning back to me. "K-e-n-d-e-r-a-double-l. You've probably never met a Kenderall before, because I invented the name myself."

Wow. She must have been a really advanced baby.

"Umm." I blink in shock at the black and pink hairy thing grunting on the floor next to her. I don't want to state the obvious, but: "Is that a—"

"Pig? Yeah. He's my pet miniature teacup pig, Sir Francis."

Without being rude, there is no *way* this pig could get into a teacup or a teapot. It's enormous.

"He's another one of Kenderall's *striking characteristics*," Cal says as the pig stares into the distance with a glazed expression.

"Nobody forgets the Girl with the Pig," Kenderall says fiercely. "Although that wannabe Pilot has just gone and got a tiny pink one, and they say she makes it wear wellies. Next time I see her at a casting we're having words."

"Sir Francis?" I say, bending down and patting him on the wiry top of his head. This is partly because I've never seen a pet pig before, and partly because Cal is studying me intensely and I need to avoid eye contact before my cheeks explode. "As in Sir Francis Bacon, famous philosopher and author?"

Kenderall's eyes widen. "There's a man called Sir Francis *Bacon*?"

"Well, not any more there isn't. He died of pneumonia in 1626 while experimenting with keeping meat fresh by freezing it. Possibly pork."

I was sort of hoping for a friendly laugh.

I do not get one.

"I named him after Sir Francis Drake. I thought he looked a bit British, no offence. Are you telling me everyone in New York thinks I have a *novelty* pig called *Bacon*?"

"You want to be remembered," Cal reminds her.

Kenderall looks totally horrified. "Not for being *funny*."

I stand up swiftly: Francis is starting to pee on the platform floor and I need to move before it hits my foot. "Are we the models for today, then?"

"*I* am," Kenderall says, pointing at her own face. "This needs recording as often as possible."

"And I'm the photographer's assistant," Cal says, shrugging. "I'm just here to carry things and make tea. It's not that interesting, but on days like this it's totally worth it."

He looks me up and down again.

There are 60,000 miles of blood capillaries in the human body, which is the surface-area equivalent of three tennis courts.

Every centimetre of mine is now on fire.

"There's another girl waiting for us at the fairground," Kenderall says, bending down and tying a little orange bandana around the pig's head. "And

OMG, she's so *yawn*. There isn't a single striking characteristic about her."

"Not bad looking," Cal says, shrugging. "If you like pale brunettes. Personally, I prefer perky redheads."

Which should be a cue for me to get even redder, but I'm not really listening any more. I heard one word, and then everything went very quiet and far away.

"F-fairground?" I stammer. "What do you mean f-f-fairground?"

"It's, like, this space that hosts fun rides, like a carnival?" Kenderall says, rolling her eyes. "Oh dear. Don't say that kind of stuff out loud, babe. It gives models a bad name."

"But..." I look around the station wildly, to where Wilbur is now showing Nancy the sketches in his art-pad. As he flips the pages, I see elaborate and surprisingly beautiful drawings of roller coasters and Ferris wheels and swings. "Wilbur said we were going to the beach."

"This is Coney Island," Cal says, stretching his arms out wide. "There *is* a beach, but it's famous for its fairground."

OK. This is the second time in a fortnight that someone I trust has taken me somewhere and pretended I'm going somewhere else.

I need to start asking smarter questions.

"B-b-but…" Sunshine. Sea. Sand. Pods of dolphins. They're all vanishing with little *pops*, like lemmings off the edge of a cliff. "It's just an elaborate set, right? A backdrop?"

"Nope, my little Chicken-monkey," Wilbur says, sashaying back towards us. "Isn't this fun? You won't even have to queue for rides."

No.

No no no no no *no.*

I start backing away in terror.

"Oopsy," Wilbur says, grabbing my arm as I manage to get one foot on the train behind me. "The fairground is this way, Bunny-boo."

In the distance, I can see the top of an enormous, brightly coloured wheel and a sign that says LUNA PARK.

Luna is the Latin word for *moon*, which is the stem for the word *lunatic* because in the thirteenth century people thought that periodic insanity was caused by changes of the moon. And as they drag me towards the single thing in the world I am most terrified of, all I can think is:

Lunatic Park.

Sounds about right.

53

I am very fond of gravity.

Gravity keeps the Earth and the other planets in orbit around the sun. It keeps the moon in orbit around the Earth. It creates tides and waves. When you drop a pen, gravity is what makes it hit the ground; when you jump, gravity is what stops you flying into space.

Without gravity, the entire world would literally spin out of control.

If I wanted that kind of unregulated, unmanageable nonsense, I'd go to Pluto where I would weigh nine pounds and could just float around like Peter Pan.

Over the last ten years, I have been to five funfairs with Nat who insists on going on the wildest, fastest rides possible while I stand, terrified, at the bottom holding her coat.

This is my punishment for running away again.

I thought I understood *karmic retribution*, but the universe obviously works faster than I thought it did.

You couldn't cook a casserole in the time it's taken for me to get my cosmic comeuppance.

"I wasn't sure about this initially," Nancy smiles as we approach the fairground. "But you might actually be some weird kind of genius, Wilbur."

"*Mais bien sûr,*" he says in mock surprise. "Who said I wasn't? Was it Stephanie at Infinity Models? I once said she couldn't pull off leggings and she's hated me ever since."

I stare at the entrance gates in shock.

It's an enormous, ten-metre clown face, moulded in peach-coloured plaster.

The eyes are wide open and bright blue; the cheeks are bright pink and the lips are bright red and also open. There's a spiky yellow crown and two brightly coloured turrets on either side. And in the gaping, wide mouth are huge white teeth: rectangular and flat, like a row of shiny headstones.

We're expected to enter Luna Park through the mouth of an insane clown, apparently.

And Nat wonders why I don't like fairgrounds.

"Look, Munchkin," Wilbur says, pointing upwards. "The teeth and eyes light up at night-time. Isn't that just *fabadoozy*? I wish mine did that."

I can feel the palms of my hands getting damp.

Since when have lit-up eyes and teeth ever made *anything* less scary?

I take a deep breath and run under the teeth with my hands over my head just in case the jaws suddenly decide to come alive and clench down. Of all the many ways I do not want to die, Eaten by a Clown is pretty high up the list.

Just underneath is having my legs chewed off by a vampire zombie-shark and being made to spend the afternoon in TopShop.

"Harriet," Nancy says, touching my shoulder as I quiver on the other side, arms still wrapped around my head. "Do you want to follow Marianna? She's your stylist this morning."

She points at a small woman with glossy black curls, shiny pink lips and an enormous black bag.

"Uh-huh," I say blankly, eyes widening even more. I've just noticed the pods revolving around the Ferris wheel. They're red and blue and green, with metal grids all the way round them. Like tiny cheerful little birdcages.

If you're being optimistic.

Swinging death prisons, if you're being less so.

"You're not afraid of heights, are you?" Nancy says, frowning. "I should probably have checked that with you yesterday."

Am I afraid of heights? No.

Am I afraid of being secured into a blue metal ball, attached to two bits of elastic and catapulted fifty metres into the air at 90mph?

Absolutely.

"Nope," I lie, tucking my hair behind my ears and grinning so hard my ears start to ache. "I am very much looking forward to this exciting and unprecedented experience."

Because I am a professional model.

Because I agreed to this job.

Because I don't want to let anyone down or for anyone else to be angry with me.

But most of all, because otherwise I'll be sent straight back home to my parents.

And frankly I think a ride called Slingshot will be absolutely nothing in comparison to what they are going to do to me when I see them next.

54

Getting ready has always been my favourite part of any fashion shoot.

It's the bit where – with a few splashes of lotions and potions – I'm transformed into somebody else.

Somebody glamorous. Somebody pretty.

It's a bit like alchemy, except that instead of turning base metals into gold they somehow manage to get a freckly, awkward schoolgirl to look vaguely presentable in front of a camera.

Unfortunately Marianna doesn't appear to have the same alchemical ambitions.

"Nobody said you'd be this pale, redhead," she grumbles as she starts emptying the contents of her black bag all over a fold-up table in the changing room. "They could have given me warning."

My face obediently starts changing colour.

"0.5 per cent of the world's population has red hair," I say slightly defensively. "That's nearly forty million of us."

"Your *hair* is not the problem." She picks up a few different pots of cream liquid and starts aggressively mixing them on the back of her hand. "*You* try covering up a trillion freckles without any preparation."

Then she starts her assault.

She attacks me with a foundation brush and three different shades of foundation. She attacks me with a coarse eyeshadow brush and stabs enormous quantities of dark grey into my eyelids. She rubs a toothbrush along my lips and applies a gel that burns. She starts back-combing my hair so vigorously I decide to put Death by Hairbrush just below Death by Clown on my list of ways I don't want to perish.

At one stage, she bends down on the floor and picks up some mud which she then starts smearing on my face.

She also adds to this physical onslaught snippy little comments, like: "God, but your eyelashes are *non-existent*," and "Have you even *heard* of tweezers?" and "What a *nose*. You could find ants with that thing."

Finally she sprays me with an enormous can of hairspray until I start choking.

"I'm *sorry*," she says stiffly. "Is the model finding

getting paid to sit still and do nothing *difficult*?"

I blink a few times in surprise. "Sorry."

Which is another huge mistake.

"*Brilliant,*" she says, getting a cotton-wool bud out and dipping it in eye make-up remover. "The mascara wasn't dry. So I'll just start again, shall I? It's not like I've got anything better to do."

Finally, when I've been satisfactorily beaten to a pulp, she goes to the corner and pulls out a bit of fabric.

It's shapeless and small and grey. It's ripped and shredded, and has bits of loose thread hanging off the edges. There's a dark smudge running across the front of it, and when she holds it out a rusty-looking safety pin falls to the floor with a *clink.*

For the first time, I *really* miss Yuka Ito.

"Do you have an *opinion*?" Marianna snaps as I blink at it.

I shake my head. "No-o-o. It's very..." *Likely to give me tetanus.* "... multi-textural."

"Just get into it."

I obediently do as I'm told. Then I'm led out of the room to where Wilbur is waiting for me.

"*Oh,*" he says, clapping his hands together. "Oh oh *oh.* It's amazing, my little cat-flip-flops! It's *exactly* what we wanted! Do you want to see your gloriousness?"

I look down at my ratty furry slippers: the kind old ladies leave outside the bathroom.

"Sure," I say doubtfully.

Wilbur picks up a cracked mirror and holds it aloft for me.

My eyes are dark grey and swollen and pink around the edges. My skin is the wrong colour. There's mud on my cheeks, and my hair looks like something hamsters make in the corners of their cage.

I don't look like I've been transformed into a glamorous funfair-loving model. I look like I've been sleeping under one of the rides for the last five years.

"Don't you just *love* it?" Wilbur says, laughing delightedly. "You look *just edible.* It's by a new designer in Brooklyn so *hip* almost nobody has ever heard of him. Never to be made again."

I can see why.

"Umm, Wilbur?" I check as I'm led back into the sunshine. "Exactly how many people read this magazine?"

"Three," he says cheerfully. "Maybe three and a half."

"Thousand?"

Wilbur shouts with laughter. "Oh my little poo-nut, where do you think we are – the Pitcairn Islands? Three and a half million, give or take one or two."

Three and a half million.

Three and a half *million* people across America are going to see me looking like somebody who gets killed quite early on in *Les Miserables*.

I guess karma isn't finished with me yet after all.

55

Kenderall is the first thing I see when I return to the fairground.

This is partly because she's dressed in a long, bright yellow silk dress, with huge gold earrings and gold bangles wound up her arms like some kind of Amazonian sun goddess.

But mostly because she yells, "*You have got to be freaking kidding me!*" at the top of her voice as I approach.

"Well," she says, stomping towards me in bright gold heels. "*Somebody* pulled the short straw, didn't they? You need a better agent, babe. You wouldn't get me into an outfit like that in a million years. You look *hideous.*"

I'm too busy staring beyond her to respond.

There's the usual group of people wearing black and holding lights and light reflectors and make-up bags and large cameras. And in the middle of this crowd is a girl.

She's tall and pale and beautiful. Her brown hair is up in a bun, and she's wearing a sky-blue silk evening gown, with silver earrings and a large silver necklace with a shimmering blue stone set in the middle.

Behind her is a winding mass of metal.

It twists and turns and spirals and dips and tangles like the strings of a puppet that's been left too long in the box.

Every few minutes there's a loud rush, and a small car zooms past at top speed, packed full of people.

Screaming people.

"That's Cyclone," Nancy quips, pointing at the giant roller coaster. "We're going to get a great action shot with this one."

If you scare a vulture, it will vomit to try and drive away its predator. It's both a peace offering, and a method of self-defence. I'm not a vulture, but I might go ahead and give it a shot.

I look down at my hideous outfit, and then at the beautiful yellow and blue silk dresses next to me. Then I look at my nasty fur slippers. When Charles Perrault wrote *Cendrillon* in 1697, he accidentally replaced the word *vair* – fur – with *verre*, meaning *glass.*

Which means I'm Cinderella.

"Hello, Fleur," I say to the least ugly sister I have seen, ever.

"Hi, Harriet," Fleur says softly. "*Again.*"

56

Obviously, *Harriet, again* can mean a lot of things.

It can mean, "Oh, thank *goodness*! I was hoping I would see you again!" It can mean, "I am so sorry I ran off without giving you my number! Let's hang out and play Monopoly as soon as possible!"

Sadly, there is no exclamation mark, so it means neither of those things.

Fleur looks exhausted.

And slightly concerned that I'm either going to try and force her into an involuntary lunch or knock her on to the floor in public again.

"How are you?" I say awkwardly as Nancy starts arranging the crowd and securing the barriers around us.

"Fine," Fleur tells the floor.

"And..." I've run out of small talk already. There really should be a class on this at school. "The clouds are nice today, aren't they? I think those are Cirrus, and they are usually just above six thousand metres high."

"Right," Fleur says as I point vaguely upwards, and I really wish I'd just stuck with fire hydrants. At least we'd be on known territory.

"Fleur?" Cal lifts the rope for the ride. "Ready?"

Her collarbone is going steadily pink.

"Mmm," she says, staring at the toes of her shoes and climbing into the roller-coaster car.

Cal hops into the back seat and winks at me.

"Don't worry about blurgh," Kenderall says in a low voice. "I did try and warn you."

"Blurgh?"

"Fleur Blurgh. She can suck the character out of anyone from a hundred paces."

I look at Fleur in surprise. She's huddled in the seat of the car with her arms folded around her middle and her shoulders hunched, as if something in the centre of her is slowly getting smaller. Where is the girl who winked at me from behind the curtain in Russia?

Fleur looks up, catches my eye and looks away, as if I'm totally invisible.

"On you get, my little Model-moos," Wilbur says, gesturing towards the train. "And let me remind you, Chipmunks, this is high fashion. No screaming. No laughing. No looking like you're having fun. I want you to appear thoroughly miserable."

I look at the tiny metal car and the spiralling mass of metal above us that totally defies gravity and logic. This is possibly the most inaccurate allocation of the word 'fun' ever.

"That shouldn't be a problem," I say, climbing in next to Kenderall and behind a woman wearing black, holding an enormous camera. "Just shoot me."

And the worst three minutes of my life begin.

57

Here are the three biggest roller coasters in the world:

- *Kingda Da,* in New Jersey. 139 metres.
- *Top Thrill Dragster*, in Ohio. 130 metres.
- *Superman,* in California. 126 metres.

They're all in the United States.

This country clearly has no respect for the natural speed, height and orientation of human beings.

For the first few seconds, I almost forget where we are. The sea is sparkling in front of us. The sand is a yellow ribbon, and – dotted like tiny stars – are people: lying on the beach, eating hot dogs, sunbathing, swimming with dolphins.

And then the world tilts and it all disappears.

"*Woooooooooo,*" Kenderall shouts next to me. "Come on, baby! Bring it on!"

The camera starts clicking, and – in what feels like

another dimension, even though she's sitting next to me – I can feel Kenderall go very still, arch back in her seat and start pouting dramatically.

When I was six, Nat had a little black gerbil called Fidget. It liked sniffing your finger through the cage, nibbling on bits of carrot and running very fast in its wheel.

But every now and then it couldn't keep up: it would end up pressed against the side of the wheel, spinning round and round until it finally got ejected on to the floor of the cage.

That's exactly how I feel.

Every time the roller coaster slows down and the world stops spinning it's only for long enough to blink back the tears and take one deep breath before it dissolves again.

I'm not just dizzy.

I'm not just disorientated.

I'm hanging on to the metal pole in front of me so tightly my knuckles look like they're about to poke through my skin, like a mini Wolverine.

I am *terrified*.

We twist and turn and roll and jolt; we rotate and warp and wind and zigzag. Finally, when I'm not sure I can handle any more, the train starts slowing down.

Thank God thank God thank God thank—

"Did we get it?" Nancy shouts over the gathering crowd around the base of the ride as I desperately try to work out which way up I am.

In front of me, the photographer peers at the camera and then shakes her head.

"One more time!" Nancy yells.

And the nightmare begins again.

We go round eight times.

We go round until there's dry saliva on my cheeks and my eyes are burning and my hands are dripping and wind has blown my hair into a wild fuzz over my head.

We go round until there's a point where I seriously consider just clambering out of the train at a high point and attempting to climb down the metal beams like Spiderman.

Finally the photographer gives an almost imperceptible nod.

"OK," Nancy says. "That's enough."

And the train slows to a stop.

I, however, don't.

As I clamber out, the world continues to buckle. The clouds continue to spin; the floor continues to warp and rotate and move up and down.

"Monkey?" I hear Wilbur say from a billion miles away. "Are you O—"

And everything goes black.

58

I've always wanted to faint.

On my list of Romantic Moments Harriet Manners Would Like to Achieve, fainting is number two.

Just under being the cause of a swordfight at dawn, and just above being rescued from a tower and then carried across a desert in a floaty dress.

I'm supposed to faint delicately and then get caught by a handsome boy who is terrified that I might be dead and tries to breathe life back into me with a well-timed and medicinally dubious kiss.

Unfortunately, it doesn't quite work like that.

When the world lights back up a few seconds later, I'm being held awkwardly by a struggling Caleb: one arm under my armpit, and the other grasping at my elbow.

It's not romantic.

It's humiliating.

I scrabble with my legs on the ground, and he loses

his grip completely and drops me heavily on the floor.

"Ouch," I say as my knee smashes the pavement.

"I know I'm charming," Cal says, smirking. "But we only met an hour ago. You weren't supposed to fall for me *that* quickly."

I flush and try to stand up, at which point I realise that Wilbur is yelling. Just as I'm automatically getting my apologies ready, I realise it's not aimed at me.

"I said *stop*," he shouts at Nancy. "I said *stop* six rides ago. What the *fiddle cats* are you playing at?"

"I didn't realise, OK?" Nancy says defensively. "I just wanted the right shot."

"Does *that* look right to you?" Wilbur snaps, pointing to me rolling around on the floor like Bambi on rollerblades. "Does *that* look like the right shot?"

"Oh, God," Nancy sighs. "All right, I got tunnel-vision. I'm sorry, OK?"

Wilbur bends over and gently helps me up. "Are you back with us, my little Frog-bubble? We haven't killed you, have we?"

I tentatively shake my head.

At any given moment, the earth beneath our feet is spinning at 465 metres a second. Right now, I can definitely feel every centimetre of it.

"So," I say shakily, and then I clear my throat.

"What's next? How about that?"

I point at what looks like a small metal bucket being swung from over fifty metres in the air towards the ocean.

Nancy and Wilbur look at each other.

"Told you," Wilbur says smugly. "My Baby-baby Panda is a total trooper."

"The big rides are over, Harriet," Nancy says, patting my shoulder awkwardly. "We'll keep you on the ground from this point on."

The rest of the shoot is completed without trauma.

We ride a tiny children's steam train with a smiling elephant painted on the roof. We sit inside enormous white and blue teacups; shoot water pistols at stuffed animals; dance on arcade games; whack plastic rats with bouncy hammers.

And yes, at some point we're put into the Wild River ride and drenched at the bottom of a fifteen-metre plunge, but after the roller coaster it feels like a sunset stroll along a promenade.

Plus at least my dress gets a good clean while we're at it.

Finally the shoot is announced a success, and we're led back to the changing rooms, dripping and exhausted and smelling slightly of stale cola.

Fleur hasn't looked at me the entire morning.

At one point she was so busy ignoring me, her bracelet got caught in my dress and we were physically attached for eight minutes before the stylist disentangled us.

But I'm still going to give friendship one more shot, because:

a) the Fleur I used to Know has to be in there somewhere and
b) now I'm in America, I don't appear to have that many other options.

"Umm," I say as she starts hastily taking off her earrings and darts with her shoulders hunched into the cubicle next to mine. "Fleur?"

"What?" She calls over the cubicle wall.

"Would you, umm..." I clear my throat. "There's an exhibition on Magritte at the Museum of Modern Art, and I was wondering if you wanted to come with me? He does pictures of pipes that say THIS IS NOT A PIPE because, you know, it's not. It's a picture."

Then as I wait for her to reply, I hear the sounds of her hurriedly getting changed.

"Sorry, Harriet," Fleur says finally as she dashes out of her cubicle. "But I've just got to get out of here."

And she starts heading back to the station without another word.

59

By the time I emerge in my own clothes, Fleur has gone.

In fact, I've been so distracted by the process of trying to clean my entire body with little cotton-wool pads, I've almost managed to forget that I'm not actually supposed to be here either.

Almost, but not quite.

I take my phone out of my pocket and fiddle with the power button anxiously.

"I'm going to take you shopping," Kenderall states as she picks up the end of Francis's lead. He snorts reluctantly. "I've decided I'm going to make you my new project."

"Umm." I frown suspiciously. "What *kind* of project?"

The last kind of 'project' I did involved Sellotape, quite a lot of glue and ended up with me accidentally attaching myself to what was supposed to be a papier-mâché fairy-tale landscape.

I'm not entirely sure I want to repeat that mistake.

It took ages to get the glue off.

"*You*," Kenderall says, looking me up and down. "I'm training to be a stylist, so you're my practice. I can't be a model forever, and anyway: I need hyphenating."

I stare at her. "You need... *what*?"

"*Hy-phen-ating*," Kenderall intones. "Some girls are a model-hyphen-DJ. Others are model-hyphen-actresses. *Some* are even *multi-hyphenators:* sculptor or painter or underwear designer. I haven't got a hyphen, so I'm branching out. I'm doing a course at college."

I try to work out what my *hyphen* is.

Geek-hyphen-schoolgirl, maybe.

Or geek-hyphen-idiot.

"Plus," she says. "You clearly need help with your *amp*, babe."

My brain quickly scans for definitions. "Like, my electricity? Or my excitement and energy levels?"

Then I remember *adenosine monophosphate* which we studied in chemistry and add, "Or a white crystalline water-soluble nucleotide?"

"*Ump*. Unique Modelling Point. We have to work out what your brand is. After all 'to love oneself is the start of a life-long romance', you know?"

I blink, slightly startled. "Oscar Wilde?"

"No, babe. It's on a magnet I've got on my fridge. I think it's from Target."

Right.

"Shopping sounds... lovely," I say, although obviously it doesn't. I clench my phone a little more tightly in my hand. "But I need to go home."

"Sure thing," Kenderall says, shrugging. "If you want to be forgotten, that's your problem. More *ump* for me."

I watch her walk away, head gleaming.

Then I press the power button on my phone. My morning of escape and adventure is over, and it's time to deal with what's coming next.

I prepare myself for a barrage of angry text messages. Messages that tell me how selfish I am, how inconsiderate I am, how worried I've made everyone. Messages that specify in excruciating detail exactly how much trouble I'm about to be in and how long I'm going to be allocated bathroom cleaning on the family rota.

I wait.

And I wait.

And then – just for good measure, because I don't

know what kind of reception you get at an American seaside – I wait a little longer.

Then I peer at my screen.

Nothing.

Not a single message. Not a voicemail. *Nada*.

A wave of relief sweeps over me so strong that the ground tilts again for the second time in one day.

I did it! I got away with it!

And then – almost immediately – a series of different waves, equally as strong, start following it. Waves that feel nothing like relief or happiness.

It's two in the afternoon.

I've been missing for *nine hours*, and neither my parents nor my boyfriend have thought to ask where I am or what I'm doing?

Nobody is worried that I may have been kidnapped, or murdered, or cut into a million pieces and fed to the approximately one million pigeons of New York City?

Don't they even *care* that I've gone?

With a sinking stomach, I'm suddenly not sure which I like less. Getting in trouble for running away. Or not getting into any trouble at all.

I stare sadly at my phone and another wave hits me. A wave so strong and abrupt it sweeps all the others away and I can't think of anything else.

"Kenderall?" I say.

She stops and spins round. "Yeah, babe?"

Defiantly, I put my phone back into my satchel. If nobody cares where I've gone, then I might as well stay away.

"I'm coming with you."

60

Here are some things I like more than shopping:

- *Everything.*

Mobile phones have eighteen times more bacteria than the average toilet handle. I would rather lick mine than spend the day making terrible decisions and being forced to pay for them. Only crazy people would do that.

It's called *retail therapy* for a reason.

Back home, Nat is like some kind of purse-carrying tiger. Within seconds of entering a shop, she'll go very, very still, quietly assessing her territory.

"What are we looking for?"

"Ssssshhhh," Nat will reply. "I'm concentrating."

She'll scan the room with eyes narrowed and eyebrows furrowed. Then she'll lift her chin.

"This," she'll say, walking forward with great

purpose and grabbing a pair of spotted trousers. "And this." She'll march over to a lime-green jumper. "This." She'll make a graceful right angle. "Obviously this." She'll pick up a silk jacket with studs round the collar.

"And this?" I'll make some kind of hesitant gesture towards a rack, just to look like I'm participating.

"No."

"But... Nat. It's a jumper. It's green. It's identical."

"It's not. It dips instead of falling straight, the neckline isn't wide enough, it's six centimetres shorter, the green is slightly too blue. What you've got there is a *Mum* jumper."

"Oh."

"Do you want a *Mum* jumper?"

"Umm... No?"

"Then come on."

And Nat will head to the till, pay for her items and emerge, glorious and triumphant, into the sunlight with her prey in shiny bags hanging from her wrists instead of her mouth.

The torture is swift, merciless and over almost immediately.

Kenderall is not a tiger.

Within minutes of entering the shiny doors of Barneys on Madison Avenue, I can tell this isn't going to be a speedy metaphorical death.

She's like an enormous brown bear. There's no urgency, no direction, just contradicting opinions. She plods around the beauty section: picking things up, putting things down. Considering, pondering. Opining.

Debating over and over and over and over and...

In essence, she holds you down with her big paws, sits on your chest and slowly but carefully begins chewing on you while you're still alive.

And the last thing you hear before certain death is: "I'm not sure, I just think this lipgloss is too *shiny*."

But you know what?

It's *still* better than going back to Greenway.

"Now," Kenderall says when we've finally made it through the beauty section. "We need to decide what kind of apparel *brand* you are."

"Huh?"

The bright lights, the gentle murmurs, the bow of the doorman in a neat little blue cap: it's all a little overwhelming. For the first time in my life, words have the power to scare me. PRADA. GIVENCHY. STELLA

McCARTNEY. LANVIN. ARMANI. RALPH LAUREN.

Everything about Barneys is expensive. The smell: leather and perfume and wood floors. The lights: perfectly coordinated and glowing in the right places. The displays; the mannequins; the layout; the staff.

As for the clothes, all I'm going to say is: I'm not touching anything.

I either need to keep my hands in my pockets for the rest of the afternoon or consider cutting them off permanently.

"*Brand*," Kenderall says patiently, prodding a pair of $3,000 velvet hotpants. "If you don't make yourself irreplaceable, somebody will replace you. Being different is being remembered. Being the same is being forgotten."

I nod. Sir Francis has been left with a man with a xylophone outside: Kenderall gave him twenty dollars to 'pig-sit'.

"I don't think I have a brand," I admit.

"No," she agrees. "You don't. You walk into a room, and nobody is going to notice. Whereas *me* –" she points at herself – "I walk into the room, I *am* the room."

That literally makes no sense. The difference between a human and a four-walled space is quite big, even to an untrained eye.

"OK," I say doubtfully.

The shop assistants are staring at my purple flip-flops. I think they might have some kind of alarm that goes off if you're wearing anything that's been recently vulcanised.

"Importance is all in the mind," Kenderall says firmly. "And you express that mind with your clothes and your mouth – understand?"

Nope. "Uh-huh."

"These people don't know who we are. I could be an heiress. You could be a Russian princess. Believe it, and it's exactly the same as it being true."

I really hope it isn't. I'd have been wiped out by the Russian Revolution in 1918, for starters.

"Gotcha," I say, trying to lift my head as regally as I can.

"Live your truth," Kenderall says. "Or whatever you want that truth to be, which is basically the same thing."

She starts stalking through the hall, prodding at things with a disgusted look on her face.

"Gucci would approve of this layout," she says loudly so that everybody can hear her. "I know his taste. We're close family friends."

"Do you *really* know Gucci?" I say in a low whisper.

I can't help feeling a bit surprised.

According to what Nat told me a few weeks ago, Guccio Gucci died sixty years ago.

"Babe," Kenderall says, "as far as everyone here is concerned, we know *everybody*."

61

We are condescending from that point on.

We are rude in Jimmy Choo. We are supercilious in Oscar de la Renta. We are disdainful in Alexander McQueen and imperious in Michael Kors.

At least, Kenderall is. I try to look as stern and Romanov-like as is physically possible.

And it works.

Not a single person glances at my flip-flops. Nobody asks me not to touch anything, or breathe on anything, or goes to the rail two seconds after me and rearranges everything with a pointedly tired facial expression.

Not a single person treats us as if we shouldn't be there.

And I have to be honest, it's quite nice being treated like you're *someone.*

"As your personal stylist, it is my *job* to make you stand out," Kenderall calls over to me as she lumbers around the clothes racks. "As difficult as that may be."

Then she holds up a black leather pair of trousers.

"You could be The Girl in the Black Leather. Everything you wear has to be made from leather. Jacket, trousers, shoes, shirt."

I look at the price tag. $2,500.

"Umm. Primitive leather was made by immersing raw skins into a fermented solution of pigeon poo and allowing germs and bacteria to loosen hair."

"OK. Ew." Kenderall puts the trousers quickly back on the rack. "Moving on."

Then she picks up a purple dress.

"You could be The Girl Who Always Wears Purple."

That sounds more doable.

Then I look at the label. $9,990.

Maybe not.

"Umm, it's called purple because it is made from the mucus secreted by the *Purpura*, a spiny sea snail. Do you really want me to look like the snot glands of a gastropod mollusc?"

"Scrap that," Kenderall agrees.

In quick succession she suggests diamante, lux-sports-wear, nightwear-for-daywear, and a dress made entirely out of paper ("although I think Molly already nabbed that one"), and I find scientifically accurate ways to reject all of them.

Finally we get to the shoe section.

"*These*," she says triumphantly, picking up a pair.

They're bright red with enormous heels. There's a pair of little white eyes by the toes and orange claws wrapped around the back of the ankle that click into place.

"Lobster shoes?" I say dubiously.

"Precisely," Kenderall affirms. "You can be The Girl with the Lobster Shoes. *Everybody* will remember that."

I blink. I happen to like lobsters very much.

Their brains are in their throats, they breathe and listen with their legs and they taste with their feet.

I'd just never considered them as a fashion accessory before.

"One hundred and seventy-eight dollars," Kenderall adds, thrusting them at me. "They're in the sale. It's a bargain. After all, you can't put a price on yourself."

Quick, Harriet.

"Lobsters are actually brown or green," I say as fast as I can. "They have a pigment called *astaxanthin* in their shells, which absorbs blue light and is the only pigment not destroyed by cooking. So red lobsters are dead ones."

Then I look at the shoes. "These are actually *dead* lobster shoes," I add, in case I haven't made that clear.

"Brilliant," Kenderall says triumphantly. "That's even better. You can be the Dead Lobster Shoe girl."

She pushes me towards the till.

My hands are shaking. All I have on me is my $100 birthday money, and the emergency money I stole from the kitty.

I swallow and look at Kenderall with big eyes.

"But—"

"Do you want to be remembered?" she says. "Or do you want everyone to forget about you?"

And that does it.

The box in my head rumbles, and suddenly everything bursts out in a series of explosions.

My birthday. BANG.

Greenway. BANG. My parents. BANG. The silence of my phone. BANG. Toby replacing me with my dog. BANG. Infinity Models. BANG.

Nick. BANG BANG.

Nat. College. *Jessica.*

BANG BANG BANG BANG BANG.

Then one last thing falls out with an enormous, brain-silencing thump: *You're a nobody. A nothing.*

BANG.

I clench my hands together.

Then I lift my chin, put the hideous shoes on the counter and – with calm, steady hands – hand my money over.

I am not going to be forgotten about any more. I'm not going to be pushed aside, or ignored, or replaced. I'm not going to be left behind.

And if a pair of lobster shoes is what it takes, so be it.

62

Kenderall takes us up to Fred's to 'replenish'.

It's a café on the ninth floor of Barneys, it's very expensive and glamorous, and it confuses me immensely because Fred has an apostrophe but Barney doesn't so I'm not entirely sure what belongs to whom.

"Now," Kenderall says as she leans back in the polished wooden chair and picks the prawns off her prawn salad, "we need to talk."

Sugar cookies.

I kind of thought we'd been doing that all afternoon. I was hoping to focus on my super-American club sandwich.

"Do we?"

"Yes. They said at college that as a stylist you have to understand the private lives of your clients so that you can properly express how they are feeling on their behalf."

"Oh."

Apparently the gap in time between the Tyrannosaurus Rex and the Stegosaurus is bigger than the time between the Tyrannosaurus Rex and us.

Kenderall can't be more than eighteen months older than me, but it suddenly feels like a similarly enormous gap.

"So, how's the love life?"

"Huh?"

"Babe, who you are dating is *fundamental* to your brand. People will judge you by the company you keep. I can't un-style you from a loser."

I flush with anger and put my club sandwich down. "Nick is *not* a loser."

"*Nick*." Kenderall tests the word out a few times. "Hmm. Bit of an unremarkable name. What does he do?"

Unremarkable? "He's a model."

She looks at me expectantly. "*And...*"

"And what?"

"What's his hyphen? I can't be expected to style him as well as you, you know."

I blink. "He's... just Nick."

As if Nick could ever 'just' be anything.

"Perhaps we should look at upgrading," Kenderall

says thoughtfully. "I know a double hyphenator who might be interested. Would you be prepared to exchange?"

I glare at her.

"I don't want to *exchange* my boyfriend. He's not a jumper that doesn't fit."

"Babe," Kenderall says, lifting an eyebrow. "If he's the wrong guy, that's *exactly* what he is." She frowns and puts another tiny lettuce leaf in her mouth. "But does he L.O.V.E. *you*? Does he send you roses and profess his undying affection for you very publicly on a daily basis? Would he leap about on the sofas on Oprah in front of the world? Would he? You don't want to put effort into a guy who's not into you. It's very unstylish."

Light is the fastest thing in the Universe. It travels at 299,792,458 meters per second.

Kenderall catches me looking desperately at the door.

Even if I was light, I *still* wouldn't be fast enough.

"This is a lovely sandwich," I say, opening it up and staring at the inside. "Did you know that the average American eats 17.9 pounds of bacon every year?"

Sorry, Francis.

Kenderall pulls my plate sharply away from me.

"How can I be expected to style you if you don't know who you are?"

I flinch.

"How do you expect someone to love you if you aren't *somebody*?"

"I don't know," I admit in a tiny voice. And suddenly I don't know which question I'm answering.

According to the little blue stickers I used to stick to the inside of my diary every morning, I have now known my boyfriend for nine months.

Which is thirty-nine weeks or 273 days, or 6,552 hours.

Or, you know, 23,587,200 seconds.

But the fact I've been trying to ignore all summer is: I *still* don't know if Nick loves me or not.

Kenderall reaches into her handbag and pulls out a magazine with a flourish.

"Then I think it's about time we found out, don't you?"

63

Suddenly I don't want to be here.

At all.

The coldest place on Earth was identified by satellite in 2010 in the centre of Antarctica. It's minus 93.2 degrees Celsius, which is nearly as far below freezing as boiling water is above freezing.

Scientists may have to measure again, because I'm pretty sure the inside of my stomach has just achieved a new record.

"Did you know," I say, peering again at the inside of my almost uneaten sandwich, "that until 1820, North Americans believed that tomatoes were poisonous?"

Kenderall flicks through the magazine, ignoring me, and then opens it stridently on the table.

In enormous pink letters, I can see the words IS YOUR BOYFRIEND IN LOVE WITH YOU? emblazoned across the top of the page.

My stomach drops a few extra degrees.

"OK," she says. "This should be easy. All you have to do is answer *Yes* or *No* and the professionals will do the rest."

On any other occasion, I would be thrilled at the opportunity to take an exam.

"Mmmm," I mumble, shoving as much of my sandwich into my mouth as humanly possible.

Kenderall makes herself comfortable. "Right. a) Does he go long periods of time without contacting you?"

I chew deliberately slowly and make the universal hand motion of *I can't answer until I've swallowed.*

Then I shake my head.

Kenderall's eyebrows lift. "This isn't going to work if you don't tell me the truth, babe."

I attempt to gulp down my sandwich. "I mean, sometimes. Maybe. Now and then."

"Right. So I'll put a little tick here. b) Is there a long gap before he replies to messages?"

Yes. "No."

"Good. I'll put a cross. c) Do you see each other lots?"

"No," I admit in a tiny voice.

"Uh-huh. d) Is he always there for you on important occasions?"

Like my birthday. Or my exam results. Or when I arrive in a brand-new country. Or now.

"N-no."

"e) Does he start fights with you for no apparent reason?"

I think of yesterday evening, and the fact that he hasn't texted me since. The ice in my stomach is starting to spread: reaching out in tiny, freezing spikes into my chest and the top of my legs.

"Sometimes."

"f) Does he compliment you?"

The cold seeps into my arms and knees as I try desperately to think of one occasion. But the only *beautiful* I can remember came from Cal.

"Not really."

"g) Is he romantic with you?"

"*Yes,*" I say emphatically. Then I try unsuccessfully to think of any single occasion since we got back from Tokyo. "But... not for a while."

"Finally, and this is the clincher, h) Has he ever *said* he loves you?"

And there it is.

The freezing cold iceberg in my chest that will take me down, just like the *Titanic* in 1912. Except that – unlike in that instance – I saw this one coming.

I've been waiting for this ship-sinker for months.

My entire body is now so cold it feels like I could put my fingers out and turn things into ice just by touching them.

"No," I say in the tiniest voice I've ever heard come out of me. "He hasn't."

And every time I try to bring it up, he changes the subject.

"*Well,*" Kenderall scans the bottom of the page, "sorry, babe, but your boyfriend is Option D: Not Emotionally Invested. Your relationship is on its way out."

I blink. "Its way out where? Where is it going?"

I suddenly have a bizarre image of my relationship opening the front door, popping out to the shops for milk and never coming back.

"Out. Done. Dead. Like, *over.*" Kenderall reaches over the table and grabs my hand. "Sorry about that."

"But..." I can feel panic rising up my throat. "What if I ring him? What if I ring him *a lot,* all at once, and maybe send him some gifts and text him and make a T-shirt with our faces on it? Maybe then he'll invest himself more?"

"Wow," Kenderall says, tilting her head to the side sympathetically. "You *really* don't understand boys, do you?"

And – without warning – the box in my head opens and the final item falls out with a *crack*.

An imaginary boyfriend. That's pathetic, even for you.

Oh my God.

Is that what Nick is? Is that what I've been doing all this time? Did I want this perfect romance so badly I painted it the way I wanted and then tried to live inside it, like the little girl in *The Witches*? Was this relationship *so* important to me I forced myself into it, whether it was there or not?

Suddenly it's as if all the lights have been switched on; I've been sitting in darkness for months and hadn't even noticed.

The fashion show, where Nick left me on my own for hours and barely acknowledged me. The roundabout, where he could have written something lovely but didn't. The lack of picnics or flowers or gifts in the post. The lack of texts and phone calls. My birthday, where he didn't care enough to read the directions properly. My exam results, when he wasn't there. Shouting at me instead of being on my side. Treating me like a child. The birthday present he forgot to bring.

The time he called me a *geek.*

In biology last year we studied osmosis and learnt that when there's a selectively permeable membrane, small molecules – like water – can pass through, but larger molecules like sugar only stay in one place.

Is that what's been happening? Am I the little water molecule, racing towards Nick, while he stays unchanged and unaffected exactly where he is?

Has my entire romance been in my head?

Was Alexa *right*?

I stare at Kenderall blankly.

Most hideous of all: am I *so* forgettable that after months and months of knowing me I can't even get my own boyfriend to fall in love with me?

"No," I finally say in a far-away voice. "You're right. I really don't understand boys at all."

Without another word, I put a twenty-dollar bill on the table. And run out of the restaurant.

64

I stare at my phone the whole journey back to Greenway station.

I sit on the train, wishing it would do something. *Anything.*

It doesn't.

And for the first time in nine months, I'm not surprised. Because for the first time in nine months, it suddenly makes sense.

Finally, I take a deep breath and write:

Nat, how are you? Hope you're having fun. Can you ring me when you get a chance? Hxxx

Then I wait.

And I wait.

The sad fact is, there are 7,220,400,641 people on this planet, and right now I haven't got a single one to talk to.

Finally, just as I'm climbing off the train, there's a small ping.

From: Alexa Roberts
To: Harriet Manners

Plan for Harriet and Nick's Most Romantic Summer Ever (MRSE)

- **Read poetry together, quoting alternate lines.**
- **Take a moonlit walk along a beach, holding hands and making interesting observations about the ocean.**
- **Write love letters to each other and leave them in a trail with a map so only we can find them.**
- **Pick wildflowers and put them in my hair.**
- **Have dinner on a roof, surrounded by candles and an appropriately positioned fire extinguisher.**
- **~~Feed the ducks.~~**
- **Find a sunlit clearing in a forest, and then slow-dance in it.**

Dear Harriet,

Even your fake boyfriend doesn't like your lame plans. At least you fed the ducks. SCORE.

A

Apparently if you shrank our sun down to the size of a white blood cell and shrank the Milky Way galaxy down by the same scale, it would be the size of the United States.

I'm not sure how tiny that makes us, but that's about the size I feel now.

My romantic summer didn't happen.

And I didn't even notice.

I start walking towards the house, and then make a decision. Or whatever it's called when there's no other option left to take.

I take a piece of paper out of my pocket, look at Kenderall's number scrawled there and then text:

OK. You're right. Tell me what I have to do. Hx

65

When the *holothuroidea* is under attack, it turns itself inside out and uses its digestive tract's toxic juices to protect itself from its enemies.

It can also turn its body into mush and slip through cracks before solidifying again: essentially the equivalent of scattering itself into pieces and then reassembling them.

As I approach the front door of my house, I wish I was a sea cucumber.

It's the only way I'm going to survive the next ten minutes.

For the second time, I have been missing *all day*.

I open the front door as quietly as I can.

"Annabel?" I whisper. "Dad?"

But the only sound in the house is a steadily dripping tap in the otherwise unlit kitchen.

With infinite slowness, I start inching silently up

the stairs. Each step is an achievement.

One. Two. Three. Four. Five. Six. Seven…

I've just reached the landing when the front door opens. With a small crash, Annabel tries to get the buggy over the step while Tabitha screams at an unprecedented level.

"Tabby," she sighs as the shrieks go up another notch. "Please. It says in the baby book that going for a long walk calms babies down. Do I need to make you read it again?"

Then, in slow motion, Annabel looks up.

We stare at each other, the way a cat and mouse stare at each other just before one of them gets eaten.

I have a strong suspicion it's going to be me.

"Annabel," I say, steadying myself against the wall with a terrified hand. "Before you say anything, I can explain..."

"What are you doing out of your room?"

I blink. "What?"

"I told you, Harriet," Annabel sighs. "You're to stay in your bedroom. You're grounded. That doesn't mean waiting until I go out and then running around the house like an escaped gerbil."

Apparently the brain generates between ten and twenty-three watts of power, which is enough energy to power a normal-sized light bulb. At this precise moment, mine wouldn't even fuel a single Christmas tree light.

"Uh?"

"Go back to your room," Annabel says tiredly. "I'll bring up whatever it is you think you need."

"OK..." I frown and start backing up the remaining stairs. "Sorry."

What the *sugar cookies* is going on? I've been gone *all day.* How did Annabel not notice?

I push open my bedroom door and stare at Miss Hall, sitting calmly on the armchair in the corner.

"Umm," I say, and start backing out again.

Then I stop.

I can either stay here and get ripped apart by a six-foot-two woman wearing Gore-Tex, or I can go downstairs and get ripped apart by a lawyer instead.

Neither are an experience I'm totally keen on testing out.

"Harry," Miss Hall says, lifting her eyebrows. "How nice to see you."

I look around the bedroom. Maybe if I quickly grab the lobster heels from their gift bag I can use them to pinch her into submission. Except… I appear to have left the bag behind.

Figures.

"I can explain," I say for the second time in under a minute, even though I have literally no idea how.

"I don't see why," Miss Hall says sharply. "If you don't want an education, it is not my job to force you."

My eyes open wide. "But—"

She holds an enormous hand up. "Yesterday, I was sent home without pay. That will not happen again. If your parents do not run a tight ship, that is their problem, not mine. As long as my wages keep coming in, you can do what you like."

I stare at her.

Shouldn't she be shouting at me, or at least giving me a long, disappointed lecture on the importance of education? Doesn't she care?

No, I realise suddenly. *No, she does not.*

"But I *want* to study," I say, clenching my hands tightly in front of me.

"Maybe." Miss Hall leans back in her chair. "But some people just aren't mentally equipped for academia. I think it is time to accept the fact that you are one of them."

My hands are shaking.

Today has just raced on to my Top Ten List of Least

Favourite Days Ever, slightly above the time Alexa made everybody in class say they hated me and slightly below the day I ate a bad piece of chicken and couldn't leave the bathroom for twenty-four hours.

"I *am*," I say in a small squeak. "I *am* equipped."

Because if I'm not equipped for academia, what else do I have left? If I can't study, who else can I *be*?

"Some of us are strong and capable," Miss Hall says, pointing to herself. "And some of us are not."

She stares pointedly at me.

Thanks to my first day of study, I know that scientists think that a *quark* is the smallest thing in the known universe.

Right now, I'm so little I could climb inside one.

Alexa was completely right.

"OK," I say quietly. I sit heavily on my bed and stare blankly at the wall. "So what do I do now?"

"Whatever you like," Miss Hall says, looking at her watch and standing up. "My shift is over. See you tomorrow."

66

Over the next three days, I am entirely on my own.

And I mean that in every sense possible. (Miss Hall sitting in the corner of my room ignoring me does not count.)

I am on my own when I eat: my meals are left outside my bedroom door. I am on my own when I study: trawling through books and trying desperately to work out what everything means. I am on my own when I wake up, and when I go to sleep, and when I go to the toilet.

I'm actually quite glad about that last one. It would be a bit weird if I wasn't.

In the meantime, Nat doesn't ring me or text back.

Toby/Hugo doesn't email me.

My parents don't talk to me. (They are taking the How to Ground Your Teenager manual far too seriously for my liking.)

Miss Hall sits in a corner and reads a book with a

man carrying a woman on the front cover, which – given her stature – might be a little optimistic.

And Nick?

He rings three times, but I'm under strict instructions from Kenderall not to answer his calls.

This is the list I've been sent:

Ways to Make Your Boyfriend Love You

- *Be cool. Nobody likes a needy cling-on.*
- *Be mysterious. Nobody likes to know everything about anyone.*
- *Optimise your appearance.*
- *Be worldly and knowing.*
- *Be breezy and happy, all the time.*
- *Ignore phone calls. Do not reply to any messages, at least not for many hours.*
- *Show him what he's missing.*

I put it in a list, obviously.

It came from Kenderall in a series of text messages with 'babe' scattered at random throughout.

I've written it down and studied it carefully.

I've also compared it to dating advice on the internet, and it mostly tallies up. Frankly, I can't believe

I didn't research this before now. Thank goodness I finally have a plan to follow.

This is what happens when you don't do your homework properly. I have nobody but myself to blame for the mess I'm in.

So I do my best.

I dutifully ignore all of Nick's phone calls. I ignore most of his text messages. And then, occasionally, eight or nine hours later, I send a reply that says:

Sorry! Crazy busy and mysterious! Will speak soon! Hx

or

Oops, I missed your call! Have you seen the interesting stuff in the news about Pakistan?! Hx

And, sure enough, Nick's phone calls and text messages get increasingly frequent, and increasingly confused, culminating in:

What is going on? Has somebody stolen your phone? LBx

Finally, Kenderall decides it's 'time to bring out the big guns'.

"Not literally?" I ask her anxiously down the phone. America has eighty-eight firearms per one hundred people, and the more I know Kenderall the more I'm convinced that she definitely has one of them.

"LOL," she says flatly. "We need to crank it up. Meet me at 81st Street and Central Park West at 4pm tomorrow. A buddy is doing a photo shoot tomorrow afternoon, and I've convinced them to use you for it. I would do it myself, but they need a girl with hair and that is *so* last season."

I blink and look at the list.

I've got just one more day of being grounded left. Do I *really* want to risk getting caught again?

"But... Which of the bullet points does a photo shoot tick off?"

"All of them, babe. Trust me."

I look at Miss Hall, nodding off in the corner. I look at the dark, slightly stale recesses of my bedroom, which still smell of pizza and this morning's breakfast Pop Tart.

Then I look at the photo of Nick I have stuck on the wall next to my bed so I can see it when I fall asleep.

I don't really have an option.

"Do you really think it will work?"

Kenderall laughs.

"Oh, babe," she says. "With boys, it always does."

67

The next afternoon, I can't even bring myself to look out of the window of the train from Greenway to New York: that's how guilty I feel for sneaking out again on my last day of being grounded.

But if ticking off this list is what it takes to make Nick fall in love with me, then that's what I have to do.

So I focus as hard as I can.

It takes four attempts at Grand Central station to get on a subway train going in the right direction, but I finally succeed and emerge into the sunshine, feeling a little proud of my map-reading skills. I *knew* that Brownie Orientation badge would come in handy one day.

Then I see who's standing at the entrance of the subway, and my smile falters.

They're not six-foot tall and they're not bald. They don't have gleaming brown skin or cheekbones you could spread houmous with or a voice that carries five miles without the aid of a loudspeaker. They aren't wearing orange and they don't have a pet pig.

Most importantly, they're not even female.

They have blond hair, and a striped shirt, and piercing blue eyes.

Laser beams are different from normal light because they have one monochromatic wavelength of light, focused in one coherent direction: each photon moving in perfectly coordinated step with the others.

And as this boy stares at me, that's how I feel.

As if a series of photons are pinning me to the spot, one after the other.

"Hey, gorgeous," Cal smiles as I squiggle like a butterfly on the end of a pin. "I was kinda hoping I'd see you again."

I stare at Cal.

Then I quickly drop my eyes to the floor because I'm slightly concerned that if I keep them wide open my rapidly rising blood pressure is going to force them straight out of my head.

"Where's Kenderall?"

"She couldn't make it." Cal shrugs. "The photo shoot has been cancelled."

"Oh," I say in disappointment. I was kind of hoping for an opportunity to wear a dress that was actually stitched together this time. "Well. I guess I'll just go home then."

I turn to leave.

"But you've come all this way," Cal says slowly. "It seems a shame to waste the journey."

He's totally right.

Nobody knows I'm here. And I'm officially ungrounded in less than twenty-four hours so I'm *almost* legitimately free again anyway. I can use the time to finally tick off a few things on my New York To Do List.

I can go to the New York Metropolitan Museum, or the Guggenheim, or the Strand Bookstore that has eighteen miles of books: new, used, rare and out of print. I can spend the rest of the afternoon buying as much exciting literature as I can physically carry.

I can go to the New York Supreme Court and enquire about branded pens for Annabel and a super-cool NYPD T-shirt for Dad.

I can visit the Museum of Comic and Cartoon Art and pick up some postcards to send Toby.

I can go to the Fashion Institute of Technology Museum and find Nat a really cool belt that she will say she loves and then never wear because I am terrible at picking out belts.

I can pick up a New York snow globe for Nick, to remind him of when it snowed in Moscow.

Except I can't.

Because I spent all my birthday money on stupid shoes that I lost before I even got home.

Because if I buy Annabel and Dad gifts, they'll know I was in New York again.

Because Toby and Nat have so completely forgotten about me, they don't *deserve* presents; Nat would probably just give the belt to stupid Jessica anyway.

And because I don't think Kenderall would consider buying your boyfriend snow globes very cool *or* mysterious. It's definitely not on the list she gave me.

So I pull my guidebook out of my satchel and quickly scan the bookmarked pages. "I could go to the Federal Hall where George Washington was inaugurated," I say with slightly less enthusiasm. "They might let me sit on the steps outside."

It's not that interesting, but at least it's free.

"Wait," Cal says, grabbing my hand as I start to walk away. "That isn't *exactly* what I meant."

My entire body suddenly feels hot and prickly, as if I've just been coated in chilli oil and deep-fried.

I stare at our linked hands. What is he *doing*?

"I thought maybe I could get to know you a little bit better?"

"Why?"

"Because every time I'm with you it feels like there's a rainbow nearby."

I look at the sky. It's totally cloudless.

"But there's no rain," I say, feeling even more confused. "You need raindrops so that beams of sunlight can refract through them and separate into different wavelengths."

"No," he says slowly, taking a step closer. "Because I've just found a treasure."

I'm not sure how you can scratch an unbearably itchy body all over at the same time, but I'm considering lying on the floor and giving it a thorough go.

"Umm," I say awkwardly. "I sort of have a boyfriend."

"Sort of?" he deadpans. "So... which bit of you doesn't?"

The itchiness gets even worse. "I mean, yes. I do. I have a boyfriend. One hundred per cent. So I'm not really interested in... umm. You. But thank you."

Cal gives me his megawatt smile and then starts rubbing his thumb along the top of my hand. "Wow, bit arrogant, aren't you? I only meant it as a friend."

I'm so embarrassed I'm considering peeling off my skin, leaving it on the pavement and starting again. Like a snake. Or an orange. "I'm so sorry. I didn't mean..."

I fade into humiliated silence.

"So? Want to hang out? As buddies?"

"I'm not sure I—"

My phone beeps and I finally yank my hand away.

Go with Caleb.

I stare at my phone, as another message immediately follows the first.

You asked me what to do. This is it.

I look back at Cal. He's now so close I can see splashes of silvery-grey in the blue of his eyes, like flecks on the foam of the ocean.

Which – as far as I'm concerned – is *way* too close.

I take a step back so they just look blue. My phone buzzes again.

You're going to tell Nick you're sorry about the silence but you're out with your new friend Caleb

and you'll ring him later.

And again.

Just DO IT.

I frown at my phone, and then back at Cal. This makes no sense. Kenderall wants me to go with Cal, and then *tell* Nick? What is that going to achieve?

Except of course it doesn't make sense. Because I clearly don't know what I'm doing.

And as doing what makes sense to me has got me absolutely nowhere up to this point, it might be time to listen to someone else, for a change.

So I nod, and obediently send Nick the text, word for word.

Then I look up at Cal.

"OK. What would you like to do?"

"Tell me, beautiful girl," he says, smiling widely, "do you like stars?"

68

Do I like stars?

That's like asking a rabbit if it likes carrots, or a bee if it likes nectar, or my dad if he likes attempting to do the Riverdance in the middle of the living room when he gets overexcited.

In other words – *yes.*

I also know quite a lot about them.

Scientists think there are one trillion galaxies in the universe, and each of those galaxies has 100 billion stars.

You would need 1,100 years to circle the largest known star in the universe at 560 miles an hour, and it would take you 35,000 years to reach the nearest next star to the Sun.

If you look at stars, you are actually looking back in time because it takes light thousands or millions of years to reach Earth.

When we study stars in physics, I get so excited that

Mr Kemp has to ask me to stop putting my hand up before he asks the question.

But I have no idea what Cal's talking about.

It's 4pm.

Either he is an extremely optimistic kind of person, or he doesn't understand how night and day work.

"I can't stay out late," I say nervously as we start walking down the pavement.

"We don't need to," Cal says, stopping abruptly. "We're here."

I stare at the enormous entrance of the American Museum of Natural History – all grey stone and columns and brightly coloured flags – and it clicks into place.

"The Rose Center for Earth and Space?"

"Unless you'd rather go somewhere else?" Cal stretches his arms out. "We could go for a carriage ride in Central Park, or take a boat around the Statue of Liberty, or go to the top of the Empire State Building, if you like?"

My stomach flips.

"No," I say, looking back at the museum. "Stars sound good to me."

The Hayden Planetarium is like an enormous bubble,

except with walls made of cinema screen instead of a layer of water molecules sandwiched between two thin layers of glycerine.

Cal pays for both of us, and we file in quietly and start heading towards the middle.

"How about here?" he says, taking my hand and pulling me towards the back row. "The view is better."

That makes no sense. Surely that's kind of the point of a three-dimensional screen?

I shrug and take my seat, and then focus on sitting with my face pointing upwards so I don't have to acknowledge how close Cal is. Armrests are there to provide a natural divide, and he isn't paying attention to *either* of them.

"Hey," he whispers in the darkness, leaning over so I can feel his breath on my cheek. It smells weird. Orange-y. As if he's been eating mandarins. "I think you might have something in your eye."

He reaches forward.

"Oh," I say, quickly blocking him with my hand. "No, it's just astigmatism. There's an irregular curve in my lens so I get a bit squinty when I'm tired."

"Are you sure it's not a twinkle?"

I turn to look at him. *What?* "No, it's definitely astigmatism."

"Right." He leans back in his seat and puts his hands behind his head. "Good to know."

The crowds are settling down with incredible slowness. Why aren't they hurrying up? When is this show going to start? How long do I have to talk to Cal for?

"Speaking of which," I say as the silence stretches out for what feels like eternity, "did you know that stars don't actually twinkle? They only *look* like they do because the light passes through different densities of the earth's atmosphere which makes it wobble."

Silence.

"And on a good night," I add, "you can see twenty quadrillion miles with the naked eye."

Suddenly Cal sits forward.

"Huh?" He pushes his hand through his hair. "You know, stars are really beautiful. Almost as beautiful as yo—"

"Will you *shut up,*" the woman behind us snaps loudly. "I came here to see the universe in all its glory, not two teenagers trying to make out."

I'm glad it's pitch-black: maybe I can slip to the floor and slide on my belly all the way to the exit, like some kind of seal.

"Oh no," I say, turning round as apologetically as

I can. "We're just friends."

"*Exactly*," Cal agrees, grabbing my hand. "*Good* friends. *Great* friends. Really, really *close* friends."

I'm still trying to work out how to make him let go without having to chew off my own hand when a loud voice booms:

"Thirteen billion years ago, the very first stars were born."

And the universe explodes around us.

69

New York has officially disappeared.

But as a piano starts tinkling, the darkness above us is suddenly replaced with a bright, vivid-blue sky. White clouds race across what used to be the ceiling as the sun sets over the spiked Manhattan skyline. People in time-lapse picnic in Central Park, then scurry and jitter across it like a thousand tiny ants in jeans and T-shirts.

Then we pull backwards, until all that's left is a silent, spinning Earth and blackness.

We hang there for a few seconds.

Then the sky shatters into colour and sound: blues and greens and yellows and purples, pianos and cellos and harps. Supernovas explode and swirling cosmic dust pulls together in huge pulses of light. Comets streak across the sky and nebulas glow blue and yellow; planets spin and pulsars flare red. Suns flash and galaxies spiral. Stars are born and die.

As drums beat and a violin lifts and soars, we rush across the known Universe, around solar systems; orbit around the moon; through the Milky Way and out again.

A gentle voice tells us how everything we are built from came from the nuclear fusion at the centre of a sun. How every element of Earth was formed there.

How we are all made of stars.

And the air in my chest swells and swells until it feels like I'm about to explode into colours and lights too.

By the time the humming, dull neon lights of the planetarium are turned back on again forty minutes later, I have no idea where I am. And even less idea what Cal's doing still holding my hand.

I'd kind of forgotten I had one in the first place.

"Are you OK?" Cal says, slipping his arm around my shoulders. "It looks like you've been crying."

I touch my wet cheeks in surprise.

"That was..." There are 1,025,109 words in the English language, and at this precise moment I cannot find a single one of them. "Beautiful."

Cal smiles. "Just like you then."

And the real world comes back to me with a BANG.

I stand up so quickly my knee smashes into the seat in front of us.

"I think..." I say, wrenching my hand from his and looking at the door. "I think I should go home."

Cal's face falls.

"Oh," he says flatly. "Sorry if I offended you." He looks at the screen around us. "I was just trying to make up for you missing the photo shoot."

My insides twist.

I am a horrible, ungrateful person. This boy has just given me forty amazing minutes of one of my favourite things ever, and my response is to run away.

"I'm so sorry," I say, flushing. "Thank you *so* much, Cal. It's just..."

You're not Nick.

"I have to get home, my parents are going to be worried, I'm supposed to be grounded..."

"Don't worry about it," he says, shrugging. He stands up and starts walking past me to the exit.

"But..." He looks so hurt. So deflated. "Cal..."

"I said don't worry about it," he snaps. "Let's go."

I follow Cal in meek silence to the exit.

I'm so ashamed of myself, but I don't know how to make it right. And now there's just this awkward space between us where something else is supposed to go.

Except I'm not sure exactly what that is.

"Well," I say nervously as we stand on the steps of the American Museum of Natural History.

The sky has clouded over and it looks like it's about to rain.

Maybe there's about to be a rainbow after all.

That's embarrassing.

"Catch you later," Cal says in monotone as I search for a suitably irrelevant fact to fill the silence with.

And without another word he turns and walks away.

70

I watch Cal leave with a guilty lump in my throat.

Miss Hall was right: I really need to work on my first impressions. And my second, and my third. Fourth might need a good hard think about too.

It's probably best if I find another subway stop to get back to Grand Central station. I don't think that awkwardness needs to be extended to standing on the same platform together.

My phone vibrates and I grab it quickly.

OK. Flying to California for a last-minute shoot. Back in a few days. Nick

Moths don't have stomachs, and I suddenly know exactly how they feel. As I stare at the message, mine disappears completely.

There's no kiss. No LBx. No PS.

Just 'Nick'.

As if his name isn't in my phone and I can't see it at the top of the message. As if I didn't learn every digit of his phone number off by heart months ago, along with his agency number, email address and precise height in centimetres.

Whatever it is Kenderall wanted to achieve today, it clearly hasn't worked. Nick is just getting further away.

I'm losing him completely.

In a burst of panic, I hit a few buttons with sweaty fingers.

"Kenderall," I say breathlessly, "I don't know what you wanted to happen but it didn't and now I don't know what to do and Nick sounds really angry and..."

"Whoa there," Kenderall shouts. "First. Are you wearing *culottes*? That is *not* a look your stylist encourages."

I thought they were pretty jaunty, as well as multipurpose: they double as both shorts and a skirt.

"You're not *listening*," I say, tugging impatiently at them. "Nick isn't happy *one bit*. He said he's gone away and he didn't call to say goodbye, and..." I stop. "How do you know what I'm wearing?"

There's a sharp whistle and Kenderall stalks towards me in bright orange leggings, silver high heels and a neon-orange crop top. She has an enormous gold bag slung over her shoulder.

"Seriously, babe," she says loudly into her phone, even though I'm stood right here, "you are making this an *uphill battle* for me. My hyphen is at risk here. These don't make me look good."

I stare at Kenderall. How did she know where I was?

"So," she adds, putting the phone down and air-kissing a metre from my cheek as per usual. "Let's see this text."

I click on Nick's reply and hold it up.

"He's furious," she agrees happily. "That is one unhappy guy, right there."

Sugar cookies.

"I should ring him and apologise," I say, grabbing my phone back. "I should explain who Caleb is. No, I should get a taxi to the airport and run through the departures lounge with I'M SO SORRY written on a big white board and he'll see it and all the airport staff will start singing and—"

"My God," Kenderall says. "No wonder you British girls lose your guys. Talk about *needy.*"

Oh. "So what should I do?"

"Nothing, babe. He gets angry, then he gets jealous, then worried. When he's terrified he's lost you, he realises he loves you. This is how it works."

That seems like an awfully long sequence of emotions to predict accurately, given that each of us has our own chemical make-up.

"Right," I say doubtfully. "But isn't that..." I try to find a word that doesn't sound accusatory. "*Manipulation?*"

"Exactly," Kenderall says cheerfully. "And while we wait for this *Nick* boy to sort his feelings out, we're going to party."

She hands me an envelope. Inside it is a piece of cream card stamped in the middle with swirly gold and silver letters saying:

LA MODE 10TH ANNIVERSARY BALL
Saturday September 9th
Gotham Hall
Dress Code: Ravishing Royalty
6pm until late

Gotham Hall? Isn't that where Batman lives?

Then I look at the envelope. It has HARRIET MANNERS written on it in huge letters, and was clearly opened before she handed it to me.

"Who gave you this?"

"That funny little stylist, William or whatever.

I bumped into him at LA MODE yesterday. I said I'd be seeing you and he asked me to pass this on. Except apparently they've run out of invitations so you'll have to take me as your Plus One."

"It's Wil*bur*," I say distantly. "With a *bur* and not an *iam*." Then I look at the invitation again. "I can't go. I need to get home before it gets dark."

"We can't *not* go," Kenderall says. "*Everyone* who is *anyone* will be there. And we *need* to be the anyones."

"But..."

If they haven't already, Annabel and Dad will surely work out I'm missing by nightfall. I've got to get back to Greenway before it's too late.

"Oh," Kenderall says tensely as I desperately search for an excuse that sounds more grown-up than *I'm grounded*. "So I do all this stuff for you, but you won't even go to a *party* for me? I thought we were *friends*."

I flush with guilt.

I am being incredibly selfish.

Again.

"I suppose we could just pop in?" I suggest tentatively, quickly trying to do the maths. If we just drop in, I can be home around 8pm. That isn't *that* late, is it?

"Awesome," Kenderall says, holding out a bag.

"Oh, and you left these at Fred's. Your *Ump* will never work if you don't actually wear them, y'know."

Inside the bag are the lobster shoes.

Sugar cookies.

"We'll just be there for half an hour, right?" I check as Kenderall grabs my elbow and starts dragging me down the road behind her.

"Babe," she laughs. "Half an hour is all we're going to need."

71

Gotham Hall was built in 1922.

It was originally the Greenwich Savings Bank, and was inspired by an Ancient Roman prototype with columns of limestone and sandstone. Inscriptions are written all over the inside: about Minerva, the goddess of Wisdom, and Mercury, the god of Commerce.

And Batman has never lived there.

None of which is of any interest to Kenderall.

As we walk through the Upper East Side of Manhattan, down Fifth Avenue, past the Four Seasons and Prada and Gucci and Tiffany & Co. and Armani, I crack out my guidebook and find out as much as I can about where we're going. Partly because I'm genuinely curious and partly because studying is what I automatically do when I'm really nervous.

But mostly because if my head is burrowed in a book, I can pretend I can't see all of the people staring at me.

Half an hour ago, Kenderall dragged me into the Bloomingdale's' toilet to get ready. I now look like the enthusiastic love-child of disco Barbie and a rainbow macaw.

My dress is bright red and yellow and blue and green. It runs in a tight column all the way down to my feet and then explodes into a mass of yellow feathers at the bottom and in a stream along the floor.

My skin is covered in thick foundation, my cheeks are pink, my lips are red and on my eyelids are fake black eyelashes so large that every time I look up I think a couple of enormous spiders are trying to attack my face.

On my feet are the lobster shoes.

And – between the extreme tightness of the dress and the highness of my heels – the only real method of transporting myself is to shuffle in tiny pigeon steps, like a traditional Japanese geisha.

Or, you know: a pigeon.

In the meantime, Kenderall looks beautiful in a simple orange minidress with a gold chain belt.

"*What?!*" she says as I look at my outfit and then at hers. "Babe, orange is my *brand*."

In the animal kingdom, colour has many uses. It can be used as camouflage or as a warning. It can be a way of communicating, of attracting or repelling, of scaring or appealing.

It can even be a way of pretending.

The Monarch butterfly has bright colours to let the world know it's poisonous. The Viceroy butterfly has bright colours to make the world think it's a Monarch.

I think I know which category I fall into.

On the upside, at least nobody's going to try and eat me. I look *extremely* inedible.

We turn the corner on to Broadway and Gotham Hall looms in front of us. It's tucked away, as only an enormous eight-column Romanesque building can be tucked away in New York: smallish and antique against the vast skyscrapers.

An American flag hangs at the front, a red carpet curves down the stairs, and blue lights are shining from underneath and wrapped in tiny sparkles around the trees outside so the whole thing looks enchanted.

As we walk nearer I realise with a lurch that New York has changed again.

Gone is the sunny tourist buzz of a New York day or the quiet calm of a New York early morning. Gone is the far-away twinkle of New York when you look at it from a distance.

At dusk, it's like the inside of a kaleidoscope. The bright reds and greens of traffic lights, the yellows and pinks and oranges of shop signs and cars flashing, the blues of fairy lights, the whites and yellows of lamps and lit offices, the purples and blacks and silvers of the people walking past.

And across the road, next to Gotham Hall, people are emerging smoothly from black cars in short bursts of colour, like butterflies from a chrysalis.

They walk up the red carpet into Gotham Hall, glittering and shimmering. A blonde with an enormous, pale pink dress with embroidered lace down her back; a brunette with dark ringlets and a green gown with sequins like stars all over it. An older lady with a silver chignon and a navy blue high-necked gown; a young girl in lilac decorated with pale blue flowers.

The men follow them: monochrome and rigid in black and white, like gallant penguins.

I look nervously down at my dress for the umpteenth time.

I still don't like parties. They terrify me. And this one looks like the most daunting one I've ever been within a mile of.

Maybe Kenderall will let me 'make an impression' from Pronto Pizza takeaway opposite. I can stand on a table and twirl round every time she points in my direction.

"Umm," I say, trying to prop myself up against a bollard. If I fall over, I suspect I'm going to go down in a straight line, like a tree. "Are you sure I look... appropriate?"

"Babe," Kenderall says. "You look *remarkable.*"

The word *remarkable* comes from the sixteenth century French word, *remarquer,* which means: observable, extraordinary, conspicuous.

But that just means I stand out.

It doesn't actually indicate whether it's in a good way or bad.

"She does," a voice says from behind us. "She looks incredible."

My cheeks are red before I've even spun round.

"Hi, Cal," I mumble. "How are you?"

"Brilliant," he says, flashing his blinding smile.

There's no sign of the awkwardness of just a few hours ago. No sign, in fact, that he remembers the planetarium, or holding my hand, or seeing me at all.

I feel myself relax a little.

Maybe I didn't offend him. Maybe he just feels awkward around girls that cry in cinemas because the solar system is really pretty.

I'm not sure I can entirely blame him.

"So," Cal says. "Do I get to walk into this party with the most beautiful girl in New York on my arm?"

I look at Kenderall expectantly.

"He's not talking about me," she says, rolling her eyes. "My God, Brits are ridiculous."

Cal holds out his elbow. "Only as friends," he says, winking.

I take it as gently as I can. I'm not entirely sure I've ever had a boy offer me his arm before. And at least if my ridiculous shoes defeat me on the stairs I won't fall over on my own.

Maybe that's what I should have been looking for.

"Now," Kenderall shouts with glee. "Let's P.A.R.T.Y."

72

The *Oxford English Dictionary* defines *grand* as:

1. *Magnificent and imposing.*
2. *Large, ambitious and impressive in scope or scale.*

The Grand Ballroom of Gotham Hall is exactly what it purports to be.

As Cal, Kenderall and I walk up the red-carpeted stairs and push open the ornate golden doors, it unfolds in front of us like an enormous, circular Aladdin's cave.

Above us is a huge gilded ceiling with a circle of blue stained glass in the middle, through which you can just see the sky. A huge gold and crystal chandelier hangs, suspended in a sparkling globe, and below it is a marble floor with gold leaf in spirals and circles scattered across its surface.

It looks like the ballroom has been overgrown by

a magical ghost forest: there are pale white trees everywhere, covered in tiny, paper-thin white leaves which seem to grow out of golden holes in the floor.

Gossamer-thin blue chiffon has been draped from the ceiling, and on the walls are the shining silhouettes of blue trees and birds, as if the entire room has been submerged under water.

Tiny lanterns hang from the ceiling, and hundreds of white candles are placed at intervals around the room, flickering and shivering.

Purple and blue flowers have been wound around everything – around white linen tables, around marble columns, around seats covered in white muslin – and in the corner a girl in a pale blue dress plays a white harp so the room is filled with a tinkling, water-like sound.

It's so beautiful, so other-worldly, that for a few seconds I can't even speak. I feel *exactly* like Cinderella.

Cal and Kenderall don't appear to be quite so bowled over.

"Nice," Cal says as he hands our bags in at the cloakroom, then grabs a tiny canapé from a silver tray gliding past.

"Not bad," Kenderall says, shrugging. "Oooh, is that the editor of *Vogue*? I must go and introduce myself."

She glances at me.

"Stay here," she adds firmly, "and try to turn around as much as possible. If anybody asks, I styled you, OK? Give them these."

She hands me twenty or thirty business cards from her tiny orange handbag.

Kenderall Angel Dua
Top Model-Stylist-Pig Owner
Bring your BRAND to LIFE
BE UNFORGETABLE

I'm not entirely sure whether to tell her she's spelt 'unforgettable' wrongly or not.

Although at least that's one way to achieve it.

Instead, I nod obediently and take them. There's nowhere in this dress to put them, so I grab a stretchy gold bangle off my wrist and strap them to my arm instead.

"HELLO?" Kenderall shouts across the room. "SUSAN? It *is* Susan, isn't it? What a *spectacular* dress. Why don't you reconsider the shoes you're wearing with it?"

And she stalks towards a woman wearing a gold gown and a darkening expression on her face.

Cal leans forward. "Can I just say," he says underneath his breath, "that of all the pretty girls in the room tonight, you are by far the most—"

"Bubba-lloo!" a familiar voice interrupts. Wilbur skitters towards me, dressed in a silver suit, covered in thin, translucent sequins. From a distance, he looks somewhat like a portly tuna. "Don't you just look..."

And then he stops and his eyes widen.

"What the *billybuttons* are you wearing, Munchkin? You look like somebody accidentally tried to play paintball with a parrot."

"Kenderall did it," I say as loyally as I can, handing him a business card. "It used to be white, but she dyed it and added the feathers for a more unique take."

"Oh, *sugarmonkeys*," Wilbur sighs, staring at the card and then looking around the room. "Nancy is going to *kill* me."

On the other side of the room, Kenderall shouts: "Babe, that dress is just *foul*. You need *help.* Call me on 858..."

Wilbur shivers.

"My mistake. I should have sealed that invitation with wax or arsenic," he says. "Or just given it to you directly, like a non-insane person."

Then he looks at the space behind me.

Cal is no longer holding on to my arm: he's lurking a few metres away, staring at a space across the room.

"And what," Wilbur says sharply, "are *you* doing here?"

"I'm *her* guest," Cal says, shrugging and pointing at me.

I blink in surprise. *Is he?* Just how many Plus Ones was I allowed?

"*Are you?*" Wilbur echoes with slightly less surprise. "Well, that's lovely, my little Mould-toes, but why don't you go somewhere else for a bit?"

Cal takes a few small steps away.

"Further," Wilbur says, gesturing with a hand.

Cal takes another few steps.

"Much further."

Cal takes six or seven more.

"Tell you what," Wilbur says cheerfully, "why don't you go to the other side of Manhattan and just keep walking until you hit the river and then don't stop?"

Cal scowls and walks over to the canapé table. Wilbur looks back at me. "Where's Prince Charming?" he says sternly. "I sent him an invite two days ago and told him you'd be here. Why aren't you together?"

Cows have four stomachs.

I'm suddenly glad I don't, because just one spinning

over is uncomfortable enough.

We could have been at a *romantic ball* together, and Nick *still* went to the other side of the continent?

"Oh," I say as airily as I can, trying to remember the list. *Be cool. Be mysterious. Be breezy and happy, all the time.* "He's in California... on a shoot." I clear my throat. What would Kenderall say? "Couples need to give each other *room to breathe*, babe."

Wilbur stares at me as if I've just sprouted feathers and am preparing to lay an egg. "Did you just call me *babe*, Harriet?"

I'm saved from the answer by a soft kiss on my cheek.

"Darling," Nancy says. "Don't you look... umm... extraordinary. I *so* want to introduce you to some people. Can I whisk her away, Wilbur?"

Wilbur frowns.

"*Certainment*," he says. "Just hang on a tickety-boo." And he bends down on the floor and – with the speed of a professional chicken plucker – rips all the badly glued feathers off the bottom of my dress, pulls the gold scarf from around his neck, spreads it out into an enormous sheet and wraps it tightly around my shoulders, knotting it at the front like a short kimono. "There," he says. "Marginally more acceptable."

"Thank you," I say, chewing my lip.

"And I'll be having words with *you* later," Nancy adds, lifting an eyebrow at him and glancing at Kenderall who is now attempting to stick sequins on the face of a lady with grey hair.

"Yes, Pumpkin-moo," Wilbur sighs. "I thought you might."

And as we walk away, I can still feel him frowning behind me.

73

All I know is I have half an hour.

Thirty minutes before I must leave this party and start heading home, or I'll be grounded for so long in ten or twenty years somebody will have to climb up my hair and let me out of my bedroom again.

Except it doesn't work like that.

After fifteen minutes, I begin to make my excuses.

"Of *course*," Nancy says sweetly, hugging my arm. "Let's just *quickly* meet the Fashion Director of *Elle*? I've told her *all* about you and she's *so* interested."

After twenty-five minutes, I try again.

"*Absolutely*," Nancy agrees. "But let's just say a quick hello to the Editor of *Cosmo*. I think you might be *just right* for this new shoot they're doing and…"

So I try again after forty minutes.

Then again after an hour.

Then after two.

Three hours later, I'm still being led around the

party, trying unsuccessfully to remember names and holding conversations I am nowhere near equipped to deal with. And I'm still handing out Kenderall's cards.

All of which get thrown straight on the floor: by the end of the third hour it looks like I'm just leaving a trail of orange rectangular breadcrumbs, like a neon-obsessed corporate Hansel and Gretel.

"Ah," a woman in a glittery black dress says as Nancy makes the billionth introduction of the evening. "The girl with the red hair. I've been waiting to meet you all night."

I look down.

Seriously? I spent nearly *two hundred dollars* on a pair of shoes that look like dead lobsters and my brand is actually something I had growing out of my head for free?

"I recognise you from somewhere," she continues. "But I just *can't* put my finger on it." She tilts her head and gazes at me. "I don't suppose you've been covered in octopus ink at any stage in the last year, have you?"

Nobody is ever going to let me forget about that, are they? It wasn't *totally* my fault. Some of it was definitely Charlie's. Not that people like it when you blame a totally ruined fashion shoot on an octopus.

"No-oooo," I lie in embarrassment, looking desperately at the exit.

"You have! I knew it! You're the girl Yuka Ito keeps going on about!"

"Umm…" I glance anxiously at the clock on the wall in a panic. It's now past 9pm. "It's funny you should say that, because in German folklore the paranormal double of a living person is called a *doppelganger* and there might be one of me wandering ab—"

Then my eyes land on a girl in the corner.

I fall totally silent.

Fleur is in a pale pink beaded dress. Her hair is tied into a side-knot, and she looks amazing.

Ethereal. Incandescent.

And also like she wants to rip my face apart with her fingernails.

"Hi," I mouth silently, lifting my hand and waving at her.

Fleur stares at me in disgust, and then turns around and starts picking at one of the canapé trays.

The woman in black sequins is still talking. "Nancy, we should set up a meeting. Who's your agent?"

I force myself to look back at her. "My agent?" I say blankly. "I don't really have—"

A hand touches my arm.

"Sorry to interrupt," Cal says smoothly. "But there's something *really* important I have to tell this girl."

"But—" the woman in black protests.

"It can't wait any longer," he says, blinding her with his megawatt smile.

And before I can object, Cal grabs my hand and pulls me into the hallway.

74

I'm so grateful, I don't even ask where we're going.

I allow myself to be led through the hallway, and then back round the other side of the party, into a corner behind some blue chiffon.

Finally.

Finally I can make my escape.

I glance at the clock again. 9.25pm. If I go *now*, I can catch the last train to Greenway.

The lights of the party are in soft focus behind Cal, flickering behind the curtain. You can still see colourful shapes of people, but they're softened: blurred by the blue sheet, as if they're under water.

"*Thank you*," I say as Cal grips my hand. "How did you know? I didn't know how to get away. Do you think there's a back door I can slip out of before anyone sees m—"

And then I stop.

Not because I've forgotten what I'm trying to say,

but because just as I shape the final syllable, Cal puts his hands around my face.

And kisses me.

75

Now, I know something about kisses.

I know that when they're right, the entire room and everything in it disappears.

That when they're right, you can't put a single thought into coherent order: everything jumbles up, as if your brain has been put in a washing machine set at the highest speed.

That the inside of you goes warm and starts tingling and vibrating, like an electric toothbrush.

I know the world stops.

Thanks to Toby, I also know that when they're terrible they can be deeply uncomfortable and deeply awkward.

This is none of the above.

The harp plays and the candles flicker and the lights sparkle and the blue chiffon floats prettily around us.

But it's *wrong*.

I know it's wrong, because I'm thinking totally

clearly. There's no warmth, no tingling. There's no happiness or excitement.

The world just keeps on spinning.

After two shocked seconds, I manage to put my hand up and push him away.

"What are you *doing*?"

"What did it *feel* like I was doing?" Cal says, raising his eyebrows.

"But..." *Now* my head is starting to tumble. "We're *friends.* You don't kiss *friends.*

Not unless you're Toby but we've talked about that.

"Oh, please. You've been wanting me to for days. It's been written all over your face."

"In what *language*?" I snap crossly. "Because it really, really hasn't."

Then I rub my mouth as a horrible guilty sensation sinks in.

Sugar cookies.

This is *my* fault, though, isn't it?

I let Cal show me the stars and hold my hand. I allowed him to catch me when I fainted. I came to a fairy-tale ball *on his arm* and then ran with him to a candle-lit corner.

What kind of horrible, selfish idiot *am* I?

"I-I didn't mean to lead you on, Cal," I stutter.

"I really didn't. You're so nice, and you've been so thoughtful, but…"

You're still not Nick. You never will be.

"Fine," Cal shrugs. "Whatever."

And without another glance he pushes past the blue chiffon, back into the party.

76

I stare at Cal's retreating figure.

Then I try to follow him.

Except I can't, because I manage to get tangled up in the blue fabric.

Obviously.

I should have seen *that* coming from the minute I entered the ballroom.

In a panic I spin myself energetically round like a fly caught in a web, and then start bleating through the chiffon: "Caleb. Wait. I can explain…"

A small white hand gently reaches down and disentangles me. "Let him go," Fleur says quietly as I emerge, flushed and puffing. "There's no point."

"But…" I stare at her, and then at Cal. He must have walked fast: he's already on the other side of the room. "I've hurt him. I need to say sorry, I need to—"

"You don't need to do anything," Fleur says. "He's done, Harriet. Tick."

My eyes widen. "What do you mean *tick*? Like... off a list? Or like a parasitic arachnid that attaches itself to a vertebrate, sucks blood and then leaves a nasty bite?"

Fleur laughs grimly. "Both, actually. Caleb is an MC."

"An MC?"

"A Model Chaser. He crashes fashion parties and photo shoots so he can get near to as many of us as possible. And now he's done with you. *Tick.*"

I look back across the room to where Cal is now talking to a very pretty girl with long blonde curls.

With a lurch, I recognise all of it.

I recognise the focused, piercing expression and the charming smile. I recognise the way he's grabbing her hand. I recognise the way he's leaning in, to see if she has a sparkle in her eye when actually it's astigmatism.

Then my stomach rolls again.

Did he ever actually call me *Harriet*? Does he actually even remember my *name*?

"I'm sorry," Fleur says as I watch him flick a bit of imaginary fluff off the blonde's shoulder and she goes bright red. "I should have warned you, but you had Nick then. And I thought you were smarter than –" she pauses – "well, *me*."

I look in shock at her ashamed expression, and realise that ever since I saw Fleur in the LA MODE reception it's been like looking at one of those pictures that can be two things: a candle or two faces, a bunny or a rat.

Except now I can only see one.

Fleur's quietness.

Her jitteriness in the reception when Cal was on the sofa. The pink flush when Cal put her on the roller coaster. Her eagerness to get away once the shoot was done. Her inability to make eye contact.

Then I suddenly replay the look she gave me ten minutes ago. When Cal was standing right behind me.

None of it was about *me*.

It was about *him.*

"But the planetarium," I say, still feeling confused. "How did he know I'd like..."

"Stars?" Fleur raises her eyebrows. "What girl *doesn't*?"

And the final puzzle piece falls into place. I bet there never was a photo shoot planned for this afternoon. I bet he just arranged it all with Kenderall.

"For me, it was a boat ride at sunset," Fleur sighs. "For Cassie it was the Statue of Liberty. He took a picnic to Central Park with Lydia, bought Rosie flowers and Rachel got a ride in a horse-drawn carriage."

My eyes widen, and I look again at Cal's back.

Ugh.

For the first time possibly ever, the biggest idiot in the room isn't me.

"So you don't hate me?"

"Why would I hate you?" Fleur says, sounding genuinely surprised. "Of course I don't hate you, Harriet." She pauses. "But I *do* hate New York, and I really, really want to go home. I've had three jobs in six months, I live with eight other models in a tiny flat where there's never any hot water and I'm hungry *all* the time."

I look at Fleur's tiredness. She looks so much smaller than she used to. In more ways than one.

"It'll be OK," I say, reaching up and putting my arm cautiously around her high shoulder. I feel like Pooh Bear trying to cuddle Christopher Robin. "You can come and stay with us, and… and…"

Suddenly I can't breathe properly.

"Had," I say, gripping Fleur's shoulder tightly. "*Had.*"

"Huh?" Fleur frowns.

"You said 'You *had* Nick then'. *Had.* Past tense."

"Oh my God, Harriet. I didn't mean you to find out

like... He'd only just got here and… I tried to explain, but he was too far away and he didn't hear me and…"

The room disappears.

And then – bit by bit – I do too.

First my ears vanish. Then my chin. Then my lips and my shoulders and my arms. Then my fingers and my knees and my feet and my elbows.

Until I'm nowhere and nothing.

I look at the blue chiffon curtain. From one side, I could see lights. I could see people.

Which means they could see me and Caleb.

No.

No.

No no no no no *no no no no NO.*

Because all I know now is this:

1. *Nick was here, and he came back for me.*

2. *He just saw everything.*

77

A cheetah's heart is capable of jumping from 120 beats per minute to 250 in a matter of seconds.

Apparently so is mine.

I spin in wild circles, trying desperately to catch a glimpse of Nick's curly head amongst the glittering crowd.

"Hey, babe," Kenderall says as I start spinning in the opposite direction, just in case that helps. "I finally met *Nick*. He's mega *hot*, babe. Probably doesn't need a hyphen. You want to hang on to that one."

I stare at her, aghast.

She has got to be kidding me.

"You *saw* him?" I nearly shout, hope rising. If I can just talk to him, I can explain everything. "He's still here?"

"Oh no," she says calmly. "He's long gone. *Told* you the plan would work. He's totally *crazy* about you now. He left this for you on his way out."

She hands me a tiny blue box.

I hold it tightly in my hand. For a second, I am a whisker away from sticking it straight down her stupid long model throat. "*This* was the plan? Getting someone else to kiss me in front of my boyfriend was the *plan*?"

This is why I should *always* get people to write their plans down for me.

"Well, I didn't *know* he'd *see* you and Cal, did I? But I was hoping he'd have his suspicions after your little 'date'. It worked out even better than we could have hoped for."

She stretches her arms above her head and yawns hugely.

The strongest organ in our body may be the tongue, but for a few seconds I can't get mine to say anything constructive at all.

"How is this better?"

"Boys don't know what they've got until they've lost it to someone else," Kenderall states. "Everyone knows that. I was *helping* you."

"But I don't *want* to lose Nick," I shout. "THAT WAS THE POINT."

Kenderall blinks. "Well it's not a *science*, babe. Jeez."

I stare at Kenderall. Then I stare down at my stupid dress through my stupid fake eyelashes and the silly orange cards strapped to my arm. I think of all the stupid texts I've been sending, and all the forced silences.

And weirdly enough my anger with her abruptly disappears.

Kenderall's not a bad person. She just doesn't know me. She doesn't know Nick, and she doesn't know what the hell she's talking about.

Unfortunately, I obviously know even less.

I have been *such* an idiot.

Trembling, I rip open the little box and pull off the tiny white note attached to it.

Inside, wrapped in white tissue paper, is a silver necklace.

It has nine brightly coloured beads on it in different sizes. Three blue, two red, one orange, one purple, one yellow and a tiny mottled blue and green one.

It's our solar system.

Nick has given me the planets.

For my T-Rex,
Happy 16th birthday.
LBx

I didn't want to lose my boyfriend.

But it looks like I just did.

78

July 21st

"So," I said, curling up next to Nick. David Attenborough was talking about sharks ascending from the cold dark depths, and I couldn't find my slippers.

"So," Nick said, wrapping his warm hands around my feet.

"So," I said again.

"So," he laughed. "Say it, Manners. Whatever it is you're fretting about and pulling apart like a puppy with a ball of tissues, just say it."

I cleared my throat.

"So, I was just wondering... Because the thing is... I just wanted to know..." I took a deep breath. "Am I your girlfriend yet?"

"Officially?"

"Yes."

"Write-it-down official? *Diary* official?"

I flushed. How did he know that I'd left a space

for this express purpose right at the back? "Have you been looking through my personal secrets, Nick Hidaka? That's not very gallant of you."

"I don't need to," he said, grinning. "I just know you pretty well, Harriet Manners."

"Well, yes then," I said, trying to stick my nose in the air. "Am I your girlfriend, *diary* official?"

"Yes," Nick said, wrapping his arm around me and pulling me into his jumper. "Of course you are."

"In pen?"

"Harriet," he laughed, and suddenly my feet didn't feel cold any more. "You can write it in permanent marker if you like."

So I did.

79

They say that life is just a blank chain, and precious moments are the beads we hang off it to make it beautiful.

As I hobble down the front steps of Gotham Hall clutching my satchel against me, I can suddenly see them all, glittering and flashing in front of me.

I see Nick under the table at The Clothes Show Live in Birmingham, offering me chewing gum. I see him on the pavement outside Infinity Models when I asked if he wanted to sniff my hands. I see him leaning against the lamp-post in the snow in Russia, and holding my hand when I was scared.

I see our first kiss, in the darkness of a television studio.

I see him leaning against a doorway in Tokyo.

I see him sitting on the steps outside a Sumo hall, and standing on the stage opposite me with a little curl sticking up like a duck tail. I see him holding me steady in the water of Lake Fuji, surrounded by stars.

I see him sitting down on the pavement next to me in Shibuya; his nose twitching as I shouted and made little T-Rex claws. I see him on a roundabout, spinning us round in circles. I see him racing me to a postbox, and writing something silly just to make me laugh.

I see him making me part of his life, and winking at me on a catwalk.

I see him ringing me from the back of an elephant and travelling two hours with sixteen purple balloons and sixteen cupcakes just to see me on my birthday.

I see him on Brooklyn Bridge, with New York lit up behind him: angry because he was worried about me.

I see him always knowing who I am without me ever having to tell him.

Being there, without me ever having to ask him.

And as the bright beads start slipping away, one by one, I suddenly realise I don't need the fairy-tale romance. I don't need the big gestures; I don't need to be shown the heavens or flowers and horse-drawn carriages and boat rides at sunset. I don't need everything to be *perfect*. For me, it already was.

And I don't need Nick to say he loves me.

Because I already know.

*

Apparently we each shed a million skin cells every day, and I must be losing mine all at once because I feel like I'm suddenly falling apart.

I ignore the protesting seams of my horrible dress and sit on the red-carpeted steps of Gotham Hall. Then I pull my phone out of my satchel. There are fourteen missed phone calls from Nat.

I stare at them, then curl myself into a tight ball.

If there was any kind of table out here, I would be hiding underneath it within four seconds.

The etymology of the word *friend* comes from the Proto-Germanic word *frijand*, which means *to love.* Love and friendship: friendship and love. They come from the same place.

I've just been too blinkered to see it.

Oh God.

Oh God oh God oh God.

Of all the messes I've ever got myself into, this is by far the worst. It's elephantine. Whopping. Colossal. Gargantuan.

Whatever word you want to pick that means:

Really, really horribly huge.

And then – as if by magic – the night manages to get just that tiny bit worse.

"Harriet?" a familiar voice says, and I lift my head.

"Would you like to explain what the *hell* is going on?"

And there, standing on the red-carpeted pavement of New York City, is my father.

80

It's funny how sometimes you can't see yourself until somebody else does it for you.

As Dad stares at me with his arms crossed, I suddenly see me.

And I mean really, really *see* me.

I'm supposed to be curled up in my bedroom in my penguin pyjamas, reading an interesting book about the Tudors and making notes.

I'm supposed to be listening to the BBC World Service and looking up facts about animals on the internet and emailing my friends witty anecdotes about them that they'll pretend to be interested in. I'm supposed to be making lists and plans and organising everything in my life down to the minutest detail.

I'm supposed to be making up choreographed dances with my Best Friend and forcing my family to watch them, even if they don't want to.

I'm supposed to be *me.*

Instead, I'm curled up on some red-carpeted steps outside a party in the centre of Manhattan on my own at nearly 10pm in a dress that's so uncomfortable I can't breathe properly.

On my feet are horrible red shoes that I can't walk in and that look like life-size dead crustaceans. I'm shivering, thick orange make-up is smeared all over my face, and one of my fake eyelashes has unpeeled and is sticking out from my eyelid like a tiny stegosaurus spine.

I've been kissed by a boy who isn't my boyfriend, schmoozed at a party I didn't want to go to and run away from home, repeatedly. I've called people *babe* and taken money that isn't mine and wasted it. In one way or another – by omission or statement – I've lied to everyone: to my parents, to Nick, to Nat.

I can see why my dad doesn't look exactly proud of me at this precise moment.

I'm not really either.

"I'm going to ask again," Dad says, except I'm surprised I can even understand him, his jaw is clenched so tightly together. "I just got a call from Wilbur, asking me to get here as soon as I could. As far as I knew, you were in your bed at home. Grounded. What do you think you are playing at, young lady?"

Did my dad just *Young Lady* me?

He's never *Young Ladied* me before in his entire life.

"Dad," I say automatically, wiping my hand across my face, "it isn't what it looks li—"

Then I stop.

Because I'm kind of done with things not being what they look like. Right now, I just want them to be exactly as they are.

"Oh, Dad," I say, putting my head in my arms. "I'm sorry. I'm so so so so so sorry."

And I burst straight into tears.

81

My dad has his arms round me before I even reach my second wail. I push my face against his suit shoulder pad the way I used to when I was little.

And I cry.

I cry and cry until there's nothing left.

I cry until my chest hurts and my nose dribbles and Wilbur's gold scarf gets completely soggy. I cry until it's all out: every bit of the last few weeks, yanked out like a splinter.

And – in between sobs – I tell Dad everything, right from the beginning.

I tell him about Alexa and my stolen diary. I tell him about Nat and Toby, and how scared I am of being forgotten by them. I tell him about Miss Hall and how much she hates me and how stupid I am, and about running away – three times – and modelling and stealing the kitty money and spending it on shoes that I hate. I tell him about Kenderall and Caleb and Fleur.

I tell him about Nick.

Then, when there's nothing left to tell him, I look up anxiously and wipe my eyes.

"You're a silly sausage, you know that?" Dad says, kissing the top of my head.

I can think of less nice ways to put it.

"Yes," I agree in a tiny voice. "I am unfortunately the silliest of all sausages."

"Why didn't you just tell us about this in the first place?"

"Because..." I swallow and my chin starts wobbling again. "Because I'm sixteen and *I want to be a grown-up*."

Those last seven words come out as a series of high-pitched squeaks, which makes them sound even more ridiculous than they already are.

Unless I'm a grown-up hamster.

Dad laughs. "Sweetheart, you could be a hundred and sixteen and I'll *still* be your dad. You will *always* be able to tell me when you're unhappy."

I sniffle slightly. "You're not *Noah*, Dad. Apparently he lived to 950 years old, but I think you might be being a little optimistic."

"I'm going to start pilates any day now, Harriet. Or yoga. Who *knows* how long I'll be around for?"

Apparently humans share fifty per cent of their DNA with bananas. My father is a constant reminder of that.

"None of this stuff means anything, you know that, right? All of this –" Dad waves his hand around at the lights, the harp music, the golden doors behind us, the red carpet beneath us – "it's just glitter."

"I know. I guess I just... forgot for a bit."

"What counts isn't here." Dad waves his arm around again. "It's not there." He points at my florid dress and orange face. "It's not on a modelling shoot in front of cameras or a party. It's in here." He taps hard on his chest. "With the people who love you."

I watch his hand wave around a few more times for no apparent reason.

"Dad, are you surreptitiously trying to use up Powers while we have a father-daughter heart to heart?"

"*No*," he says indignantly. "But if I *did*, tonight would've used about –" he presses the little button and green numbers flash up – "452. I was very angry when I walked here. I did a lot of arm swinging."

I look at my father, and realise I haven't seen him in days. In fact, I've barely seen him since we got to America. And neither has Annabel.

"Where were you tonight, Dad?"

"Another client party. There was this big orchestra, and these little lights, and this really awesome cocktail that had a little umbrella in it and they gave me a new silk tie and…"

He stops.

"Oh, bloody hell," he adds. "I've done it too, haven't I?"

"Great minds," I say, smiling sadly. "Or, you know, exactly the opposite."

We both sit in silence.

I think about how tired Annabel looks all the time. How far away from home she is. How she gave up a job she loved to wipe up baby sick in a lonely house on her own while Dad and I gallivant around New York.

I'd never even considered that of everyone in our family, this move was the hardest on her.

And neither – judging by the look on his face – has Dad.

"I think we should go back home," he says, standing up and putting his jacket around my shoulders. "Today's rations of Manners idiocy are all used up."

I nod. I could not agree more. "I need to go somewhere first. Is that OK?"

My father tucks me under his arm and starts walking me back down the pavement, and for the first time New York doesn't feel too big.

It feels so small I could put it in my pocket.

"We can go anywhere you want, sweetheart."

There's a silence, and then I put my head on his shoulder.

"Dad... I think... I just wanted to be *somebody*. Just for a little while. Does that make sense?"

"And that's why you're a silly sausage, Harriet," Dad says, scruffing up my hair. "Because you already are."

82

Brooklyn Bridge looks precisely the same as it did a week ago, with one noticeable exception.

This time I'm on my own.

Dad gives me a hug and then waits with my satchel at the edge of the bridge while I start walking slowly across.

As I get closer, I can see Nick exactly where I knew he'd be: sitting in the shadow of the tower with his head against the wall. I can see the edges of his curls, lit up in the lamplight. He's wearing his army jacket: the one with pockets so big they fit both our hands at once. There's shadow across his face, but I can still see the little mole on his cheek and the way his cheekbones curve inwards just by his ears.

All I have to do is tell the truth.

I just have to pull it out in exactly the right way, so it doesn't get all tangled up and confused.

It shouldn't be this hard.

"Hey," Nick says quietly as I get close enough to see a tiny early autumn leaf stuck to his coat.

OK: he just stole my opening line. That was pretty much all I had.

"Hey," I swallow nervously, pulling Dad's jacket a little tighter around me. Never mind roller coasters. Never mind Slingshot. I have never in my life been this scared. "Nick, I..."

"I'm sorry, Harriet."

I stare at him. "*What?*" Then I flush. "I mean, pardon?"

"I'm sorry." Nick stands up slowly and puts his hands in his pockets. "I wasn't here, Harriet. I should have been here."

My stomach goes cold.

Is Nick trying to say that if he's not directly in front of me, all of the time, I'll just let any boy start kissing me who is? That is *not* what I intend to do.

"No," I say desperately. "He was a friend, and Kenderall told me if you thought I was with another boy then..."

I stop and feel my cheeks glowing red under my half-cried-off make-up.

You'd be so jealous and angry you'd like me more.

It sounds so ridiculous I can't even finish the

sentence. I've spent twelve years of my life reading books, and when has that *ever* worked for anyone?

I mean, just look what happened in *Othello*.

Everybody ended up dead.

"Harriet," Nick says calmly, and he takes a couple of steps towards me. "I know."

"You know what?"

"I know all of it: the texts, the weird silences. I worked it out. And I also know Caleb."

I stare at him. "You know *Cal*?"

"Well, I know his type. And I guessed what was going on when I read back your weird message again – it just *wasn't* you. So I cancelled my flight and came straight back to Manhattan."

"So..." My brain is spinning in slow circles, like the ballerina on top of a music box. "Are you saying you know I didn't want to kiss him? Because I didn't, Nick. I never would. It was horrible, and I got all caught up in the blue chiffon, and he smells of oranges and..."

Nick smiles. "Why would you? The boy smells of oranges. That's just weird."

They said in the planetarium that we are all made of stars: that every atom in us came from a sun exploding.

Now I can feel it.

My whole body is suddenly full of a million lights,

burning and sparking and firing inside me.

Without another word, I throw myself against Nick's chest and bury my nose into his coat before he can even open his arms.

My boyfriend.

My perfect, non-perfect, green-smelling boyfriend.

I think I've just crushed one of his elbows. It made a weird clicking sound.

"So we're OK?" I say, pushing myself into him a bit harder regardless. "We can go back to normal?"

Everything's going to be exactly as it was, except better.

There won't be lists and plans; there won't be expectations of boat rides in Central Park, or an elevator up the Empire State Building, or flowers and chocolates. I won't try and make us jump in and out of fountains in a romantic fashion, or kiss in front of firework displays, timed to perfection.

I'll just let us be *us.*

The way we always have been.

"Ooh," I say in excitement. "There's an exhibition on Italian Futurism and Reconstructing the Universe at the Guggenheim! Maybe we can go, and stand in front of the paintings and kiss and—"

"Harriet, I need to talk to you."

I smile and snuggle in even more.

"I know you do," I say happily. "About anything. Anything at all."

There's a silence.

A silence so long you could climb it with a pickaxe and a rope, should you be interested in climbing up silences.

And suddenly I realise that Nick's arms aren't wrapped around me. He hasn't grinned since I got here. There hasn't been a laugh, or a twinkle or a joke.

He hasn't even tried to kiss me.

I've been so busy seeing the romantic reunion I wanted, I didn't even notice.

Again.

"R-right?" I prompt nervously.

"No," Nick says, pulling back slightly. "This time I *really* need to talk to you."

Then I look up and see his face.

It's as if somebody is trying to pull it apart from the inside. As if it's taking every bit of energy he has to keep himself in one piece. And, one by one, the stars inside me start flickering and switching off.

I don't think I'll need to visit the Guggenheim.

My universe is going to be reconstructed much sooner than I thought.

83

Scientists say that every year, ninety-eight per cent of the atoms in our body are replaced.

In the following five seconds, mine are all exchanged in one go.

And as the atoms in my face shift and change until they're unrecognisable, all I can think is:

This isn't how things are supposed to end.

I know stories, and I know romance, but this isn't how mine is supposed to end at all.

"You're breaking up with me, aren't you," I say, sounding strangely calm. Strangely quiet.

Strangely like somebody else.

There's another pause, and then Nick sits down heavily on the path. "Do you know *why* this is my favourite place in New York, Harriet?"

I look at the top of his curly head for a few seconds, and then sit down next to him. "Because it can bear the weight of quite a few elephants?"

Nick smiles, but it doesn't reach his eyes.

"A little bit. But mostly it's because it's the only part of this entire city that feels like *me.* I'm always nowhere. Between two places. Seeing everything from a distance. Never part of it."

I stare at the profile of a face I know better than my own. I stare at the ski-slope curve of his nose, and the dark length of his eyelashes, and the little line next to his mouth that shouldn't be there yet.

"What do you mean? You're always *everywhere*, Nick. You're like some kind of magic genie."

"I'm not magic," he says, rubbing his eyes. "And I'm definitely not a genie. That's kind of what I'm talking about. Always being everywhere means never being anywhere. I've been a model for more than three years, and I've spent most of my teens living out of a suitcase."

I don't know what to say.

It suddenly hits me that Nick has always felt slightly other-worldly to me. It hadn't occurred to me for a single second that he's just a normal seventeen-year-old boy, and to pop up around the world constantly must take quite a lot of effort.

"I'm tired, Harriet," he admits, finally looking at me. "I'm tired of photo shoots where no one knows my name. I'm tired of flights and taxis and waking up in the morning, not knowing where I am. I'm tired of parties I don't care about. I'm tired of having to pack my bags. I'm tired of having my life broken into little sections that don't join up. I'm tired of always leaving."

I can suddenly see his face on the catwalk again. The blankness, the anger, the resentment. Every time he called to say he couldn't see me because he was in Africa, or in a casting, or in California or at a fitting. I didn't see his frustration for what it was, because I thought it was aimed at me.

And it wasn't. Nick doesn't like being a model.

He *loathes* it.

"You're tired of not having a home," I say as finally I begin to understand.

He nods. "And you kept running away from yours, and that made me angry. I'm so sorry."

I duck my head in shame as the truth hits me: my family don't just *ground* me. They are the things that keep me *grounded.* They're what I've run from, but they're what I come back to every time. They're how I know I'm *me.*

And I didn't understand until right this moment that Nick might need that just as much as I do.

"The falcons," I say, looking up and remembering his silence.

"As you said." The corner of his mouth twists down. "Peregrine means *wanderer*. But even they have somewhere to come back to."

I've never seen Nick like this before. He looks so... lost. I shuffle a little bit on the pavement so my knees are touching his.

"I haven't been home for more than ten days in three years," he says quietly. "I miss being shouted at by Mum because I haven't taken my shoes off at the front door or because my dirty laundry is in a smelly pile in the corner of my room. I miss my friends. I miss surfing and sunshine and playing the piano and waking up knowing where I am and who I am. I miss being in one place."

After the last few weeks, I think I can finally understand that.

"You play the piano?" I say in surprise.

"Used to. They're not that easy to fit on an aeroplane."

"You could have got a mini keyboard. Or one of those electronic piano T-shirts."

Nick laughs. "Should have thought of that." Then he frowns. "But I'm not tired of you, Harriet. I can't imagine *ever* being tired of you. So what can I do? If I stop modelling, I can't be physically with you. But if I continue, I'm never here either. I don't know what to do."

And suddenly I know just how much I love Nick.

I love him with every single atom of me. With every one of my thirty-five billion cells; with every skin cell, hair cell, liver cell, kidney cell, heart cell and bone cell.

I love him with every single one of my old atoms, and I know I'll love him with every one of my new atoms too. However many times I'm replaced, whoever I become, I will still love him.

Because I love him enough to say this:

"You need to go home."

Nick stares at me for a few seconds, and then his face twists up. "But I *can't*, Harriet. Because that means—"

"I know what it means," I say, because Australia is over 9,000 miles away and Nick can't be there properly if I keep any part of him with me.

"*Shoot,*" he says, putting his head against mine.

I laugh. "You really have choice moments of using that word, you know."

There's a long silence while we sit with our heads together.

That's the thing with breaking up. There's no need for language. No need to reduce emotions to basic words, to limit the immensity of how you feel to the paltry confines of the English—

"I love you, Harriet."

Oh. So, maybe there is.

"I love you too," I say, nudging my nose against his. "No biggy."

84

Dad and I sit in silence all the way back to Greenway.

He puts his arm around me, and I curl up tightly on the leather seat and stare blankly out of the taxi window.

I watch the bright lights of New York getting smaller, the buildings shrinking, the noise fading and the world I thought I wanted evaporating behind me.

It's way past 11pm when we finally get back, staggering with tiredness up the driveway.

The front door swings open before we even knock.

"Hello."

"Hi, Annabel," I say without meeting her eyes. "I think there might be a few things I need to tell you."

"Yes," she says, stepping back into the hallway. "I would imagine there probably are."

Like with Dad, I make no excuses.

I don't fantasise how the story was supposed to go,

or how I wanted it to go, or what I thought my role in it should have been. I don't dramatise, and I don't paint it in a way that will get me out of trouble.

I just tell Annabel the truth.

All of it.

Then I stand anxiously on the carpet in front of my stepmother and clutch my hands tightly together.

There's a long silence while Annabel takes in the state of me: the smeared and tear-swollen face, the ridiculous outfit, the blisters on my bare feet, the fact that I'm so tired I can barely stand up straight.

Finally, she says, "Take your sister, Harriet," and holds out Tabitha. "My bicep muscles are nowhere near as developed as I'd like them to be and after a while babies are *really* heavy."

I hold out my arms and Tabby immediately curls into my chest with a little squeak. I bury my nose into her milky curls and a wave of love abruptly washes over me. I hadn't realised how much I'd missed my little sister.

"This is all very illuminating," Annabel continues calmly. "Considering I thought you were in your bedroom the whole time."

I look at the floor. I am going to be locked in my bedroom so long this time there will be thorn hedges growing around the house like Sleeping Beauty, except I'll be wide awake.

"So let's address the first point, shall we?" Annabel leans back on the sofa. "You are not stupid, Harriet. Or *academically challenged*, or *weak*, or *unremarkable,* or whatever it is you were told. Your tutor was a fraud."

"What do you mean a *fraud*?" A rush of guilt washes over me. "No, Miss Hall was only covering for me, Annabel, and it's not fair if she gets blamed for—"

"She was covering for herself, actually, Harriet. And I mean a *fraud.* A fake, a sham, a charlatan. A trickster, a hoodwinker. The woman doesn't have a single real qualification to her name. Not one."

I stare at Annabel, and suddenly the relief is so huge I have to sit down before I drop my baby sister.

"So I'm not –" I swallow – "totally failing?"

"Harriet, nobody can be expected to teach themselves advanced A level physics. If they *could*, there probably wouldn't be schools in the first place."

Oh thank *God.* I *knew* damping was quite a tricky topic to grasp completely in ten minutes.

"But how did you..."

"She popped over to drop off some books for you this afternoon but I found her in my bedroom instead putting my brand-new leather Filofax into her backpack. Let's just put it this way: Miss Hall won't be 'teaching' in America again."

I blink.

My admiration for Annabel just climbed another notch. Miss Hall must be at least a foot taller than her and several times wider.

"And second of all," she continues gently, "I think you've had punishment enough, don't you, sweetheart? I forgot your sixteenth birthday. I forgot to do a background check on your tutor. I was too tired to make sure you made new friends here or to notice how miserable you were. I can't blame you for feeling forgotten about and I'm incredibly sorry that you do. And I promise you, this will never happen again."

Of all the things I predicted Annabel would say – which was quite a few – this wasn't even in the Top Ten List. I'm starting to think I should probably stop writing them in the first place.

"Does that mean I'm not being grounded again?"

Annabel grimaces. "No. We were too harsh in the first place: five days is far too long. I guess we're new to this as well. Plus we've made some rather large mistakes too." She sighs. "Perhaps you would like to ground me instead?"

I shuffle slightly closer on the sofa. "OK. But you can use the kitchen."

"And the bathroom?"

"I might even allow you to take turns around the garden, like a Victorian lady with consumption."

"You're so very generous."

We smile at each other, and I suddenly realise that maybe the reason I've never missed my mum is because I've always had one.

"So what happens now?"

"Well," Annabel says more brightly. "I'm glad you asked because I've made this." She pulls a piece of paper out of her briefcase and crosses off the first thing on the list.

WHAT HAPPENS NOW

1. ~~APOLOGISE~~
2. FIND A NEW TUTOR FOR HARRIET
3. RING EVERY SINGLE ONE OF THEIR REFERENCES AND INTERVIEW THEM PERSONALLY
4. TRIPLE CHECK THAT THEY AREN'T GIANT-ESQUE KLEPTOMANIAC MEGALOMANIACS
5. CALL THE LOCAL SCHOOL FOR INFORMATION ON EXTRA-CURRICULAR CLUBS FOR HARRIET SO SHE CAN

MAKE NEW FRIENDS

6. DO THE SAME FOR ANNABEL

I look at the list with a swell of admiration and approval.

If there's ever been an argument for nurture versus nature, Annabel and I would be it. We're like non-genetically related peas in a pod.

And, yes, I'd have preferred a double-lined heading and maybe a different-colour pen, but I can't just go around forcing my plans on other people.

Ooh.

Maybe I've learnt something in the last few weeks after all.

I smile. "Do you think they have a Paleontology group? They've just found a fossil of a brand-new miniature T-Rex in Alaska."

"Let's pop that on the list."

Annabel gets out a pen and starts scribbling at the bottom of the paper.

At which point Dad clears his throat.

We both look up in surprise. He's never normally this quiet. In fact, I think we'd kind of forgotten he was even in the room.

"That list won't be necessary," he says calmly.

"I think it will," Annabel says, glancing at it again.

"Harriet isn't a little girl any more, Richard. We can't just make her sit in Greenway with nobody to talk to except for her parents and a baby. It's not fair."

"I know. And that's why we're going home."

85

I've never seen Annabel speechless before. Today is just packed *full* of unexpected firsts.

She stares at Dad for a few blank seconds, and then says, "I'm sorry: *what*?"

"We're going back to England. You're exhausted and miserable, darling. You shouldn't be stuck out here on your own any more than Harriet should."

"But... what about your job?" Annabel objects. "I thought you loved working in New York."

"It's OK," Dad says, shrugging. "But I love you both more."

Apparently it takes seventeen muscles to smile, and forty-three muscles to frown. I have no idea how many Annabel is now using: her entire face is crumpling like a piece of paper.

"Really?" she says quietly.

"Really really," Dad says.

"We can go home? Back to our house and our

friends? You're serious?"

"I have never been serious in my entire life," Dad says indignantly. "But yes."

Annabel puts her hands over her face.

"Oh.... thank *GOD.* I *hate* it here, Richard. *Hate* it. I love Tabby but I'm so bloody *bored.* Sometimes when nobody's looking I put on my suit and make fake appointments in my Filofax and pretend to sue people on the phone. I even brought a little hands-free set so I could call up my office receptionist while I was out on buggy walks."

She pulls a little earpiece out of her pocket and holds it up guiltily. "Audrey's getting really sick of me," she adds sheepishly.

"My lovely lawyer wife," Dad says, grinning and kissing the top of her head. "That's why I'm going to freelance. When Tabby's on the bottle we can take working in turns. After all, I did it with Harriet and she's turned out OK."

"*Hey,*" I object. "What do you mean *OK*?"

Dad lifts his eyebrows. "Don't push it, kid."

I obediently close my mouth.

I've never seen my father look so in control. So... wise. So... *knowing.*

I think I may have underestimated him.

"Because here's the thing," Dad says, reaching into his pocket and pulling out a little purple sock, "we aren't three separate colours, Annabel. And if one of us isn't happy, none of us are."

OK, maybe I didn't.

"*Seriously?*" Annabel says, mouth twitching slightly. "You just have to take the red and the blue things away from the white things, Richard. It's not that hard."

"Yes," he says, lifting her chin with his hand and kissing her. "When they're stuck together, it is."

They smile at each other and something unspoken passes between them. And – for the first time in my entire life – I think I might know what it is.

"Now," Dad says, flinging an arm out. "Thanks to my probationary period, we can be out of here in a week. So let's get moving." He flings his arm the other way. "We have curtains to bring down." He starts pointing madly at them. "Plates to pack." He pretends to pack up plates. "Driving to do."

He energetically mimics driving.

"Give me your Powerband," Annabel says drily. "All these hand gestures are making me feel seasick."

Dad grins, takes it off and hands it to Tabitha

instead.

"That's my girl," he says proudly as she starts shaking it up and down. "Earn Powers for Daddy. A few more and I should be able to fly us home on my bare shoulders."

Annabel stands up and takes off her dressing gown.

Underneath it she is wearing a pinstripe suit.

"Don't say anything," she says as Dad and I stare at her in amazement. "Just... don't."

And as we start to pack our bags, I can't help wondering if after all our adventures, maybe the biggest one is going home.

86

Tabitha screams all the way back to London too.

It turns out she just really doesn't like planes that much.

I'm so delighted to be back in England, I don't even mind when my face is crushed into a patchouli-scented left breast seconds after entering the arrivals lounge.

Even if it does mean I now have a permanent embroidery elephant outlined on my cheek.

"Darlings!" Bunty says, letting me go and kissing everyone vigorously. "Look how tanned you are! Doesn't the exotic beach life suit you!"

"The exotic *beach* life?" Annabel says, clicking Tabitha back into her car-seat. She's worn herself out and is sleeping 'like an angel', according to the airport security guard who clearly wasn't on our flight. "Mum, we were in Upstate New York."

"Were you?" Bunty says. "I thought you'd emigrated to the Bahamas."

Dad looks at Annabel hopefully.

"No," Annabel replies. "We are not emigrating to the Bahamas, Richard. But nice try."

"I can understand why you've come back in that case," Bunty says, retying her pink bun and sticking a loose twig into it. "But *what* an adventure. You'll have to tell me all about it in three or four or five months' time."

We stare at her. "Where are you going?"

"Rio," Bunty says, gesturing at her tasselled leather bag. "I've done my bit, and I'm off again. Not a big fan of this staying in one place malarkey. Bor-ing."

Annabel leans forward and gives her a kiss. "Thanks for looking after the house for us, Mum."

"You're welcome, darling. Just don't look at the curtains in the living room too closely." Bunty pauses. "Or open the cupboard under the sink. Or the store cupboard. Or the shed. I may or may not have set just a *little* bit of it on fire during a very spiritual experience with an incense stick."

Dad and Annabel say nothing.

I am very impressed by their serenity and calmness.

"Also," Bunty adds cheerfully, "how many cats did you have when you left?"

"One," Annabel says, putting her hand over her face.

"You have three now." Bunty swings her bag over her shoulder. "See you at Christmas, lovelies!"

And my grandmother disappears as abruptly as she arrived.

For the first few minutes after opening the front door, our house feels strange.

This is partly because it smells of patchouli and vanilla, partly because there are mirrored, feathered objects hanging from every wall.

And partly because I know every single inch of it.

I know the squeaky sound of the first stair.

I know the bit of flaky paint behind the door where it rebounds when I slam it.

I know how many steps it takes to get from the living room to the kitchen; I know exactly where to angle the shower controls to get the perfect temperature; I know the round greasy stain on the ceiling from where Dad threw a pancake too enthusiastically, five years ago.

I know where the light switches are with my eyes closed, and how the tree outside makes different noises with every month of the year, and just what angle I have to roll out of bed to land on the fluffy rug.

I know the warmth of the beam of light, pouring

through the front door. I know the sound of our neighbour's lawnmower, and the stain on the carpet Annabel still doesn't know was Nat, laughing Fanta out of her nose four years ago.

Dad puts our suitcases down and I start walking round the house with a lump in my throat.

I touch the walls. I touch the stair banisters. I touch the doorframes and the sofa. I touch the remote control and the kitchen taps.

Dad is doing the same thing.

Except a lot more energetically.

Then he runs back into the driveway, opens the car door and kisses the steering wheel. "It's on the right side!" he shouts, giving it a hug. "It's *so good* to be back!"

Finally, I walk in slow steps up to my bedroom.

And then I stop.

Because sitting on the bed, grinning at me, are a boy, a girl and a dog.

87

I suddenly feel even weirder.

As if nothing has changed at all, but at the same time everything has.

Hugo, in the meantime, has leapt off the bed and is running backwards and forwards, his bottom wriggling so hard there's a strong chance his head is about to rattle off.

I kneel down and he throws himself clumsily on top of me and starts trying to clamber over my head. I have no idea what the odds for Death By Licking are but it looks like my dog is giving it his best shot.

When Hugo's finally calmed down, I take a deep breath and look up.

"Did you know," Toby says amicably, "that dogs are capable of understanding up to two hundred and fifty words and have the average intelligence of a two-year-old child? Watch this, Harriet."

He clicks his fingers. "Two times three, Hugo."

Hugo wags his tail and then snuggles a bit further into my arms and ignores him completely.

Toby sighs. "It turns out two-year-old children aren't that smart at all," he says sadly. "And also that I am not very popular with animals."

I stand up cautiously and look at my friends.

Nat is in a bright blue dress that seems to be unravelling slightly around the ruffles. Toby is wearing a black and white T-shirt with a little bow tie drawn on it and a ring with a built-in laser which he's currently shining into the middle of my face.

"Hi," I say awkwardly, putting my hand up to block it. "How are you?"

"Awesome," Nat says slightly stiffly. "How was New York? Are you disappointed to be back?"

I clear my throat. "New York was, um. Well… Spectacular. You know, big and… How's, umm, Jessica?"

"She's *OK*," Nat says, biting her lip. "Very... you know... cool and stuff."

We stare at each other uneasily, and it suddenly hits me just how much I haven't told Nat over the last few weeks.

Like literally anything.

She thinks I've been living the New York dream in a huge mahogany skyscraper, with celebrities cluttering up the pavement, and eating hot dogs out of vans with the boyfriend I no longer have in tow.

"Nat," I say weakly. "The truth is..."

"Harriet!" Nat cries, suddenly jumping off the bed and lobbing herself around my neck. "Oh, Harriet, I'm *so* glad you're back. I've been *trying* to be happy for you in your new glamorous life but it's been *so hard*. College sucks and I never have time for anything any more and, and Jessica's a total pain in the backside and she doesn't have any lists or plans or *anything* and, and..."

Nat squeezes me tighter. "She's not even a *little* bit like you, Harriet. Even if she *has* got the same hair colour. It's like... *trickery* or something."

I blink into her shoulder. "Y-you..." I start, and then swallow. "You missed me?"

Nat pulls away and stares at me. "What are you talking about? Of course I missed you. You're my best friend."

I can feel my eyes starting to prickle. "You didn't want me to go?"

Nat frowns. "Of course I didn't. I was trying to be excited for *you.* Because you're my *best friend*."

My nose is tickling now, as if miniscule spiders are crawling up and down inside it.

"And you're not planning on replacing me with a college girl who knows all about shoe colours and handbag shapes and doesn't have any interest in coordinated dances around the living room?"

Nat laughs. "Harriet, if I wanted those things, I'd have made friends with Alexa years ago. I *love* our dances. They're *ace.*"

Oh my God. For the billionth time in a very short period, I have been very, very stupid.

Nat's not going anywhere. She's my white pigeon.

And I, obviously, am her monkey.

I wrap my arms around her and then mumble into her shoulder, "If it helps, I didn't see any celebrities, Nat. Not one."

"And if it helps," she laughs, "it turns out I hate coffee. Like, *really* hate it. It tastes like cat poop."

I laugh.

"Natalie is right, Harriet," Toby says, standing up and awkwardly trying to cuddle us both at the same time. "It's been super-boring without you. We're so very glad to have you home."

"Me too," I say, shutting my eyes and smiling.

Because now I really, really am.

88

Anyway, I have come to a recent conclusion:

If you're the kind of person who makes plans for anything and everything – and I am – you might as well focus them on the things that really matter.

Things that you can actually do something about, instead of the things you can't.

So on Friday afternoon after school, that's exactly what I do.

I meet Nat on our bench at the corner of my road, and together we walk to the school gates and wait for Toby.

Apparently our new form tutor announced my intention to return to school on Monday morning with some scepticism, as if I was a nineties pop star and he wasn't sure I would make it.

"I feel *immensely* non-conformist," Toby says proudly as he sneaks out of the school with the sideways step of a ninja, or a crab. "The bell doesn't ring for another..." He looks at his watch. "Three and a half minutes. The teachers think I'm in the lavatory but I went at 2pm instead."

"Gross," Nat says, scowling at him. "*That* goes on the list of things I never, ever want you to talk about in front of me again, Toby. Are we clear?"

"Yes," Toby says firmly. Then he looks confused. "Do you mean bells? Or non-conformists?"

Nat rolls her eyes and plonks herself down on the wall.

And together, we wait.

Finally, the school bell rings and Alexa walks through the gates exactly when predicted, minions close behind her. Let's just say that extra-curricular activities have never been high on her list of priorities.

Then she sees me and stops.

"Oh." Alexa clearly wasn't expecting to see me for another few days. I've surprised her, as was the plan. Then she rallies. "Look who's back early. How delightful for the whole British population."

"Hi, Alexa," I say calmly. "Are you enjoying sixth form? I really hope so."

She blinks a few times.

"Good to see the New York sense of style hasn't

made a single dent on your appearance," she snaps, looking me up and down. "Are your shoes made out of rubber?"

I look at my faithful purple flip-flops. "Yes."

"Shame," she laughs. "If lightning hits you, you'll probably be quite safe."

"*Right*," Nat says, jumping off the wall with pink cheeks. "I've had just about *enough* of—"

I put my hand out to steady my best friend. Alexa is rummaging in her bag, just as I knew she would. With a flourish, she pulls out the purple diary, and – with it – a handful of paper.

She *has* made photocopies, after all.

Hearts and equations and flowers and doodles; badgers I attempted to sketch; facts about stars and manatees and almonds. My biggest secrets, my most precious memories and my silliest ambitions.

All cut out and pasted together, with my face in the middle and the word

GEEK

written across it in thick red marker pen.

By Monday morning, these would have been spread around the common room, for all the new students who don't know me yet to see.

But she hasn't got round to it.

"Nice, huh?" she says, handing me a bundle and then distributing a few around. "I also checked out *Nick Hidaka*," she adds, turning to look at the girls behind her. "Are you kidding me? He's an actual model. You just got him off Google."

I touch the planets around my neck. "So?"

Alexa's eyes widen. "So, it's *pathetic.*"

"Is it?"

Her eyes are now so big they look like they're about to pop out. "Whatever. You're clearly either *insane* or *delusional.* And I'm not giving the diary back, so don't even ask. It's nice to have a bit of fantasy bed-time reading."

For the first time in ten years, it finally hits me how sad it is that Alexa's life pivots on trying to hurt me.

"Keep it," I say. "There's nothing in that book I'm ashamed of."

Because there isn't.

Every single bit of it is me. The good stuff and the bad stuff. The geeky stuff and the girly stuff. The silly stuff and the serious stuff and the embarrassing bits and the bits I'm proud of.

It's all me.

Because I am, and always have been, *somebody.*

"Wait," Alexa says as I start calmly handing out the photocopies to students coming out of the gates. "What the hell do you think you are *doing*?"

"Helping out," I say, shrugging. "You want everyone to know who I am before I start sixth form, don't you? I mean, you obviously don't want them to forget about me."

And I spin round and hand out another two to students I don't recognise.

"*Leaflets*, Lexi?" one of her minions says in a low voice. "You photocopied her diary and made *leaflets*? That's a bit much, isn't it?"

"Yeah," another girl says, frowning and looking at one. "Talk about getting carried away, Lex."

And – though it's barely noticeable – the group around Alexa take the smallest, tiniest step away from her.

Alexa's entire face slowly drains of colour.

"It was a *joke*," she says loudly. "What's *wrong* with you people? God, hasn't *anyone* got a sense of humour these days?"

"Oh, I do," Nat says, taking a few steps forward and snatching the diary out of Alexa's loose grasp with a threatening growl. "How about *this* for a laugh?"

And then she holds out a huge roll of paper.

"I got it made into an A2 poster last week," she says, winking at me. "Thought it might come in handy at some point."

Nat unrolls it and holds it up high.

It's an enormous photo of me and Nick. He has one arm around me, and he's laughing so hard his head is thrown back and you can see the little mole at the base of his throat. His curls are matted, his canine teeth are pointy, and his eyes are shut so his dark lashes are throwing shadows across the top of his cheeks.

I've got my eyes crossed and my tongue out, because Nat kept telling me to 'work the camera, babbbyyy' and it was really irritating me.

"Funny, huh?" Nat snaps. "Isn't that just *hilarious*?"

Alexa is still staring at the picture.

"Photoshop," she says briskly, face now ashen. "You can fake anything these days."

I think about New York.

I think about Kenderall and her oversized miniature pig and her undersized knowledge of relationships, and Caleb and his artificial charm. I think about Miss Hall and her fraudulent CV, and Fleur and her brittle unhappiness.

Then I think about my family, and my friends, and

the boy in the photo in front of me.

And how I feel about all of them.

"No," I say, looking straight at Alexa. "Not *anything*, you can't."

And then, with Nat and Toby on either side of me and the giant photo tucked safely under my arm, I start walking home.

My phone beeps and I pull it out of my pocket.

It's not the end, Table Girl. We're just hitting pause.
LBxx
PS ILY

I smile.

Apparently a butterfly's wings are actually transparent, but thousands of tiny scales reflect light at different wavelengths. In my stomach now, I can suddenly feel them: glinting and flickering inside me. Every colour of the rainbow.

I kiss my phone, put it back in my pocket and hug my friends a little bit tighter.

Because that's the thing about love.

You can plan it, and schedule it, and map it out. You can tell it how you want it to be, and where you want it to go, and what it's supposed to do. You can try to make it fit you.

But it won't listen to any of it.

Love puts itself first, and makes its own plans. It maps you out instead.

Maybe that's what makes it perfect.

Acknowledgements

Thanks to my editor, Lizzie Clifford, who has understood Harriet completely from the start: these books would not be the same without you. Thanks to my agent, Kate Shaw, my very own army of one, and to Em Manchee, for helping the numbers make sense.

Thanks to my darling grandma, who was always so proud of me, despite not being Agatha Christie. Thanks to Grandad, for believing I can do anything and making me believe it too; to Mum, whose support and kindness are never-ending (and whose scrapbook-making skills are exemplary); to Tara, my little sister, my best friend, my non-kissing soulmate, and to Dan, for looking after her for me. Thanks to Dad, who can always inspire and make me laugh: your pies (and patios) are really something.

Thanks to Caro, Vero and Louise, for giving me a home in another country, and to Aunty Judith, who will always be there too. Thanks to Lucy, for not putting her hand up, and to Anna and Lucie: you have made long days at a computer seem so much shorter.

Thanks to everyone at HarperCollins for working so

tirelessly and creatively behind the scenes: in particular Rachel, Sam, Abby, Geraldine, Nicola, Hannah, Lily, Kate, Elorine and Mary. You have made me a part of the team, and I am so very grateful.

Finally, to everyone I have ever loved, or been loved by in return. It is – and will always be – the thing in the world most worth writing about.

Thank you. x

Coming Soon!

Harriet Manners has high hopes for the new school year: she's a Sixth Former now, and things are going to be different. But with Nat busy falling in love at college and Toby preoccupied with a Top Secret project, Harriet soon discovers that's not necessarily a good thing. . .

Look out for Geek Girl's World Book Day drama!

Harriet Manners knows lots of things.

* Dolphins shed the top layer of their skin every two hours

* Shakespeare invented 1,700 words, including *puking, assassination* and *eyeball*

* A raindrop that falls into the Thames will pass through the bodies of eight people before it reaches the sea

And she knows just how badly auditions can go, especially when you're a model. But she has no idea what to do when arch-nemesis Alexa decides the school play is the perfect opportunity to humiliate her. . .

Can Geek Girl survive the bright lights of the stage?

And go back to the beginning to see where it all began...

Harriet Manners knows a lot of things.

* Cats have 32 muscles in each ear
* Bluebirds can't see the colour blue
* The average person laughs 15 times per day
* Peanuts are an ingredient in dynamite

But she doesn't know why nobody at school seems to like her.
So when she's offered the chance to reinvent herself, Harriet grabs it.
Can she transform from geek to chic?

Harriet Manners also knows:

* Humans have 70,000 thoughts per day
* Caterpillars have four thousand muscles
* The average person eats a ton of food a year
* Being a Geek + Model = a whole new set of graffiti on your belongings

But clearly she knows nothing about boys. And on a whirlwind modelling trip to Tokyo, Harriet would trade in everything she's ever learnt for just the faintest idea of what she's supposed to do next. . .

Photograph © Georgina Bolton King

Holly Smale is the author of *Geek Girl* and *Model Misfit*. She was unexpectedly spotted by a top London modelling agency at the age of fifteen and spent the following two years falling over on catwalks, going bright red and breaking things she couldn't afford to replace. By the time Holly had graduated from Bristol University with a BA in English Literature and an MA in Shakespeare she had given up modelling and set herself on the path to becoming a writer.

Geek Girl was the number-one bestselling young-adult fiction title in the UK in 2013. It was shortlisted for several major awards including the Roald Dahl Funny Prize and the Branford Boase award, was nominated for the Queen of Teen Award and won the teen and young adult category of the Waterstones Children's Book Prize. Holly is currently writing the fourth book in the *Geek Girl* series – *All That Glitters*.

www.facebook.com/geekgirlseries

For my dad.
My rock. My hero. My Richard.